THOMAS J GREER, PI

Carl Spence

Published in Australia in 2019 by Carl Spence

Website: www.carlspenceauthor.com

ISBN 9780648334828 (paperback)

A catalogue record for this book is available from the National Library of Australia

This book is a work of fiction. Names, characters and incidents portrayed in it are the product of the author's imagination. Any resemblance to actual persons, living or dead, is entirely coincidental.

For those loved but lost ...

CHAPTER ONE

Near on a year had elapsed before Tom started to consider whether he had made a mistake and should never have become a private investigator. He wondered whether he really was, in fact, an investigator at all.

The Diploma of Private Investigation was fittingly enough displayed on the wall behind him, encased in museum glass. The glass was bordered by a red cedar frame matching the wooden bowl he had bought at the Eumundi markets almost two years ago. Now, each time he thought about the cost of that special museum glass, he winced.

Tom swivelled on his desk chair in his tiny office on the first floor of Eugene Aspinall and Co. Investigations and stared at the paperclips in the bowl, repeatedly glancing at his watch counting down the minutes to knock-off time. Everything signalled it was time for reflection. And action, it all seemed so perfectly clear now.

The hypothetical cases covered during the private investigator course were engaging enough in some sort of artificial way, but there was simply no question the real cases would be better. Surely, that was to be expected. But it certainly hadn't turned out that way.

Home study had seemed ideal at first but he soon realised it cut him off from social contact and, cooped up in his childhood bedroom in Norwich, sometimes weeks went by without seeing anyone apart from his mother. Contact with his tutor had been mostly by phone. A sizeable age gap existed between Tom and Alister McBrierley. The day he handed his last assignment in to him, he turned twenty-five and although Alister never disclosed his age, from what he had told him about his long career, it seemed he was at least 75.

After tutoring, Alister had stayed on as a temporary mentor. The Institute had promised as much, despite intimations Alister may retire.

That afternoon, Alister was due to make his weekly call to touch base with his newly qualified man and Tom had already prepared in his mind, while he swivelled despondently on that chair, the exact words he would say to Alister about why he had decided to quit and move back to Norwich. After all, he deserved an explanation.

Eugene Aspinall and Co., or 'EAC Investigations' as it was in the process of converting to, took its name from its founder who had passed away several years prior to Tom's employment. Now owned by a partnership of three men and a woman, it continued its base in London with a satellite office in Canterbury. To take the job, it had meant moving to London and Tom could not help but feel that his dissatisfaction was partly linked to his aversion to this city. His good friend Paddo shared a similar feeling, although he too had moved from Norwich to London with his wife, Bessy, for work.

Alister had told Tom that he loved London and had made it his home for over forty years. 'That's where the great cases are,' he had reassured him. Tom would need to explain to Alister that the reason he was deserting his post early after only a year in the job boiled down to the job itself – the crazy clients and the absence of any decent cases to keep him motivated.

It was now 3.30 pm and leaving early was a serious option. Alister could reach him on his mobile, as he sat in a pub somewhere, knocking back a pint and thinking about his next career move. No need to hang around, not when Jason and Robert, two of the four partners, had gone for a long, boozy lunch and said they wouldn't be back.

Seeing the in-tray empty except for yet another court document to serve upon some scurrilous soul, it was yet another reminder of the extent to which things had not really panned out as he'd expected. Tracking down debt defaulters and fraudsters and serving them with some sort of summons was hardly what he wanted to be doing. Alister had told him to expect a lot of it at his stage. And not to complain, as it 'kept bread and butter on the table'. He thought about the wine that would be on the table at the restaurant where Jason and Robert sat. That he wasn't invited and it was only he who was allocated the drudgery of that type of work.

When an appointment had been made for him to see Brian O'Bryen, a prospective client, from South Kensington almost six months ago, he realised now that had been the start of a journey leading to an ever increasing desire to find an exit.

Sometimes during the day, the experience he'd had with Brian, even though it was a mere fifteen minutes, would re-enter his mind in times of inactivity, almost like a detailed flashback. Sometimes during the night when he tossed in bed, he could still feel the pain in his rib.

No one told him that Brian had called the office many times and spoken at length to Jason, Robert and finally Stephanie, all to no avail. The general rule was well known – initial consultations were to be by phone. An appointment might then be scheduled, only if considered appropriate. Jason was always the most vocal about the need to cull time-wasters before they even got in the door. It seemed to make sense. Alister had explained to him that some people think they're in a crisis when in fact there is no crisis at all, and when you tell them you can't help them, they find it very hard to understand. It was important to remember that investigators were not counsellors or therapists. But a good private eye, he wisely observed, will recognise not only the difference between a real and perceived crisis, but how to quickly deal with a person exhibiting the signs of one or the other.

Involuntarily, Brian made his appearance in Tom's mind once more. It was likely Alister's impending phone call that had triggered it and he started a slow 360 turn on his chair hoping he could spin into some other universe. He picked up a pencil for company on the first spin, twirled it in his fingers, then tapped the eraser against his brow. If that eraser could rub out the memory of Brian, it would help but not provide a fix.

Tom could still see Brian's face that day, that disturbing expression in his eyes. He relived the experience from the moment he walked out of the office that day he went to visit him to the time he walked back into the office. It was almost as if he'd died and then somehow floated above the whole scene, watching himself and the deranged Brian on playback – commentary included – yet with no ability to press fast forward.

"Has he been in to see someone before?" he'd asked Cathy, the office receptionist, the day he found out that she had made an appointment for him to visit Brian at his flat.

"No."

"Has he spoken to anyone?"

"Not sure," she replied. It was a lie he would later forgive.

"Why doesn't he come into the office? Or make an appointment to see me? Or call me first? Why am *I* going to see *him*?"

"I believe he's in a wheelchair, Mr Greer. He would have difficulty getting up the stairs."

The train to South Kensington station that day had not taken long and it was a short walk to Brian's ground floor flat. When he pressed the doorbell it only took a split second to be greeted by him and he had barely the opportunity to look at his watch to see if he'd arrived on time.

"Come in, Mr Greer," he said immediately and gruffly. "Take a seat in the kitchen, down the hallway, that way!" Carrying a walking stick in his right hand, Brian used it to push the front door wide open. The door bounced against the side wall, rattling the locks. Backing up his wheelchair, he let Tom pass.

"Thank you," Tom said. A mere two feet down the hall, he jumped as the door slammed closed behind him. It was one swift jab of the stick. The hall had fallen into darkness where light was so desperately needed.

"Stop!" Brian said, wheeling by him, stopping at an archway from where he lifted his stick and used it to flick the switch, again using the end like an extension of his arm. "In there," he pointed, the rubberised end showing the way.

Tom stood still for a moment, taking note. Everything was suitably fashioned low. He could see a kettle and a teapot and his favourite tea bags. Perhaps Brian might offer a cuppa.

"Sit over there!" Brian said, the stick again showing where.

"I'm pleased to meet you, Mr O'Bryen," Tom had said, courteously, upon taking the seat and extending his hand to be shaken.

Brian turned his chair away and then re-positioned himself directly facing Tom, up so close Tom had to tuck his legs underneath the seat. No handshake, so he took his arm back and scratched his nose instead.

"It's taken a bloody while! I haven't been able to get an appointment you know!"

"I understand it would be difficult. We're on the first floor and the stairs are ..."

"What are you talking about? I'm disabled, not incapable! I can get out of the chair when I have to climb stairs! Easily drag myself up one step at a time, if people ... *if* I'd got the bloody chance!"

Tom realised that being pleased to meet Brian had been patently premature. "I'm sorry about that. It's an old building. We've been looking into upgrading our access ... for people ..."

"For people like me, you mean?"

Bitterness, anger, frustration – they were all there. Understanding, empathy and professionalism – must duly follow. A deep breath didn't help and Tom had tried so hard to stretch out his legs, but it wasn't possible, not with that chair right up against him. After a pause and waiting for Brian to come to the topic of his enquiry, asking seemed the right thing for Tom to do.

"In any event, I'm here to help, if I can. What can I do for you, Mr O'Bryen?"

"How long have you been at that firm?"

"Six months or thereabouts."

"Not very experienced then."

"It doesn't mean I can't help you."

"Hmm. I don't know."

"I'm here, Mr O'Bryen."

At that moment, Alister's advice had entered Tom's head. *Work on your patience, my boy, it's a weak point for you.*

"How old do you think I am?" Brian asked next.

Tom found that question difficult to answer. It seemed that Brian's hair had gone grey earlier than he might have hoped. The last thing he wanted was to make a mistake about this. Regardless of whether

Brian was in a mood or it was his usual manner, he was already upset. Upsetting him further was to be avoided.

"Have a guess," said Brian, seeing his difficulty.

"Thirty-seven."

"You're good. I'm impressed."

"Is age important?" Tom asked.

"They think so. The mongrels."

"Who are the mongrels?"

"The committee, the panel or whatever. The selection association."

"Which one are you talking about?"

"This one." Brian reached for a piece of paper and took it from the kitchen table and handed it to Tom, as if it would be self-evident exactly what he meant.

Tom examined it. It seemed to be in the nature of an information sheet and related to competitions for selection in sporting teams. He couldn't see any reference to people's ages.

"You can keep that," Brian said, as he read it. "It was a pre-selection of sorts for the bigger events, even the Paralympics. Not *exactly* the Paralympics that time, but teams that might end up being in various games and events."

"I see. Did you participate in any of these sports?"

"I most certainly did."

"In what events?"

"Wheelchair Curling."

"And how did you go?"

"I was the best player, by far."

"Then what's the problem?"

"I didn't get selected. And I *never* get selected."

"Why not?"

"I was told I had a poor attitude. That … I wasn't … that I'm not … I didn't have the right sportsmanlike approach, team mentality, or some such rubbish. Can you believe that?"

Still swivelling on his desk chair, thinking of the events of that day with Brian, words he would now have to say to his mentor entered his mind. *Alister, I avoided saying yes in answer to Brian's question. I was the professional you taught me to be …*

Tom's mind returned once more to that day.

"And you disagree?"

"Of course I do!" Brian said. "I want you to look into the whole damn thing. I think I've been discriminated against on lots of levels; certainly on the grounds of my age, for one. That they think I'm too bloody old, when I'm not at all. I want you to investigate because I suspect there is something much bigger going on with the whole show that's seriously not right. Not when I'm the best player and I keep getting overlooked."

"Right. Did the panel or association give you any formal reasons, like in writing?"

"Look, I had a pending doping offence. I admitted that. It was minor. I have a letter somewhere. But it's not …"

"A drug offence?"

"Just a one off. I had one years ago as well, but it's ancient history. Nothing too heavy. It wasn't like it was Ice or Crack, that time."

Tom started to hand the piece of paper back to him.

"I told you to keep that!"

Tom folded it in two and held it in his lap. "Is it the first time you have tried out for the team?"

"No. I've tried out many times. And, quite frankly, I'm over it! Over them!"

They had arrived at the point where Tom needed to break it gently that he was not going to take the case on. There was no case. There was clearly a problem, but not with the associations or organisations he was dealing with. Their procedures and policies would be of the highest standard. Tom felt sad for Brian but there was no merit in pretending otherwise.

"I don't think we can help you." Alister had told him to bring out the royal 'we' when it seemed appropriate to depersonalise a response. "It's not something that I think … that well, not to put it in a way that *I* don't understand your frustration – I do – but sometimes there are processes that are just that – processes, procedures and …"

"Excuse me?"

I should have just got out then, Alister.

"You damn well have to help me!"

"Well, no, *I don't*."

"Yes, you do!"

Brian had held the walking stick in his hand the whole time, and he clenched it now like he was prepared to squeeze any remaining sap out of it.

It was time for Tom to get up, apologise some more and politely make his way out. But before he was a few inches off the seat, Brian quickly lifted the stick and jabbed the end hard into his ribs, forcing him straight back down. For a second that seemed like an eternity, speaking or breathing seemed impossible.

Looking at Brian's face – seeing it now again – inflamed desperation in his cheeks, twitching eyebrows, bulging bloodshot eyes acting as windows to a twisted brain, Tom's own face turned a shade of purple. Brian had inflicted his punishment for being turned down yet again with one skilful blow.

"You stupid fool …" Tom forced himself up, pushed his chair back roughly so that it toppled over, then staggered around the wheelchair. Soon, but not soon enough for his liking, he was out the door and on the street.

Back at the office, the others told Tom about *all* the calls they had already taken, and how they had *all* told Brian the same thing.

Tom's rib was broken. His spirit was next in line.

"I feel like calling the cops and getting charges pressed against that weirdo for assault," he told Jason later that afternoon.

Jason smiled at Tom, seemingly amused. "I'm sorry about what happened. We all are. But I don't think you can. We just can't have that sort of terrible publicity."

"What are you talking about?"

"I can see it now: 'Private Investigator assaulted by man in a wheelchair after refusing the man's request for help!' Think about it. It would hurt and embarrass us. You're going to have to take it in the guts, I'm afraid. You've taken a hit for all of us," Jason said, still smiling and looking at Cathy as if she was in complete agreement.

"In the ribs, actually. You should've told me, or at least warned me!"

"We knew you would handle it and get him off our backs. The guy was busted a month ago with his third shoplifting offence. If I had told you, he would have immediately seen you'd already made up your mind. He wouldn't stop calling, but he will now. Excellent work, Tom."

Excellent work, my bloody …

The spinning chair came to a stop. Getting out of the chair and out of the office for good might just stop his spinning head and allow the images of that day to dissolve. He dropped the pencil on the desk, took a paperclip out of the bowl and began twisting it.

No; if it was just Brian, Alister, maybe, but it wasn't …

There was the veteran of the first Iraq war expecting me to investigate the war, calling each week for a progress report. The old man who insisted on telling me at his first appointment that his mission in life was to eradicate all cigarette smoking in London. Exactly what were the best strategies for ambushing people at their morning tea breaks, to catch them in the act? Gary, the serial criminal, refusing to discuss anything over the phone, taking half a day to insist that it was the way that he'd been first treated in prison, when he was only 22 years old, serving time for a vicious assault on his girlfriend, well, that had been the real cause of his life of crime. Time to investigate the nasty, bully guards.

The tipping point you ask, Alister? I never told you about Gerhardt A Stemmer. German Gerhardt we called him. You might think it's funny, but I've lost my sense of humour now, and it was all utter nonsense …

With the paperclip in his hand, the chair began to spin again.

"I've not long to live," Gerhardt had explained one morning as he sat in the conference room. Stephanie had sat in as well. "But I need answers, serious answers, before it's all too late. And I need you to investigate my doctor. I have plenty of money to pay you."

"We can talk about fees later, Mr Stemmer. What's the issue with your doctor?"

"I believe, no, I *know* in fact, that he's given me cancer. I just can't prove it."

"Well, that's a very big claim, Mr Stemmer. Why do you say that?"

"Why do I say it? Because I know it. Simple as that."

"How do you know it?"

"Because *I* am sick and, *he* is evil. And, just plain stupid."

"Do you mind if we ask, what was your diagnosis?" It was a duel inquisition.

"I have advanced bone cancer."

"I'm sorry. Is it …?"

"Don't be! I'm not after your pity! I'm after your investigation techniques. *That's* what I want to hear."

"With respect, Mr Stemmer, how is it possible to … for a doctor to give someone such a thing?"

"They have their ways. That's for *you* to find out."

"Were you ill before you saw the doctor? You don't look that ill."

"Yes, but not with that disease. I'm sure of it."

"We could ask to see the doctor, I suppose."

"You'll have trouble getting anything out of him."

"Well, I would have thought so, given your highly unusual accusation."

"No, you don't understand. He has a stammer."

"I beg your pardon?"

"Stammer! He's a doctor who can't speak properly."

Alister, I looked at Stephanie, and she looked at me … seriously, I mean … please!

"Mr Stemmer. You're saying your doctor has a stammer? Is that right?"

"Yes! A stutter. A very bad one."

"That must be difficult for him, I mean, being a doctor and all."

"Well, yes. And it's damn annoying. I mean, I'm a very patient man. But, I'm telling you, he drives me crazy!"

"Is he a specialist?"

"Yes. And a surgeon."

"Really? I wonder how that works?"

"I've heard he doesn't stutter, apparently, when he performs surgery, thankfully. But he has a problem, and I don't trust him."

"When you want to be handed a scalpel, I suppose, it would need to be delivered in a timely manner. 'Scalpel, nurse …'"

"That's not the point!" Gerhardt shouted, banging on the table with his fist.

"It's all very interesting, Mr Stemmer but …"

"Listen to me, would you, Mr Greer! And shut up with your wise cracks, just for a moment! Please! When he told me I had cancer, he couldn't get it out. I think he felt guilty. He got all nervous. He said to me, 'I am *sooo* sorry … but the results show you have ca-ca-ca-ca-cancer.' I was devastated of course. And then, and *then*, when I go to see him since, he makes me so angry! Like, 'Listen, Mr Doctor, I don't have much time left, damn it! Get … what … you … need … to … say … out … Just, GET IT OUT!' I don't want to sit there and hear him say, 'Well, you need to take this or that d-d-d-drug!' By the time he gets it out, I'll be dead!"

"With respect, Mr Stemmer, Gerhardt, if I may – just because he has a stammer, doesn't necessarily mean he's a bad doctor, does it?"

"That's what I want to pay you to find out! Apparently, he has a good reputation. But I don't believe it. And now I have cancer."

"Thank you for this, Gerhardt. I think Tom and I need to discuss this and *we* will get back to you," Stephanie said.

"When? I told you, I don't have much time! When are you going to get back to me? When?"

"Tomorrow."

Stephanie refused to speak to Gerhardt further.

It was me, Alister, who had to tell him no, we're not taking your case. I'm over the loonies.

Now the time had come not only to leave early, but to leave for good. The paperclip was well and truly bent out of shape now, its condition a reflection of how he felt and, when the phone rang, he was sure Cathy was going to say it was Alister. He was ready for him now.

Not that I don't appreciate everything you've done. Every single thing you've taught me. But I'm done …

Of course he would be disappointed. *So be it.*

"It's a Mrs Morrow on the phone. She wants to make an appointment. I told her you are the only one in the office today and she wants to see someone this afternoon," Cathy said.

In that moment he thought about telling Cathy to say he'd left for the day and 'someone' will call her tomorrow. Someone else. But before he thought it through, he said, "Put her through."

"Hello," the lady said.

"Hello. Tom Greer. Can I help you?" When he said that, he knew he'd lost the desire to help anyone. Anyone but himself.

"Thank you for taking my call, Mr Greer. I was wondering if I could see you this afternoon. I'm not too far away. I could be there in half-an-hour, if that is at all possible."

Her voice was gentle and clear, refreshingly polite. Tom paused and said slowly, "Perhaps that might be alright."

"If it's inconvenient, or …"

"No. No, it's fine. Do you mind if I ask the general nature of your enquiry?"

"No, not at all. But it's a little difficult for me to talk right at the moment. I will not take up much of your time. And I'm very happy to pay for an initial consult. I don't want to waste your time. And, I really don't know where I stand. But I would greatly appreciate your advice. If it's too short notice, please let me know when you can fit me in."

Looking at his watch, he knew he had nothing to lose now. One more go.

"What about 4.15? You know where the office is?"

"Yes."

"Okay. I shall see you this afternoon," he said, and threw the broken paperclip in the bin under his desk.

CHAPTER TWO

Staying back late at the office was never a problem if he had to, but for some time there had been no need to stay late. The office was on Edgware Road, and a little over a fifteen minute walk to his flat in Paddington. The flat was a small but adequate abode he shared with two girls from Poland. It was an entirely different proposition getting home each evening without stopping at one of the half dozen pubs along the way. Ever since he started to feel the way he did about his chosen line of work, his drinking had increased from its moderate level to the next level, although it varied from week to week. The Polish girls were usually more than happy to drink with him, either at a pub or at home and usually at most any hour, if he wanted. The fact that they both worked in a pub made it all the more difficult for him at times, and while they never drank on the job of course, he would regularly stop in to the pub where they worked for an occasional free ale and stay for a session. He felt he could not escape it outside work hours. It was taking the shine off his personality and he knew it.

Right on time, Penelope Morrow introduced herself at reception. Cathy let Tom know and informed her Mr Greer would be with her in a moment.

Reception and the door to his office were a mere few steps apart. It was the only office that didn't have a window and as the most junior investigator and last man in, that part he understood.

"Please, come in," he said, shaking her hand in front of Cathy who watched Tom as he led her in then closed the door behind them.

"Thank you for seeing me on such short notice," she said, as she removed her coat.

Penelope Morrow was not much older than he was – thirty, perhaps, was his first impression. Her dark-brown, almost black, short hair curled slightly around the bottom of her ears, framing a thin face. She stood a little taller than him. She folded her long beige coat, then took the seat opposite his desk and sat with her legs crossed, resting her coat on her lap.

"Would you like me to hang that up?" he asked, before he took his seat.

She didn't respond, but he moved to the door and removed his coat from the hook, placing it on the floor over some files. "Thank you," she said, handing it over.

Her cheeks glowed red on her otherwise pale skin. He knew it was very cold outside but maybe she had been walking quickly, possibly to get there on time. Not quite flustered but hardly at ease, it seemed.

"Can I offer you a cup of tea or a glass of water?"

"No, thank you."

Tom reached for a notepad, put it to one side on his desk, then sat back to look at her. There seemed to be an unmistakeable grace and charm there, if not a raw beauty. Sitting opposite her was the last thing he had expected that afternoon. He felt his mood improve and his curiosity rise.

"My husband doesn't know I'm here," she said, after a moment's silence.

It was not the first time he had heard a female client say this to him. And he instinctively felt he was able to predict one of the several things she might say next. But instead of any of those things, she said something altogether unexpected.

"I will tell him tonight and he too may want to come and see you."

"Okay. That would be fine." He noticed a large diamond wedding ring on her left hand and that her nails were glossy and clear, manicured to perfection.

"This is not about your marriage?" he said, now aware his first thought had been wrong.

"No," she replied softly, shaking her head as she did so, avoiding his eyes.

He waited. It was always best to wait at the beginning, Alister had told him. There would be plenty of time later for questions. The first meeting was sometimes the most important and not everyone would know what to say or how to say it, yet a lot could be gleaned very quickly from how someone expressed themselves at this early stage. This meant allowing them to say what was on their mind, untouched by leading questions, as far as possible, he had wisely observed.

"It's about my brother." Again, he didn't expect that, her tone slow and deliberate, like she was thinking, almost forcing the words out.

"I see," he said.

"He's my younger brother. I have another brother, older."

He nodded.

"I've come to you because ... well ... because, I walk by here every day on my way home. It's not as if you've been recommended or I saw an advertisement or anything like that. Just the sign, at your entrance. It was almost a spontaneous thing, to come here. I knew ... Mr Greer, I've reached the stage where if I hadn't come in today, I may never have. I've put it off far too long. Maybe it's already too late, I'm afraid, probably far too late." Her eyes wandered from his, then returned. "I really don't know."

"That's perfectly fine. There are no rules about this sort of thing."

She bowed her head and fixed her gaze on her hands resting on her skirt, then she took a breath, as if relieved now that she had said something. She lifted her head. "I said I wasn't going to waste your time. I sincerely hope I don't."

"Please, by no means are you wasting my time. I would like to hear when you're ready. Please, feel under no pressure here at all. Just take your time. There's no rush, Mrs Morrow. I don't have any more appointments. I don't have to be anywhere."

"Thank you."

"Should we start with some of your details?" He took hold of the pad and pen. A laptop seemed impersonal to him at a first consultation and Alister's old-fashioned methods had rubbed off.

"Of course," she said, sitting upright, ready to start. "My name is Penny Morrow. My full name is Penelope Tarryn Morrow. I live in Marylebone, not that far from here. I work, well I own, with my husband, some shoe stores. One in Mayfair, or near there, and the other in Soho."

"I see," he said, scrawling some notes. "Your phone number?"

She gave him two and her postal address and email. "You can reach me on the mobile usually any time. I'm not in the shops every day but even if I am, I can usually take a call."

"You mentioned your brother," he said, placing the pen down.

"Yes. His name is Benny Longmire. Benjamin Berthold Longmire. My maiden name is Longmire."

"How long have you been married?"

"About seven years. Our anniversary was the week before, no, two weeks before he went missing."

"Benny, your brother?"

"Yes."

"I see."

"I *will* have a glass of water if I can, please," she said, seemingly agitated now.

"Of course." He buzzed Cathy for two glasses of water.

When the water arrived, Penelope took a sip and continued. "Benny had a shop. It was a second-hand LP record shop of sorts, memorabilia, that sort of thing. Not just records. All sorts of music things. I think he'd got into trouble with the bills, the rent. He didn't have the shop for long."

"Where was the shop?"

"It was in Norwich."

"I grew up in Norwich!" he said, excitedly, almost too quickly and he realised, now with heightened curiosity, it was irrelevant to her. This wasn't a chat in the pub and he didn't expect her to engage with him about all things great about the place. But she could tell now he was very interested.

"I've only been there once – the week after he went missing. I regret not going more."

"Where in Norwich exactly was the shop?"

"I can't tell you, except, well it was in the main part of town or near there somewhere. It's been some time. I have the address at home."

His mind canvassed the shops that might fit the category, but as he was never that interested in music, his thoughts failed him.

"How long did he have the store?"

"About six months."

"Did he set it up?"

"How do you mean?"

"Did he establish the shop or was it already there when he started it?"

"It was there. I think he bought it from an older fellow who wanted to retire. I'm not exactly sure."

"Why Norwich? Did he have some connection there?"

"I don't think so. I think he just found an advertisement regarding the sale. He had a friend from there, again, exactly when, I'm not sure, but he mentioned he knew someone from Norwich before he moved there."

"You said he went missing?"

"Well, he *is* missing. It's been more than four years, Mr Greer. The police have not been able to find any trace of him. I have exhausted all the things, all the people …" she said. Her eyes filled with more than just sadness now; despair was evident in her voice as it trailed off. Blinking slowly, she paused. "I've wasted too much time, thinking the police would do something. But they haven't."

"Was it news at the time? Was it reported by the press? I was in Norwich at that time, but I don't recall hearing about it."

"I'm not sure how much. Some, I think. I wasn't in Norwich for very long. The police didn't get involved for some time, almost a month after. I've spoken on the phone a lot to the police since then. Not so much recently. They didn't think there was anything suspicious at first."

"Why was that?"

"They told me it was not unusual for people who owed money to go underground for a while."

"And he owed money?"

"Some, apparently."

"To whom?"

"The landlord, some business people. Suppliers."

"Did the police interview them?"

"They said they did."

"Four years seems a long time to go underground. Even if one goes bankrupt, four years is plenty of time to choose not to be found. What do the police say now?"

"I haven't spoken to them for probably three months. And when I last did, they assured me he was on their case list. They first started to tell me they have a lot of missing persons. And most show up. But it started badly with them, in the sense they thought he just got up and left. That he abandoned the shop, rather than trade out of his financial difficulties. I tried to convince them that he was not at all the type to run away. It just wasn't in his character."

"You are close to your brother?"

"Yes. I would say, yes. I know who he is. He would not have just left without telling me what he was doing."

"Do you have the names of the police officers you've been dealing with?"

"My contact at Norwich was initially Sergeant Dorling but he retired and in the last few years it has been PC Donovan. I think he reports to Inspector Crossthwaite. He has recently transferred from Manchester."

"The inspector, Crossthwaite?"

"I believe so."

He looked at the clock on the wall and made some more notes. She checked her watch and then her phone. "I don't have any faith in the police, I'm afraid, Mr Greer. I'm sorry to say it. The fact that Benny's account has not been touched since the day, that day ..."

"How much is in the account?"

"The bank would not say originally but the police have told me it was less than two thousand pounds."

"What age is your brother?"

"He would be thirty."

"So, he was twenty-six when he went missing?"

"Yes."

"Was he married, or in a relationship? Any children?"

"No."

"How old are you, Penny? May I call you Penny?"

"Yes. I'm thirty-four. Mr Greer, do you think you can investigate, help somehow? I have no idea, anymore," she said, sighing and dropping her head momentarily, before lifting her eyes.

"Please, call me Tom. I'm certainly willing to try. I'm not that experienced with missing persons. But, look. What I lack in experience, I want to guarantee you I will try and make up in dedication. Plus, well, I know Norwich. Although for some reason, I can't place that shop. But I will find it. Is it still there?"

"No, I don't think so. I think the landlord sold off all the stock, or someone did. I don't know what it is now."

"Right."

"Mr Greer, Tom, it's been terrible. A horrific thing for our whole family. I can't begin to explain. It's been an overwhelming strain on my mother, my marriage and I lie awake at night wondering where he is, what has happened to him. I just … I can't … I just don't understand it. Just to come here today has taken all my courage. I'm constantly thinking about it, but I haven't been up to, I don't know, up to coming and seeing a private investigator."

When he saw tears welling in her eyes and there wasn't a tissue in sight, he felt he'd let her down already. She reached into her purse, pulled one out and blew her nose.

"I'm sorry," she said. "I should be going."

"Penny, please know that you don't need to rush away. I know it's very upsetting. Perhaps we should leave it there for today? Things should be easier from here and …"

She nodded and smiled so briefly it was near on undetectable.

"I'm able to get onto the case straight away, as it turns out. My workload at the moment is light. I will have Cathy email the fee documents and some information sheets and questionnaire. Fill out as much detail as you can, including the date he was last seen. Call me or Cathy if you have any questions with the documents. The first day will be free of charge."

"Thank you, Tom. I … I feel so much better, I think, for having come to see you. I was very anxious about it."

"No, thank you for choosing me. It will be an honour to help you and your family."

When she got up, he moved quickly to take her coat off the hook and opened the door. Pulling her coat on, she turned to him and held her arm straight out and shook his hand, steadying herself with some sense of minor relief.

"I will be in touch," he said.

* * * *

Determined to put all the nonsense of Brian, Gary and Gerhardt behind him, invigorated by the enchanting yet deeply saddened Penny and the connection to his old home town, the next morning he could not wait to get out the door of his flat and straight into the office. Shortly after walking into Edgware Road his phone rang.

"How's it all going, my boy?" Alister asked.

"Pretty good," he replied, the spring back in his step.

"You sounded a little down in the mouth about it all when we last spoke," Alister said, surprised but clearly delighted.

"Things have improved, somewhat."

"That's good. Listen, I've a new case for you. They originally wanted me to do it, but I'm too bloody old. I think it will suit you. And I said I wanted to talk to you and I'd get back to them."

"That would be brilliant. Thanks. What is it?"

"Look, I'm going to be in your part of town next week. Can we get together then? I will tell you all about it."

"Sounds fine. What day?"

"Let's say Wednesday. Would that suit?"

"Fine and dandy."

"I'll see you at the office. But I'll call before."

"Do that. See you then." As Tom hung up, he'd already decided to be out of the office until the middle of next week.

When he arrived at work, Tom hung up his coat and went straight into Jason's office. "Do you have a minute?" he asked.

"Sure, what's up?" Jason asked, not taking his eyes off his laptop. "Sit down."

Jason's large office was able to cater for three seats. Tom sat in the middle chair.

"I'd like to take a week off, but combine it with some work. I haven't taken any leave yet, as you know. I'd like to go home, to Norwich."

"Okay, it's not been very busy, so sounds fine to me."

"That's what I thought."

"You want to combine it, you said. What for? Why not just take a break? What the hell would you combine it with, in Norwich?"

"I saw a new client yesterday. A Penny Morrow. Very nice lady. Her brother's missing, last seen in Norwich, as it turns out. Very lovely lady, did I say that?"

"You said she's very nice. A missing person?"

"He's been missing for four years."

"Hmm, can she pay?"

"She owns two shoe stores."

"Have you checked her out?"

"I think she's fine."

"I've mentioned to you before, Tom, it's very important to check your clients out. It's the first thing you should do. Particularly, check out if they can pay our bills."

"I will."

"Get some money on account. These are time-consuming cases. Or at least get a bill to her fast, to see if she'll be a payer."

"I will." Sometimes Tom thought Jason was more a business owner than a private investigator, but he was conscious of the fact Jason had two roles whereas he needed to only focus on the investigation side of things, at this stage anyway.

Later that morning Tom followed up with a car dealer about a tidy little black Volkswagen Polo he had inspected a few weeks ago. By noon he had picked it up and got the dealer to throw in the cost of a reserved parking space for two weeks at a carpark not that far from where he lived, plus a month's fee for a resident parking permit in Westminster. Very pleased that he didn't have to catch the train to Norwich, he was soon on the road. This car was vastly different from the big vehicle that he had driven thousands of miles in Australia a couple of years ago. He felt low and close to the road in the Polo; perfect for the city. Tom was also perfectly pleased with his negotiation skills with the car dealer. He'd come a long way.

Before he was out of London proper, he realised that he'd forgotten all about serving the court document sitting in his in-tray. There wasn't much alternative now but to ring Cathy to ask her to delegate it to Jason or one of the others. More likely Jason would give Cathy the afternoon off to do it, rather than doing it himself he figured. He was glad he wasn't going to be around to hear Jason complain that he'd neglected it.

Wet weather had been forecast for Norfolk but by the time he reached Norwich, the rain clouds spreading to the east had cleared along with his mind. Patches of blue sky appeared and things were looking up now in more ways than one. Surprising his mother, and seeing his sister Rebecca, was all going to be a bonus. He might even visit Paddo's mother, Mrs Paddington-Smythe, before he returned to London, just to see how she was getting on.

But his impatience would dictate the very first thing he would do once he got to Norwich.

CHAPTER THREE

Tom flicked through the LP records from the £3 pile. He was really timing his approach to the counter, ready to pull out any random record to buy. A man stood behind the counter who he assumed was the owner.

"Thanks," Tom said, as he handed him the album and the money.

"It's in nice condition for the price," the man said.

"Yeah. You've got some really good stuff here," he replied, taking a step back to look at the pile behind him as he waited for his purchase. In truth, he had no idea what the difference was between the good stuff and the rest. This wasn't about the records.

"There are some more bargain bins up the back. Did you see them?" asked the man.

"No. I might come back when I have a bit more time. Have a real good look then. Listen, wasn't there another second-hand record shop in Norwich? I haven't been here for a few years and I can't seem to find it. Has it closed?"

"You mean, oh … what was it called? It was a bit out of town. Um … Excuse me." The man turned to serve another customer who handed him three albums with a twenty-pound note.

"I can't remember the name either," Tom said, scratching his ear.

The other customer turned to Tom. "Anti-Vale Vinyl," he said. "It was further down a bit. It's long gone, though. A shame, really. Pretty good store. And cheap," he added, looking at the owner as if he wanted him to take note.

"Right," Tom said, with a casual nod of acknowledgement.

"There's another shop," the record shop owner said. "It's been here even longer than I have. It's not as big as this and it's not far from here. You may want to see what he has. It's only a few lanes away."

"Where was Anti-Vale Vinyl again? I thought I had my bearings but …" He turned his head left then right as if checking his present location within the city, pretending he didn't know Norwich at all.

"I can't remember the street name," the customer replied, as he was handed his albums and change.

"Well, thanks. I'll drop in again," Tom said, as he collected the bag and headed out.

Instead of waiting for Penny to send the email with further information, including the address of the old record shop, he decided to see if he could employ some old-fashioned skills now that he was back in his old home town. Alister was always remarking about not having the internet in his day and that Tom would do well to learn the basics of deception and not rely too heavily on it. Soon he was in a tourist information centre asking for directions to Anti-Vale Vinyl, playing dumb as if it still existed. He approached an elderly gentleman, the older of two serving, in the hope he might have worked at the centre for some time and known of the shop. The man quickly confirmed it had closed about four years ago, much to customers' disappointment, including himself.

"It's a shoe shop now, quite fancy. A little expensive but my wife loves it," he said, and gave him the address after Tom said he might buy his girlfriend some shoes anyway, as a surprise. He didn't have a girlfriend. He'd never had a girlfriend. But there had been a few fleeting romances, mostly lasting less than two weeks.

Fifteen minutes later Tom was outside the shop. He looked at his watch and realised it wasn't far off closing time, but he wasn't interested in going inside and looking at shoes. Instead, he took a photo on his phone and sent it with the address to his mapping contact, who sent him back the title particulars of the freehold. He then sent the lot number and plan details to his title searching agents who then sent him details of the owner of the land and building.

He sat on a bench opposite the shoe shop and read the reports. It was a company owner, so he did a company extract search and within a matter of five minutes, he had the names of what was clearly the husband and wife directors and their residential address. Handily, the address was in Norfolk, but somewhere with which he was only vaguely familiar. The man was born in London in 1943 and his wife was born in Belfast in 1944. Not only were they in their senior years, but the freehold title had been owned by the company for more than 28 years. He sat thinking about that information for a minute and by the time he got up and decided to go back to his car, he'd concluded that whilst Mr and Mrs Cable warranted a visit, they were likely conservative, held the property as a source of income and perhaps had more than one investment property. But, he surmised, they would know nothing of the whereabouts of their tenant of four years ago.

On the walk back to the car, the thought crossed his mind to call his mother, deciding instead he would stick to his plan to surprise her. Hungry and with his mind starting to turn to food, he grew pleased with himself that his timing for dinner couldn't be better.

When he got to his mother's house, he wandered around the side to the window near the kitchen. He'd always hoped that one day he would have grown tall enough to peer clearly inside, but it never eventuated. Rosemary was in the kitchen and she was indeed surprised to see her son's blonde curly hair and his face peering up with a big smile.

"Hi, Mum!"

"Tom! What are you doing out there?"

Late afternoon; it was almost but not quite too late for tea and scones with strawberry jam and cream. A childhood favourite. Rosemary whipped them up in what seemed like no time and soon they were in the kitchen chatting.

"I'm sorry I didn't call you. I thought about it though," he said, scoffing his second helping down.

"That's fine. It's just so lovely to see you! I was going to call you today."

"Is Rebecca home soon?"

"No. She's working late tonight. How have you been? Is everything okay? I haven't heard from you for ages. Sometimes I worry you're alright."

"It's all good. I'm on a job in Norwich, in fact. I thought I would come and stay, if that's alright. It will just be for a couple of nights, that's all."

"Well, yes. Of course. A job! What sort of job is it?"

"I probably shouldn't say, Mum."

"That's perfectly fine. Just so happy to see you! I don't think I really want to know, anyway. If you'd told me you were coming, I could have taken some meat out of the freezer."

"Let's go and get some from the supermarket, shall we? We can go in my new car. Come and see."

On the way, he asked her whether she still had the special dripping she kept in the freezer, frozen from previous roast dinners. Of course she did so he asked if she could do one of her special roast dinners. Soon after their return from the market, the familiar smell of the roasting meat and vegetables simmering away filling every corner of the flat reminded him he was home. As he sat at the kitchen table, occasionally looking at the oven, he told her about the Polish girls he lived with, the pubs he went to, and eventually, the people he worked with.

"When are you going to meet a nice girl and settle down, like your friend Paddo? Do you see each other much? What's his lady's name again?" she asked, getting in as many questions in one mouthful as she could think of asking.

"Bessy. I saw them a couple of weeks ago. Settling down is not in my nature, I don't think. I'll leave that to the settlers. People don't settle down anymore, anyway. That's what you did years ago. My lifestyle would not suit a relationship, at the moment."

"How's Paddo's mother doing since all that sadness involving her husband?"

"Paddo said she seems to be doing quite well. Better than he thought she would. She was disappointed that he took the job in London. Kind of ironic, as she was once very keen on him moving there. Things have changed a bit for her. I think she's possibly a bit lonely. I might go and visit her before I go back."

"That would be very thoughtful of you. Where is Paddo working?"

"He's studying and working. The job is with the Department for Environment, Food and Rural Affairs."

"Bessy was a lovely girl. What's she doing?"

"She's studying nursing."

"Lovely."

Rebecca arrived home after dinner and gave him a hug. She kept him up late talking. It was always good to sleep in his old bed in his old room. His mother's bedroom used to be his parents' room before the divorce. After that, his father moved to Canterbury where he set up a bakery. There had been no contact for at least five years. He thought about that and how the years had slipped away quickly as he rested his head on the pillow and dozed off.

* * * *

Up early next day, he fixed himself bacon and eggs and asked Rosemary if he could leave the washing up, eager to get on the road.

"That's fine. Where are you going this morning? Oh, sorry, I shouldn't ask, should I?"

"I'll see you this afternoon. Let me take you out to dinner. Tell Rebecca to keep it free, as well, when she gets up."

A kiss and a hug and soon he was on the road heading in the direction of Cromer on the A140. The directions told him it was near, but not actually in the village of Sustead where he would find the Cables. The navigation did not lead him easily and directly to their house. Eventually he found it and drove up what seemed like a never-ending driveway. When he rang the doorbell on the front door he was by no means certain that Mr and Mrs Cable would be inside. But he was dead certain the yapping little dog that had been set off by his arrival would surely greet him first.

Sure enough, when the door opened, the Norwich terrier sprang out and asserted itself, continuing with its barking. Although as soon as the man said, "It's alright, Kepler, calm down," it seemed friendly enough.

Before Tom could utter a word, Kepler obeyed his master's order and reverted to a sniffing session around his shoes.

"Sorry about that, can I help you?" said the man, slowly. Tom noted his facial whiskers were similar to that of Kepler's, except they were a tad lighter grey. His eyes seemed kind. Certainly not the kind that would be part of something untoward, on first impression.

"Thank you. Good morning. I'm awfully sorry to disturb you. I'm trying to track down an old friend of mine. I was wondering whether you may be able to help me?"

"An old friend?" the man said.

At this time an elderly lady appeared and stood next to the man. They were both shorter than Tom, very short indeed and almost identical in height and width. Kepler ran off into the front garden through the open door.

"Yes. So sorry to bother you. It's just that, I thought you may be able to help."

"How would we be able to help? Who is your friend?" the man asked, seemingly confused.

"Sorry. I should introduce myself. My name is Ed. And you are the Cables? Yes?"

"That's right," the lady said.

"He told me, my friend, he was renting from you, some years ago now."

"He did?" Mr Cable said, and in such a way that it seemed interesting and surprising news to him. Perhaps his eyes were not just kind but showing some kind of vacancy behind them. On the other hand, Mrs Cable seemed more in tune with what was going on. She stepped to the front.

"What's his name?" she said.

"Ben Longmire."

"What did he say?" asked Mr Cable, as he turned to his wife.

"He said Ben someone," she said.

"Longmire," Tom said.

"I don't know a Ben Longmire," she said.

"Ben who?" Mr Cable said.

"You said he was a tenant of ours?" Mrs Cable asked, ignoring her husband for the moment.

"Yes. In Norwich. He had a second-hand record store several years back."

"The what?" said Mr Cable.

"Oh yes, now I remember him. We haven't seen him in years. He just walked out, I think. Just left the premises. We were surprised. He was a bit of a strange one," she said.

"Well, he's a good friend of mine. To be honest, I'm worried about him. You have no idea where he might have gone?"

"No dear, I'm sorry. The police came and asked us that years ago. We only met him a few times."

"Did he leave you out of pocket, rent-wise I mean?"

"I think he did, from memory," she said. "A good few thousand pounds. We had to get an agent in and sell his things. I thought he would have shown up by now."

"The record man," Mr Cable said.

"Yes. This man is a friend of his."

"Oh."

The dog seemed to be enjoying a stroll around the front garden. Apparently, the dog didn't get out much and perhaps neither did the Cables. Tom knew there was no merit in bothering these kind people any longer.

"I thank you very much for your time. And I appreciate your courtesy," he said.

"Well, I hope you find your friend," Mrs Cable said.

"Thank you, and good day to you."

"Good day," Mr Cable said, calling Kepler over, letting him in and gently closing the door.

* * * *

As Tom took the drive back to Norwich, he decided to test the radio. When the first song was a heavy metal classic, it reminded him that he'd had a friend at university who was in a band called 'Tickled Pink

69'. And he remembered that his friend had a large collection of LP records that were mainly heavy metal. Before the song had finished it also occurred to him that it was highly likely he would have known Anti-Vale Vinyl, and he too was worth a visit, if he could track him down.

Tom parked the car on the street that Steve Rubis used to live in with his other band members. It was only a few miles from his own street. He realised that he hadn't seen Steve for a good two years at least and the chances of him still living in the same place, knowing Steve, seemed remote. Steve had not been popular with landlords. His feeling proved right when the lady who answered the door said it was no longer rented but that 'Stephen' had moved around the corner to a small disused warehouse. She told him exactly where it was.

The jam session was well underway. It seemed he had the right place and Steve hadn't changed. When his knocks on the door went unnoticed, he realised getting inside would be another matter.

"Who are you?" said a girl five minutes later after a pause in the music and several more bangs on the door.

"I'm a friend of Steve's. Is he in?" She didn't answer, leaving the door wide open and went back inside. After no one appeared for a good while, he took a few steps in anyway, and Steve then appeared.

"Hey man, what's up! Great to see you, stranger, what are you doing here?" Steve said, bounding up to him like a lost puppy and giving Tom a massive bear hug. Tom's face was squashed under Steve's armpit, then he received a hard slap on the back, almost knocking the stuffing out of him. He'd always liked Steve, even though it was apparent Steve didn't seem to like showers much.

"I'm in Norwich for a bit and I thought I'd stop by. How are you, old son? Great to see you!" he said, although his enthusiasm in saying it masked some degree of insincerity. Time had passed and it occurred to him that whilst it had, things may have stayed still for Steve. They'd had drinking and partying in common and that's not what he was here for.

"Sweet. I'm bloody fantastic. Come in, come in to the parlour!" He led him down through a narrow space filled with bicycles that opened into a large living area converted to a session room, full of musical equipment, tables, couches and junk.

"Jen, this is Tom," Steve said to the girl who had opened the door.

"Hi," Jen said in a mildly patronising tone and with apparent disinterest as she sat on a couch and studied something on her phone.

"Tom, this is Kino." Tom held out his hand to a young man of Asian appearance who held an electric guitar and wore a bandanna on his head. "He's a good lad. Been in the band for the last year. Kino gives our music a Korean, wicked, slashed edge."

"Nice to meet you," Tom said, and shook Kino's hand.

"Hey, dude, would you like a drink, a bourbon, a whisky, what about a smoke? Kino has some good shit." Tom thought he could smell the 'good shit' as soon as he walked in.

"No, I'm fine, but thanks anyway."

"Are you sure? I'm going to have a whisky." He went into another room that looked to be a kitchen of some sort and told Tom to follow him.

"Pretty neat space, what do you think?"

"Pretty cool, man," he replied, looking at the empty beer cans on the floor, the ashtrays filled with butts and a garbage bin that might just fit another empty bottle on top. Another landlord's agony. Steve lit a cigarette and rested his back against the sink.

"Lad, what brings you to town? Are you hanging around for a while? We got a gig tonight. You should come and see us. It's gonna be a hoot."

"I've just come back for a few nights to visit my mum."

"Sweet." Kino strummed a few chords that would have made further conversation impossible.

"Hey, Kino! Knock it off, would ya!" Steve said, as he went back into the other room. When he returned to Tom he told him to come out to the courtyard where they sat down.

"What have you been doing anyway? I heard you moved to London or something." Steve took an enormous drag on his cigarette and Tom noticed that he had substantially added to his tattoo collection and bulked up.

"Yeah, I did. I have, a year ago."

"Cool. What are you doing there?"

"Working with a private investigation firm."

"Wow! You private eye, you." He took a swig on the whisky bottle. "You sure you don't want one?" he asked, pointing the top of the bottle in his direction. "I can get you a glass."

"No, I'm good."

"How does that pay, anyway? Any good? Are you pulling in the big bucks?"

"Just employee's wages at the moment. London is bloody expensive. I don't have much left after paying the rent and for my daily pint intake."

"Ha! Yeah well, we did our first tour of America last year."

"Really?"

"Yeah, it was just small bars and shit. Hovels really, but it was awesome fun."

"Great. How long did you go for?"

"Two weeks. We mainly hung around in LA. Man, there's some wild shit there! Nothing like Norwich. Full on, all the fuckin' time."

Trying to figure a way of getting to what he'd come to see him about proved naturally difficult. But he had time.

"We're making our first album. It'll be out in a month."

"Brilliant. What's its title?"

"We haven't decided yet. It will probably be 'Prisons of the Mind'. That was Kino's idea. But I like 'Bringing Back the Barbarian'. That's the first track on the record."

"They're both cool. Speaking of records, are you still into collecting albums? LPs?"

"I was, but some bastard stole my entire set. It pissed me off big time. Don't remind me."

"That's a shame."

"It was more than a shame, man. I mean, I'd been doing it since I was a kid! Some of that shit was irreplaceable. Priceless. If I ever get my hands on the prick who did that to me, I'll kill him."

Tom shook his head. "Yeah, that's really low, to do that. I've actually started to get into collecting myself," he said, thinking that was not entirely a lie, given he had purchased his first vinyl LP the day before. He made a mental note to get it out of the backseat of the car, someday.

"Keep them safe, man, that's all I can say."

"I was looking for that place, actually, that LP shop called Anti-Vale Vinyl. But it's closed down."

"Yeah, it's gone. Lots of stuff is gone. I don't much like Norwich, anymore. We'll probably move to London soon. Or Canada, something like that."

"The guy who owned that shop apparently really knew his stuff. Did you ever buy stuff there?"

At that moment, Jen walked out into the little fenced yard. She walked by Tom as if he didn't exist, grabbed Steve's pony tail and twirled it sensuously. "Babe, I need to go and get some cigarettes," she said. "Do you want anything?" Her denim cut-off shorts left little to the imagination and Tom tried hard not to stare at her long, smooth, brown legs.

"Get me a bottle of cola," he said. "Cold," he added. Tom was pretty sure his last question didn't register with Steve and he didn't want to spook him by repeating it, exactly.

But as soon as Jen left, Tom was surprised when he said, "I only went there a few times. I didn't like him. The new owner. The old guy before was okay, but the new guy, he was a know-it-all. He had some albums you couldn't find anywhere else but he was arrogant as all hell and expensive."

Some information was always better than none. It seemed to contradict what the customer in the store had said yesterday about it being cheap. But now, he had someone he actually knew who had been to the store, and even had an opinion about Benny. If he timed it right, he may even be in a position later to get some more detail, if Steve had any. But pressing on about an out-of-context topic of conversation for too long was a sure-fire way of raising suspicion. He had committed that error once before. And he didn't want to let on that he was making enquiries. That he was on a job.

"What are you doing tonight?" Steve said, almost immediately after that.

"Taking my mum and my sister out to dinner."

"Well, why don't you come to the gig after that? Bring them along, at least your sister."

"Where is it?"

"At the Zephyr."

"What time?"

"We usually come on about 10, maybe a little after. It depends if Fratto Boy is running the show."

"Fratto Boy?"

"Our new manager. He's another bloody know-it-all."

Keen to leave now, but knowing it was wise to be polite, Tom made small talk for another fifteen minutes until Jen returned. He watched Steve fill a pint glass with one-third whisky and two-thirds cola. Stories of the parties thrown by his Polish flatmates seemed to entertain Steve who said he would pay him a visit as soon as the album was released, bringing him a signed copy. Going to the gig was not out of the question, and if he played his cards right, finding out something more about Benny might be possible.

When he got back to his mother's place, he pulled his shoes off and sat on the corner of his bed, closed the door and called Penny.

"Did you get the fee agreement?" Tom asked her.

"Yes."

"Are you happy with it?"

"Yes. I am."

"And what about the questionnaire? Did Cathy send that to you?"

"Thank you, yes. I have sent it all back to Cathy, signed."

"It's probably best that you come and see me again when I get back to London. I'll be back from Norwich on Wednesday. When you get off the phone, book in with Cathy at a time that suits you. Any time Thursday or Friday would be good for me."

"Okay. I'm scared to ask whether you have found anything. I know it's early days."

"Well, not really. I went to the address of the old record shop and paid a visit to the landlords. They live in another part of Norfolk. I don't think they can help us. Did you know the place is a shoe store now?"

"No. I didn't. I put the address in the questionnaire answers, but you found it already?"

"It's now an upmarket shoe shop. I didn't go in but I took some photos."

"That's odd," she said.

"What, that it's a shoe store?"

"Well, yes. I didn't expect it, I guess. Given I own shoe stores."

"Where did your brother live in Norwich? Did you ever go to his place?"

"Yes. I do have that address. I put it in the answers on the form as his last known address."

"That's good, Penny. You said you only went to Norwich once, after he went missing. What about his possessions and things at his house? Where are they now?"

"It was a flat. My brother, my other brother, took care of all that, some months – two or three months – later."

"And does your brother still have his possessions? Or do you have some?"

"He has most of them. He gave me some things. Benny didn't have a lot."

"Where is your other brother?"

"He lives in Camden."

"Did Benny live with anyone?"

"No. He lived alone. His flat was a small, one bedroom."

"Would you describe your brother as a loner?"

"No. I don't think loners could run a shop, do you?"

"Probably. Maybe not very well," he added as an afterthought.

"Why do you ask?"

"No particular reason. I will have to ask a lot of questions. Some may sound odd to you."

"I understand."

"What about arrogant?"

"Benny? I wouldn't say he was arrogant. He knew what he knew. Sometimes he had a short fuse and wouldn't suffer fools. Independent, a bit single minded, rather than arrogant. He knew a lot about music, its history. Ever since he was a kid, he had a strong interest in it. I saw him get annoyed a few times with people who thought they knew more than he did, but you'd be hard pressed to find someone who knew as much."

"Do you think that's why he bought the shop? Because it was a hobby, a passion?"

"Yes, probably. He hadn't told us he was thinking about it. I was a bit surprised because he never had a lot of money."

"He was working before that, in London?"

"Some odd jobs in retail here and there. He'd enrolled in a university course in his early twenties but dropped out."

"Okay. We can talk more next week. I'll see you then, Penny."

* * * *

At dinner that evening Tom asked Rebecca had she heard of the band 'Tickled Pink 69'.

"Yeah. I saw them a couple of weeks back at the Zephyr," she replied.

"What sort of music do they play?"

"The rubbish sort."

"Oh, you didn't like them, I'm gathering."

"No. It was loud and it was impossible to hear any of the lyrics, not that I wanted to. Long distorted slash, I couldn't really say what you would describe it as. Why?"

"I have a friend in the band. The lead singer. They're playing at the Zephyr again tonight. He invited me."

"You might think they're okay."

He left his mother and Rebecca at 9.30 and was at the Zephyr in time to catch the first set but left after that, making sure Steve had seen him there. Conversation was going to be difficult and the timing didn't seem right to try.

* * * *

First thing the next morning, he checked his email from Cathy and headed straight to Benny's old residential address. Finding it in a suburban street with a regular row of housing not that far out of the main part of the city, it was largely what he expected. He had an early lunch in town before visiting Paddo's mother, then headed back home in the late afternoon for another of his mother's roasts.

As he took the exit out of Norwich the next day, it crossed his mind to turn back and drop in to the police station to see if he could have a chat with PC Donovan, but there would be plenty of time for that later. Pleased that he'd made a start and had a break, he felt ready to start some serious investigation concerning the missing Benny Longmire when he was back in London.

CHAPTER FOUR

Despite Marzena and Helena, Tom's flatmates, doing their utmost to convince him to come out drinking with them to celebrate his mini 'holiday' and life in general – there didn't always have to be a reason – when he got back to the flat the only thing on his mind was getting back to work. With his passion reignited, he wanted to have two alcohol-free days and perhaps do some exercise. This was most unlike him and the girls giggled, and told him they were mildly impressed, albeit surprised.

For exercise, it was a stroll around Hyde Park, thinking. Thinking about Benny and what type of person he was from the limited picture he had, and what things he could do next to assist Penny.

The questionnaire clients were asked to fill out could be tailored to some specific things that might prove relevant and just may provide some insight into factors to consider. Most of it was seeking detailed information about the client themselves. He wasn't familiar with whether other firms had this approach, but he thought it was a good idea. The addresses for the shoe shops owned by Penny and her husband, held as assets in their personal names, were given in the answers and he decided to extend his exercise by walking from the park to both shops.

Similar in size and almost identical in layout, at least to the extent he could see from outside peering in, both shops seemed largely what he expected. Even the store in Mayfair seemed less up-market than the shop that had taken over the old Anti-Vale Vinyl site. But he knew he was certainly no expert on shoes and hadn't gone into the store in Norwich. It was obvious the stores stocked female shoes only. Making an appearance in one or the other might be a good idea, but he decided it was better to wait until his 9 am appointment on Thursday to see Penny. It was the first time he could recall he was actually looking forward to seeing a client.

By the time he had arrived at the office on Wednesday he'd forgotten all about Alister's intention to see him that day. Cathy was already in his office filing and told him that Alister had called the afternoon before and made an appointment for 10 am. "I didn't let you know because he said he'd spoken to you already," she added.

"That's fine. He had but … it's fine. Thanks," he said, as she handed him a cup of black coffee.

"What's up?" she said.

"Nothing. I'd just rather not see Alister today, that's all. I'd best though."

"You're always telling me how good he's been to you, Tom."

"Oh, he has. He's been very helpful, in every respect. In fact, I'd like to talk to him about Penny Morrow's case, just to see what he thinks. He's got some other matter for me."

"That's good, isn't it?"

"Sort of."

Alister had lost most of what Scottish accent he had first possessed and despite his age, was a man young in appearance and at heart. When he arrived, he was dressed exactly the same way as always – brown wool trousers, smart white shirt, a good-quality patterned vest, and tweed jacket.

"How have you been, my boy?" he asked, as he sat down in Tom's office smiling broadly and leaned back on the chair.

"Better of late. I've just had a couple of days off. Feeling loads better than I was a few weeks ago. I won't bore you with why. Not necessary. How have you been?"

"I'm fine. Look, you're going to get your ups and downs in this crazy job, just like any other, as I tell all my students. You can't let it get to you. You need to get used to riding the waves and not get all down about it. There's always something around the corner that will keep you going." Ever the counsellor and voice of experience, it all didn't seem that significant now, as finally a decent case had arrived, just like Alister had promised. Amazed from the beginning just how kind and upbeat Alister was, despite some of the nasty things he might have witnessed over the years, he was an inspiration and now a friend, not just a mentor.

"It seems you might be right," Tom said.

"I am right, my boy! Now listen, I have this job if you want it. I'd like you to take it, if you could. They're dear old friends of mine. I haven't seen them in a few years but we speak regularly. Whenever I am up in Inverness, which sadly isn't very often anymore, I always see them."

"Inverness?"

"Ah huh," Alister nodded, and sat more upright on the edge of his seat. "Broden and Coira Paterson. They're dog breeders. Pedigree, in fact. Mainly beagles, I believe. They go to shows. Have done so for years. In fact, I went to one of their shows once, back in the late eighties. In their prime, they were, then. They've been doing it for a very long time. Love it." Now resting his elbows on the desk with fingers intertwined, he could see Tom had a blank look on his face. "You may want to take some notes," he added, pointing to the desk.

Hardly enthusiastically, Tom withdrew a fresh notepad from his drawer and placed it on his desk.

"Anyway, there has been a bit of trouble of sorts lately. It's apparently been going on for some time. The police have been called but it's the usual bloody story. Not that concerned, not a priority and short staffed and all the usual guff. Sometimes the police get obsessed about things they shouldn't but this isn't one that they're much interested in."

"What's the trouble?" he asked, wondering what beagles and trouble could possibly have in common.

"I'm getting to that. Anyway, one morning about six months ago, they found one of their beagles dead in his kennel. Then another died about a month later. Since then, there have been another two, or perhaps three. I don't know exactly how many. A lot. All deliberately killed."

"How many dogs do they have?"

"I don't know. But they're breeders, not puppy farmers."

"What's the difference?"

"A lot, apparently. Certainly, to them. Whilst they breed, it's a side business. It's not really even a business to them. They're into show dogs and owning for companionship. The numbers vary. The puppy farmers just supply to the public, they run it as a business. According to Broden, the issue of puppy farming is very controversial."

"Why?"

"Well, as far as I've gathered, because of the treatment of the dogs – welfare and care issues. I mean, Broden and Coira treat their dogs like members of their family. In fact, they *are* members of their family. So, you can imagine when they lost several. Generally, the puppy farmers, who don't call themselves that, have no attachment to the dogs, nor do they want to. They just meet the demand."

"Maybe the puppy farmers have a point, provided the dogs are treated properly?"

"Don't say that to Broden and Coira when you meet them, whatever you do! They think all commercial breeders are just puppy farmers."

"I'm sure like any industry there are people who are there to exploit and do the wrong thing but …"

"Yes," Alister interrupted him. "But remember, when emotion gets involved, things can be seen differently. Take that on board, my boy. Very differently. Broden and Coira are elderly. They're in an absolute state about all this and they've asked me to look into it. I can't do it, but you can. What do you think?" He sat back in his chair.

"You think they're being targeted? Being thrown in with the puppy farmers?"

"Possibly. It needs to be considered. Something you need to look into. There's a lot of extremists out there and do-gooders. Some are misguided."

"That means I would have to go to Inverness."

"Yes. Of course. But you can stay with them. They live in a castle, well, almost a castle. They've got a huge estate. You'll love it."

Tom ran his hand across his mouth. The last thing he felt like doing was leaving again. Just when he was ready to sink his teeth further into the case of Benny Longmire. Scratching his scalp he said, "I've just got a new matter, Alister. Just been to Norwich investigating. It's just beginning. I've got some commitments here. I'm really eager to progress *that* if I can. It's the best case I've ever had."

"What sort of a case is it?"

"I was going to mention it to you. A missing person."

"Who and how long missing?"

"A thirty-year-old male. Four years."

"Alright, well, he'll still be missing by the time you get back."

With one eyebrow raised, he gave Alister his trademark cheeky smile, but this wasn't funny. Alister held his stare and smiled too. "Look, it would mean a lot to me if you could leave straight away," he said.

"You're sure you can't go? Wouldn't you like to see your friends?"

"To be honest, yes and no. But, look, not under these circumstances. It's very hard to mix this type of business and pleasure. As I said, they are in a state. Grieving, confused and frustrated. It's not very compatible with sitting around enjoying a glass of sherry and talking about the good old days, if you get my drift. Not when their dogs are being killed and the cops won't help."

He had taken no notes as there was only one thing he needed to note. It would hardly be fair to let Alister down, and it would be more than a tad imprudent to refuse this job, one given directly by his mentor. The firm could also use the money.

"I'll do it," he said.

"Thank you, my boy. I knew you would." He sat back up. "I'll get in touch with them. They will pay for your flight and your hire car. I'll email all the details. They're loaded. So, you will not need to worry about the money. Do a good job. I would be very grateful, my boy."

Tom would have to tell Penny that he had to go to Scotland for a while – exactly how long he was not sure. He was pleased to be busier but disappointed to be leaving. After he got back, he would concentrate on her matter. That was a given and she would understand. The dogs would take priority for now, but he wouldn't tell her that.

* * * *

By the time 9 am arrived the next day he was already booked on a flight to Inverness at 10 am the following day. Cathy was thrown into a spin to get it all arranged and after Jason found out, he decided he would dump several court documents on her desk, to be served on people spread across the city, that he had intended to give to Tom.

"Penny Morrow is here to see you, with another gentleman," Cathy said, as she arrived in his office with an extra chair.

"Another gentleman?"

"Yes. I didn't get his name."

"Cathy, could you please get the names … never mind."

"Sorry, Tom. I've got to get out the door. I'm overloaded!"

When Tom went to the waiting area to greet them, Penny and the man with her stood up. "Please meet my husband, Edgar," Penny said. Edgar shook his hand firmly with a parcel tucked under his other arm, a box that looked like a shoebox – a good-quality, large, red cardboard box with a black lid.

"We thought we would come together. I hope that's alright," Penny said, as they entered his office and he closed the door.

"That's fine. Very good idea. Please, take a seat."

"I've brought you all the papers and documents that we have relating to Ben," Edgar said, as they all sat down.

"Very good."

"There are some photographs in there as well. Maybe it's best we show them to you," Penny said. "I haven't shown you a photo of Benny yet."

Tom moved some items away to clear a space for the box which Edgar placed in front of him.

"This is the very last photo we have of him," Penny said, as Edgar handed a framed photo to Tom. "It's not the original. I had it enlarged from the original. It was taken in his shop." Clearly visible from behind the counter, Benny was looking directly at the camera, smiling. A happy man.

"I think it may have been taken the day he took over the business," Penny said. "There's a copy of the lease in the box as well. It was a three-year lease."

"He looks very pleased," Tom said, studying the photo.

"That's what we thought," Edgar said. "It was his first business. I think he was very proud."

"Who would have taken this photo?"

"We think maybe an employee or a friend," Penny replied.

"He only had one employee we think, but she may not have started straight away," Edgar added.

"Right," Tom said, still looking at the photo. "You have some others there?"

Penny picked up a whole collection of others from the box. "Some of these are quite old. They're all copies. I have the originals at home. Some, like this one," she said, handing it to him, "are when he was a teenager. This one is in my parents' yard." She handed him another. "This one here is on his school graduation day. That's my parents standing next to him."

Looking carefully at each photo, even studying them for their exposure and composition, he was naturally interested. "I studied photography in Norwich. Actually got a degree. These are all quite beautiful photos. And who is this?" he asked.

"That's my brother, Michael," she replied. He looked at the box. It was filled to the brim with many more photos and documents.

"The other items are a mixture of paperwork and things that we found at his flat and at the shop," Edgar said. "I don't know if you will find any of it useful. Unknown to us, the police collected some other items from his shop. It was a while before they gave them all back."

Edgar was obviously older than Penny, perhaps five years or more. Tom noticed he was casually dressed, but quite smartly, as was she.

"Penny mentioned you've already been to Norwich, Mr Greer," Edgar said.

"Yes. Please call me Tom."

"Something about seeing the landlords?"

"Well, yes. Have you met them?"

"No. Should we?" asked Penny.

"I don't think so. I took a drive out to their property. They're quite old and the man, well, he's a little hard of hearing. It didn't strike me they could be of much help. They've moved on."

"We haven't moved on, Tom," Edgar said. He put his hand on Penny's which was resting in her lap and looked at her.

"Yes. You can't move on from this sort of thing," Tom said, regretting his choice of words.

"It's been years and quite frankly, it's torn us all apart. We can't tell you how hard it's been. It simply doesn't make sense to us. I would really like to put in some sort of complaint about the police." Edgar shook his head and turned again to Penny, before looking back at Tom. "But I've been told that's not a good idea as we may need them. They've been useless, I have to say, Tom."

"Penny mentioned it took them some time to get serious about it."

"The time that was lost was unforgivable, simply unforgivable," Edgar replied. "I'm quite annoyed with them and how they approached it from the beginning."

"The police, I'm sure, would have got around to asking you a lot of questions that I'm going to ask you. I want to make some apologies for that, at the outset."

"We understand," Edgar said.

"The obvious one is, did Benny have enemies? I mean, you said he owed money, Penny. The rent. The old couple confirmed that. But they weren't an enemy. They seemed to have no malice towards him at all, in fact."

"Not that we know of," Edgar said, and Penny shook her head in agreement.

"As far as the money is concerned, this is another mystery," Penny said. "I know for a fact that Benny used to borrow money from my mother. She never had a problem in giving it to him."

"Would lending money leave your mother short?"

"No. Not at all. She is quite wealthy. She could have given him thousands. And she was never principled about it. I would refuse to take it … I would never allow her to give me money but she gave it to Benny freely and he wasn't like me. He had no problem in asking my mother. So, I don't quite understand why he would be short of money. I tried to explain that to the police."

"What did they say?"

"They said it was clear he owed money. Not a lot, but some."

"Didn't he get the original money to buy the shop from your mother?" asked Edgar, turning to his wife.

"Some of it, otherwise he couldn't have done it," she replied.

"You will find a letter of demand from the solicitor for the landlord in the box," Edgar said. "For the rent."

"My brother, Michael, has some of his other possessions. Mostly furniture and household items and the like. My mother has some other paperwork but I don't think you will find it of any use," Penny said. "She still has his birth certificate."

"What about a car? Did he have one?"

"Yes. It's in storage. It's a Renault of some sort. Small," Edgar said. "There was no money owing on it."

"Did he have a passport?"

"No," Penny said. "He never travelled. Not out of the UK."

"In what state was his flat left? Was there evidence he had packed a bag?"

"No. It's like he just vanished. He even left his toothbrush."

"Do you think you can help us, Tom?" asked Edgar.

"Well, as I mentioned to Penny, I'm most willing to try. I need to think a little bit more about where we go from here. Are you happy for me to talk to the police, if they will talk to me?"

"Yes. Most definitely. We want you to talk to anyone, anyone at all you think might assist," Penny said.

"Can you remember the last time you spoke with him?"

"Yes. It was just a matter of days before this all happened. He was thinking of coming to London for a few days. I remember it because I was with Mum at the time."

"On the phone?"

"Yes. He called me on my mobile on the Saturday afternoon. He said he'd finished work for the day."

"Did he say why?"

"No. I don't think so. He said he was busy but just thinking about it. I think at that stage, he hadn't seen her since he'd bought the shop. My mother doesn't travel anymore."

"To visit your mother, possibly?"

"Possibly, I don't know. I so wish I'd asked why he was thinking of coming to London, but of course I didn't think anything of it."

"What day of the week did he go missing? I know you've given me some dates, but what day of the week was it again?"

"It was the following Friday after that phone call. He was last seen closing after work on the Thursday."

"By whom?"

"By some customers the police interviewed. And, also the lady next door. She owns a small book shop."

"What about the employee?"

"She wasn't the last to see him. She always left earlier than he did. He'd stay and close up," she said.

"And you said you went to Norwich? And when did you find out he was missing?"

"We went to Norwich for about a week," Edgar said. "The police contacted Penny and notified her he was reported missing. That the shop had failed to open after several days and they'd knocked on his door after the employee had called them. We got into his flat, tried to reach him on the phone. Talked to some neighbours. Spoke to the lady who worked for him. Nothing. Penny rang him a few times before that. Just to see how he was going. When she couldn't reach him on his mobile, she rang the shop but there was no answer, so we had already started to wonder what was going on. Eventually we went to Norwich to see what was going on."

"I see," Tom said. "And when did the police get more involved?"

"From about that time, but they hardly did much, not immediately," Penny said.

"Did they examine his flat?"

"Yes."

"Were there any signs of anything? Food on the counter, things left undone?"

"No. My brother is quite a tidy person. His flat was immaculate."

Tom glanced at Edgar, whose gaze was fixed on him, and opened his laptop. He noticed that Penny had the same sad look on her face as the first time he'd met her. He typed some notes and said, "Unfortunately, I have to go to Scotland tomorrow on another matter. I'm not exactly certain how long I will be. But when I get back, I will be in touch again and give this matter utmost priority. If either of you can think of anything that might be relevant, and I mean anything, no matter how trivial you think it is, email me. I would also like you to email me a list of past employers, the name of the employee you referred to, if you have it, any contact details you have for her, and the contact details for his close friends. And, was his phone ever found?"

"No. It wasn't in the flat. It was the only thing missing. His phone was disconnected by the provider weeks after he went missing and no one has ever seen the phone. He doesn't have a lot of friends. Would you say that to be a fair statement, darling?" Edgar said.

"There are some friends. He had no social media presence. I keep saying 'had' instead of talking in the present. It gets me down." She paused as if to gather her thoughts and bowed her head, pressing her hand against her brow. She sighed and looked up, attempting to refocus on the task at hand. "The business didn't even have a website, though he mentioned he wanted to set one up. He only had a work computer at the shop. The police have that. In fact, that's something we don't have," Penny said, looking at Edgar.

"I forgot about that. I asked the police why they kept that when they gave everything else back," Edgar said.

"What did they say?"

"They said they wanted to hang onto it, at this stage."

"Did he have a computer at home?"

"No."

After entering some more information into the laptop, he closed it. "We may leave it at that for today. I'll have a good look at that box soon. I know we've only scratched the surface. And I will keep you informed. It may not always be in writing but it will be very regular, even if it is to say I have nothing to report. I'm very sorry you both have had to go through this. I understand the police have a difficult job. I don't want to be too critical of them because I often have to work with them. Missing person cases are not always treated the same way. It often doesn't fit into the crime category and doesn't always attract the top officers. A lot of police are reluctant to take it on; they get more into the serious or obvious crimes. I imagine seeing a private investigator is the last thing you want to do."

"It is, Tom," Edgar said.

They all rose from their seats together. Tom couldn't help noticing their lovely, eye-catching shoes as he walked them out. Penny was in high heels and Edgar had on leather, dual-tone brogues. "Thank you for coming in. I'll be in touch as soon as I possibly can."

* * * *

Tom had never been to Inverness or any other part of Scotland. He was fond of dogs, yet with no special affinity, when it came down to a choice between Benny and the beagles, it wasn't hard for him to know where his own priorities sat. A pang of frustration returned as he flicked through the in-flight magazine that featured the beauty of Norfolk and the 'hidden secrets' of Norwich. Reclining in his seat as the plane levelled off, Tom's optimism returned. At the very least, once again he was off to a new land and, no doubt, some nice highland scenery. He was happy that he had packed his camera; dusting it off and shooting landscapes would be an opportunity not to be missed. Even a photograph to hang on the wall of his office might be possible, if only he could get a decent one.

It was an easy drive from the airport to the Paterson estate. The weather was cool and the sun shining as Tom turned into the wide drive-way in his hire car. A beautiful grand entrance marked by an almost ancient rock wall extended to a cobbled section which wound its way some distance leading him to a large old building. A sign read 'Paterson Heathcroft'. He half expected to be greeted by a whole bunch of welcoming beagles, but then he remembered the poor little creatures' numbers had taken a hit of late. On the drive over, he'd already thought about being 'most distressed to hear such news' as of course beagles just happened to be his 'most favourite breed' and he'd 'had one as a child'. But then reconsidered in case they asked questions that only a beagle owner would know the answer to. Rehearsing helpful white lies sometimes helped when they were really needed.

He parked right in front of the entrance, got out and decided to await instructions as to where to relocate the hire car. A doorbell adorned the middle of the large, heavy front door which, like everything else, seemed to be old. No sounds emanated from within when he pressed it so he used the oversized iron knocker affixed to a gargoyle's nostrils. After two firm taps that seemed to resonate more outside than in, a lady wearing an apron opened the door and greeted him.

"Are you Mr Greer?" she said.

"That's right. Good afternoon."

"Good afternoon, Sir. Could you please wait here for a moment? I'll see if Mr Paterson is available." She closed the door but not fully. Soon, an elderly man returned and opened it. He was very tall and thin.

"Mr Greer, please come in," he said. "If you follow me, I shall take you to your room." He paused in the entry area and held out his hand to shake. "Lovely to meet you, please call me Broden. My wife is out visiting one of our neighbours at the moment. I'm sorry she isn't here. She will be better to show you around than me. How was your flight?"

"It was very good, thank you," Tom replied, shaking his hand.

Broden set off with Tom trailing behind until they reached a stairwell that spiralled to the other two floors.

"I'm afraid your room is on the third floor," Broden said, as they approached the first step. "It's really the second floor but my wife likes to call it the third floor, ignoring we have a ground floor then a first and second. In any event, it's at the top level." His large legs enabled him to take two steps at a time. "We have to go up one more. Do you have a bag?"

"I've left it in the car."

"No bother. This place is far too big for us, you know. Ever since our daughters married," he said as he reached the top of the stairs first.

"I've been instructed by my wife to show you two bedrooms. I'd best do that. There are eight all up. One bathroom is there," he continued, extending his long, thin arm and finger. "There is another in one of the rooms. I expect you will want that one. I shall show you that first."

They went right to the end of the hallway and Broden put a key in the door and opened it. He opened the curtains, letting a stream of golden light fill the room. It was the biggest bedroom Tom had ever seen, half the size of his flat. There was a slight musty smell, but it was truly grand, if not opulent.

"The bathroom and shower are in there," Broden said.

"This is brilliant. Thank you." The high, exquisitely ornate ceiling took his eye. Artwork was everywhere. The bathroom was big enough for a party; he'd actually been to parties in smaller rooms.

"I should show you the other bedroom," Broden suggested. "My wife will ask me as soon as she gets home."

"This is fine," Tom said. "Really."

"Come with me."

At the other end of the wide hall, Broden opened another door that wasn't locked. "This has no ensuite, but the bathroom is just there." Hovering over Tom from his great height, he smiled and raised his bushy eyebrows. "I expect the first one?"

"Yes, that'd be great. They're both brilliant, though."

"Right then. Well, here is the key. Do you need help with your bags?"

"No, I only have the one."

"Very good. I'm going to tend to the dogs for a minute. I'll be asked about that too, when she gets home. Afternoon tea is at 4. Coira will be home by then. We will see you downstairs, Mr Greer."

Broden returned down the stairs with a slight degree of urgency about his step, or perhaps it was just efficiency, as if he'd ticked off yet another task from a list that his wife had given him. Tom went back into his room and grabbed his car keys so he could move the car and fetch his bag. Given he'd forgotten to ask where to park the car, he moved it next to the garages. He'd packed lightly so his bag was only small. When he returned to his room, he peered out the window and could see Broden in boots and a hat, striding across the lush lawn, heading in the direction of what looked like kennels. As Tom watched, several beagles appeared and hovered around Broden as he let himself into a large fenced yard with a locked gate.

CHAPTER FIVE

With no internet, Tom set his laptop aside, kicked off his shoes, stretched out on the bed and rested until it was time for afternoon tea. Just before 4 pm, feeling hungry as usual, he got up, put on a fresh shirt and wandered downstairs. There appeared to be two living rooms and he peered in one and then the other. The larger of the two had some cups and saucers set out, so he entered it and peered up at the walls, admiring framed photos, sketches and a whole series of oil paintings of beagles. The room was deadly quiet and peaceful, and as he stepped from one image of a dog to the next, he could hear the sounds of his sneakers squeak on the highly polished parquetry floor. Most of the images had names under them and others held a summary of what appeared to be past glories or championship achievements.

"That's Sir Gilroy," a voice said behind him, breaking the silence like a whip crack. Tom almost jumped out of his skin. He turned to see a young lady around his age, certainly not more than twenty-five, standing just inside the living room. She was tall and very slim, wearing a cream flowing dress that stopped below her knees. Her dead straight hair was dark brown and fell down to her waist.

"Hello," he said, stopping himself from saying she had frightened the wits out of him. "I'm Tom. Tom Greer."

"I know," she said. "My grandfather mentioned you were arriving today." Standing perfectly still with her arms beside her, she seemed to him almost like a statue forming part of the room's decor. After a brief awkward silence, she nodded at the photo he'd been examining and said, "He was the son of a bitch that had an unusual amount of redness in her coat. Did you know that the name Gilroy indicates you are the son of a redhead?"

"Oh, that's interesting. I didn't know that," he said, as he turned back and took a closer look at the photo of Sir Gilroy. "Is he still alive?"

"No, but he lived a very long life for a beagle. He died almost a decade ago."

When Tom moved to the next photo, she said, "That's Moibeal. She was the sister of Sir Gilroy's mother. She was the finest show dog of her generation."

"Right. Yes. I can see from this inscription here she won many awards. What a beautiful looking dog."

At that moment, an elderly lady shuffled into the room wearing slippers. She was not quite as tall as Broden and her frame was a little wider.

"Oh, hello, Mr Greer. I'm so sorry I wasn't here when you arrived. I'm Coira. I see you have met Fenella," she said, holding out her hand to shake.

"Ah, yes. Tom, please call me Tom." He shook her hand and turned to Fenella with a smile and a nod. "You have a lovely place here. I've just been admiring these pictures."

"Yes. They bring me happiness and sadness, I'm afraid. *So many* memories there. Please, take a seat. Our maid, Ellen, will be here in a moment. Have you seen Poppa this afternoon, Fenella? I can't seem to find him anywhere."

"I saw him walking one of the dogs about half-an-hour ago. I think it was Agador."

"Well, he knows that afternoon tea is …"

"Don't fear, my dear. I'm here," Broden said, as he entered the room. For a large man, his entrance was almost stealth-like; he was very light on his feet for his height.

"Oh good, let's all take a seat then. Mr Greer is most likely much in need of refreshment after his long journey," Coira said.

Soon Ellen had made several trips to and from the room until there was tea and coffee, shortbread biscuits and scones, butter, jam and teacake all placed on the large table. Tom ran his hand over the table admiring its rich walnut finish. With rounded ends, it had to be over 15 feet long and looked as good as the day it was made.

"I prefer tea in the morning and coffee in the afternoon," Broden said.

"Just to be difficult," Coira said.

"Not at all. To the contrary it is a balance which I highly recommend," remarked Broden.

"I will have some coffee to join you," Tom said.

"Good choice."

"I should say at the outset, Mr Greer, that I wish to apologise for the stress you will no doubt perceive in this household. The last six months have been the worst," Coira said, as Ellen poured her tea. "I honestly can't remember a time that's been so dreadful. We have lost our best friends and it simply can't continue. When we lost Agador's brother last month, after losing his mother before that, I think that was the final straw. We need to get to the bottom of who is doing this to our family."

All eyes were now on Tom.

"Were they poisoned?" he asked.

"Without question," Broden said, picking up a biscuit. "No doubt about it."

"With what?"

"There's been a variety of things. The vet determined a whole range of things poisonous to dogs have been used. All absolutely ghastly. Chicken wrapped in rubber bands laced with antifreeze. Rat poison. Snail baits. One had a cocktail of both," replied Coira, shaking her head, pulling out a handkerchief. "The last three have all had high traces of antifreeze in their system."

"Dear me," Tom said. "That's dreadful."

"It is truly awful," Fenella added. "We all witnessed poor Cranbero's death last month, all of us, regrettably," she said, sipping slowly on her tea. "At first, he started walking around the yard like he was drunk. Like he'd been drinking whisky. Then, in the afternoon, just after lunch it was, he went into a huge fit of convulsions. Oh, it was awful to see that. He went from being ..."

"I'd prefer you didn't talk about it, Fenella. I think Mr Greer has the picture," Coira interrupted. Fenella returned to sipping her tea, her eyelids down.

"What have the police said? Surely, they've investigated. You seem quite isolated here. What about the neighbours? That would be an obvious line of enquiry for the police," Tom said.

"They've all been questioned and have denied knowing a thing. We have two on that side. We know them. And then, there is one further down there," Coira pointed out the window, "and one up behind. They are quite a long way away."

"How well do you know them?"

"Broden has known the McNamaras a long time. Before they even moved here. The Tysons have been neighbours for years and are quite lovely people. We don't really know the people behind. The ones closest to us have their own dogs and are dog lovers."

"I have apologised to them for even being questioned by the police," Broden said. "We don't want to cause bad blood, unnecessarily. It's been hard to be delicate about this whole thing. I've paid them all a visit, all except the people behind us."

"Why is that?" asked Tom.

"You mean why I haven't apologised to them?"

"Yes."

"I haven't got around to visiting them. I can't say that I know them that well, anyway."

"Perhaps you and I should visit them tomorrow," Tom said.

"You and I?" Broden said.

"Yes. I could introduce myself as your nephew. And tell them I'm looking at buying some land in the area."

"Perhaps that is a good idea, Broden," Coira said. "You have left it too long to go and see them and have a chat about the whole thing."

"I suppose we could. What day is tomorrow?" Broden looked at his watch, as if it might show a date.

"It's a Saturday, Poppa. Nanna has her bridge meeting in the morning. You could go then and I will fix some lunch for us all for when you get back. It's going to be a sunny day. Perhaps we can eat outside," Fenella said.

"That would be lovely, dear," Coira said.

"I shall take a drive into town this afternoon and get some things," Fenella said, and drained her teacup.

Coira picked up the plate of teacake and offered some to Tom who took a slice. "After that, take Mr Greer for a walk around the property. Let him meet some of our family. Do you like dogs, Mr Greer?"

He decided he was not going to insist on being called Tom when it came to Mrs Paterson.

"Absolutely. I'm particularly fond of the smaller ones." Just stop there. He had decided this was the wisest move.

Coira offered him another slice of teacake which he demolished in two bites, commenting on how delicious it was.

"Would you like to come for a drive?" Fenella asked him. "If we leave now, all the shops will still be open. It's not far."

"Sure."

* * * *

On their approach to the village after minimal conversation in the car, Tom asked, "Do you live with your grandparents?"

"No. Well at the moment, I am."

"Just temporarily?"

"Yes. I'm actually going to be leaving in a couple of months to begin my course. I'll be studying literature at the University of Glasgow. It's one of the oldest universities in the English-speaking world, you know."

"Really? I didn't know that."

"Oh, yes," she said, as she pulled into a parking space.

"That's interesting."

"I'm on a gap year, of sorts," she said, as he got out of the car.

"Well, it is a lovely place to be spending your time, despite the terrible events," he said, as they made their way into a shop.

"My thoughts exactly," she said.

It was apparent Fenella shared her grandfather's efficient way of going about things, moving from shop to shop and aisle to counter with

very little pausing, collecting the things she wanted with a certain precision. They were back in the car with fresh bread, cheese, ham and
various other items in no time at all.

"Should I get something?" he said, as he sat in the passenger seat
before she started the engine. He'd wanted to ask her about that when
inside the shops but as she was always a step or two ahead of him, he felt
he didn't quite have the opportunity.

"What would you like?" she asked, turning to him with a smile.

It surprised him that it was such a big smile when his question was
merely an attempt to be polite. "I mean perhaps a bottle of wine, for
dinner?"

"You can do that, if you wish."

Tom got out saying he would be but a second and returned with a
reasonably expensive bottle of red wine and they were back at the estate
within half-an-hour.

"Do you have some other shoes?" Fenella asked him as she placed
the bags in the kitchen.

"Yes. Why?"

"Are they boots? It's boggy in parts where we're going to walk."

"No."

"Never mind. You can borrow some. Follow me," she said, heading
out the side door.

She led him inside a shed. "Here, put these on," she said, handing
him a pair of black wellington boots. "They're Nanna's spares. They
might be too big for you. Try them on."

Sitting on a bench he pulled them on. "They're a little big but they're
fine, I think," he said, and stood up.

Off she went in the direction of the kennels. As he followed, the
boots began to swim on him, but there was no turning back now.

"A lot of this is new. Well, relatively new," she said, when they arrived
at the structure.

Wandering around the outer perimeter, Tom could see the whole set
up was large and sophisticated, at least to his untrained eye. Four dogs
were enthusiastically wagging their tales in the gated yard space. A wire

fence surrounded an area the size of perhaps a third of a football pitch. At the middle rear section there was a small timber Victorian-era building that appeared, nonetheless, to be newly constructed. It was the main dog house. A timber deck was divided into seven individually fenced and gated small runs. A separate smaller house outside of the fenced area matched the style and architecture of the main dog house.

Fenella could sense Tom's curiosity. "That's where mummies can have special time with their puppies," she said. She unlocked the gate to the larger yard. "Would you like to see inside?"

Tom nodded and followed her in.

"How can you tell these dogs apart? They look almost identical," he said. Subtle patterns differentiated the coats but in a pack, he would not be able to identify one dog from the other.

"No, they are all very different, both in looks and personality. You will need to lift your game," she said.

He was uncertain exactly what she meant, but assumed he needed to get his observational powers in order if he was to solve this mystery.

The decking was slightly raised and she used the keys again to open one of the runs. Every second space had a neatly framed window in the little individual houses, way above dog height but he figured this must have been for light and ventilation, or just aesthetics.

"Look inside," she said.

"Wow! Even air conditioning," he said.

"You can imagine how cold it gets."

They went back into the yard space and Fenella let one of the dogs out before they both stepped outside. She locked the gate behind her. The dog stood next to her, overly excited to be chosen. "Agador, now you be a good boy and if you are, you can come with me," she said.

Tom felt like at that moment that the same might apply to him.

She gave a little click of her fingers and bent down. "Have you ever seen the classic pose?" she asked, still dealing with an enthused Agador and looking up at Tom.

"The pose?"

"Agador! Settle." He immediately calmed down.

She held the dog gently under his chin and Agador held his head slightly cocked with his tail perfectly erect and his body still. She caressed his raised tail before pausing near the top holding the very tip with two fingers and looked up at Tom. "The pose. Impressive, don't you think?"

"Yes. Very."

"Come on, Agador," she said, getting up. "Let's go and visit your mother."

They trekked up a small hill, then down another and across into a wooded valley. Flap, flap went the boots, concerning him he was going to get a blister under his thin business socks.

"Is this all part of your grandparents' property?" he asked.

"Yep."

"It's truly beautiful."

They crossed a fast-flowing creek and Tom thought it was a shame that is was too far to go back for his camera. Agador splashed in and out of the water, revelling in his afternoon treat.

"Is Agador your favourite?"

"Not really. I don't have one. I just like to bring him up here."

When they got to the top of the next hill, there was a series of small headstones. At first he expected to see the graves of family ancestors, but soon noticed there was a row of them and they all looked far too recent. As they approached, it became obvious from the plaques on the stones that this was a beagle burial ground.

"Sorry to bring you to this sad part of the property. However, I thought you may have wanted to see it for yourself," Fenella said, stopping in front of one of the graves.

The castle-like structure of the house was way off in the distance and the sun had almost gone.

"This is still a very beautiful part of the property, despite the sadness," he said, taking in the view. "A very fitting place, it would seem, for this."

He moved along the row of graves, slowly admiring each one and pausing to read the inscription. Agador trotted ahead, cocked his leg on the very last headstone and took a pee. Fenella seemed not to notice or if she did, let him go unchastised.

"This is his mother," she said, as they got to the very end of the row. Agador chased a bug down the hill, snapping at it but only catching air. If he had been in mourning, it seemed he'd now moved on.

Tom read the date, exactly two months ago to the day. No expense had been spared on the headstones. Each contained something unique, almost works of art unto themselves. A glossy photo of Agador's mother was affixed on her stone under a clear glaze.

"She was such a handsome creature," Fenella said. "But I think we should go back now." Without waiting, she headed down the hill.

When they arrived back at the yard, Broden was feeding the other dogs inside the perimeter. Agador was most pleased to be let in and be given his share.

"Have you thought about CCTV cameras?" Tom asked, standing outside the fence. "It seems to me that might go a long way to stop the attacks. I mean, one there and several along that side. The culprit must be baiting the dogs with a single bait, even just throwing it over the fence."

Broden came out and locked the gate behind him. "We have a man coming out next week to put them in. I'm quite upset with myself that I haven't acted earlier, to be honest. I hope cameras will help put a stop to this dreadful crime." As they strolled slowly back to the house he continued. "I still can't imagine who would be sick enough to do such a thing. They obviously come at night. Either from the road or through a neighbour's. There are only two ways, really."

"Have they left any evidence, tracks, anything noticeable at all?" Tom asked when they got to the house, as he pulled his boots off and ran his hand down the back of his ankles to see if the skin had come off. One ankle was red and ready to let go of its first layer.

"Not really," replied Broden. "It was exceedingly dry and the ground was hard leading up to the first two. The police thought there might be some tracks after the third, as it had rained just before but then it rained for three days. Any tracks that may have been there would have been washed out. They could simply come up the road and be in and out."

"What do you think about this neighbour we are visiting tomorrow?" Tom asked.

"I doubt he's involved. I don't think Coira likes him but you don't have to like someone. Let's go inside and have a sherry, shall we, before dinner."

When they got inside, Tom went upstairs and put a jacket on, the most formal item of clothing he had. He expected formality but perhaps not quite as much. They all met down in the other living room that Coira referred to as the sitting room. Fenella had changed into a tight-fitting red dress and it took his eye as soon as he saw her come into the room.

"Would you like sweet or dry?" Broden asked Tom, opening the large glass cabinet.

"Sorry? The sherry, you mean? Dry, thank you."

Broden handed him a glass and said, "What are you having, Fenella? Ginger ale?"

"Nanna is bringing me an apple juice," she said, and took the seat by the bay window.

"Actually, while I'm thinking of it, are you able to give me online access?" Tom asked Broden.

"Of course. Fenella, what's the password? I can't say I use it much. Coira is always on it, keeping up with the journal. She edits the beagle literature for our region," Broden said.

"It's called *beagleparadise*."

"Oh, that's right. Hardly," replied Broden, shaking his head before taking a sip of his sherry.

Coira arrived with the apple juice. "Sherry, my dear?" Broden asked.

"That would be lovely, darling," replied Coira. "Please, let's all sit."

"Tell Tom what you think about David, the neighbour behind us," Broden said to Coira.

"Well, he's not a friendly person but I suppose I was used to the previous owners. They ran a B and B but gave it away when it wasn't making much money. Lovely people, both of them. They had a few token horses and sheep, mainly to give it that authentic farmstay feel. David uses the property quite intensively for sheep. He keeps to himself mostly. He has a wife but I think I've only ever seen her once. Whenever I have seen him in town or in the neighbourhood, he will say hello. But that's about it. He refuses to stop and talk." She took a sip on her sherry, adding, "Unlike everyone else in our area."

"I would imagine he would have dogs of his own then, as herders?" asked Tom.

"Yes. He has at least two beautiful Shetland sheepdogs. He brought them across from Lerwick, so I am told. They are a very smart breed of dog," she said.

"I don't think he's the type," said Fenella.

"Most likely not, but that's where we need Mr Greer's expertise," Coira said.

When she used the word *expertise*, he wondered if he actually possessed any and exactly how long they expected him to stay.

"What about wayward kids, pranksters, vandals, anything of that sort over the last year?" he asked.

"No," Broden said. "We've never had so much as a break-in. As far as we know, no one in our neighbourhood has."

Conscious to avoid anything unsavoury at dinner, Tom figured now seemed a better time to ask some other things.

"Is there much jealousy in the dog show world?"

"This is something I've mentioned to Coira, haven't I, dear?" Broden remarked, looking at her, thankful it had been raised. As yet, he had not taken a seat and he slowly paced the room, glass in hand.

"Of course there is! It's just like anything else," Coira said a little dismissively, as if it wasn't worthy of further discussion.

Broden stopped pacing, turning to face her. "What about all those arguments you've had over the years! When was the last one? Just last week wasn't it? Some of *those* women—"

"Broden! I don't think it's one of them," she said. "Yes, they can be difficult at times. But, we share one thing in common."

"Being difficult?" he said, raising his eyebrows in the direction of Tom with a smile and took another sip.

"Now *you* are being difficult! Elsie and Terra and even Barbara may not like me. That's their problem. But we all love the dogs. Every single one of us! *That's* the difference. This person is sick," she said. "Not sick like Elsie is; not in that way. This person is far worse."

The maid came in and asked when 'madam' would like dinner to be served. Coira said that 7 pm would be satisfactory. It was served exactly on time and Tom's choice of red wine went very well with the venison and baked vegetables. Everyone had a glass except Fenella. Earlier in the evening, when Tom offered her a glass, she said she did not drink.

Over dinner, Broden asked Tom to tell them about himself. "I studied photography, initially, at the university in Norwich, where I'm from. I then travelled to Australia," Tom said.

"Did you enjoy Australia?" asked Broden.

"A lot. It was not a very long stay. My friend and I did a road trip. The weather was fabulous, the people were very friendly and the beaches, they were simply brilliant. I got the idea, in fact, of becoming an investigator whilst I was there. I'd go back in a heartbeat."

Tom chatted a little bit more about Australia and Norwich and living in London. He held their interest for some time, and steering the conversation away from dogs seemed a welcome relief, especially to Coira.

Fenella, who sat opposite, mentioned that her mother lived in London.

Dessert arrived – a large apple pie. As Tom placed a scoop of whipped cream on his pie, he contemplated asking a question about the dogs that he thought might be relevant but sufficiently low key enough not to upset the apple cart. But then, he felt Fenella's big toe rub the inner part of his leg, reaching his inner thigh. At first, he wondered if it was accidental. But when she left it there, he turned a shade of red, felt his face heat up and avoided looking at her.

Broden wasn't interested in dessert and suggested port wine and asked Tom if he would like to taste it. "Thank you, Broden. I certainly would." Broden delivered it to him, then lit a pipe and took a seat at the far end of the room.

Tom fought the urge to move for some time. He felt glued to his seat and the question he'd considered asking vanished from his train of thought. He sipped his port slowly and tried not to look at Fenella, but could feel her eyes on him. Eventually, he gave into his urge and moved his leg ever so slightly but then, Fenella rested her foot in the middle of his crotch. When the inevitable happened, she pressed harder and looked at him. She smiled, then, holding her smile, slowly turned her head to listen to her grandfather tell stories about the good old days.

After a good twenty minutes of telling stories, almost as a monologue, Broden got up. "Shall we meet downstairs at 9 in the morning and go and see David then?"

Ellen appeared almost immediately and cleared the table, as if she knew it was the end of the evening.

"I must say," Broden said to Tom, "he is such an unfriendly chap, I'm not at all looking forward to it. I'm glad you'll be there, Tom."

"Sounds good to me," Tom said.

"Right, I'm tired, too. I think we should call it a night, then," Coira said.

Tom pushed his chair back and got up from the table. "Thank you for a lovely meal," he said. "I hope we can make some progress tomorrow."

When he closed the door to his room, he immediately stripped and had a shower. Jumping into the king size bed, tired was not entirely what he felt. But the light went out anyway. Soon after he closed his eyes there was a knock on his door. Three tiny taps. He pulled his pants on, switched the light on and opened it.

"Can I come in? I have something to tell you," Fenella said. She didn't wait, walked in and sat on the bed. Her sheer white night gown extended from her shoulders to her bare feet.

"Sit here," she said. "Next to me," She patted her hand on the bed. He did as she asked.

"Tom, I think I know who might be doing this dreadful thing. I didn't want to mention it downstairs. But I've had my suspicions for a while."

"Go on," he said.

"Well, Angus is a strange fellow. He comes and cleans the kennels out every so often. Mostly once a fortnight, depending on the weather. His brother, who's a fine man, used to do it for years. But Angus, well, you should grill him. He's untrustworthy in my view."

"Why do you say that?"

"He's only been doing the job for less than a year. He's got access to the property. Some of the deaths have coincided with his visits."

"But why would he kill the dogs? It's his living, isn't it? His job?"

"He doesn't like dogs. I can tell. He's just doing it for the money."

"Isn't the money dependent upon the dogs? I'm not quite following."

"I can see that. But, there is something off-putting about him."

"Do your grandparents find him odd too?"

"They just think he's quiet. They don't see what I see. And they are influenced by the fact that he is Richard's brother, who was a gentleman." She put her hand on his thigh and kissed him on the cheek. "I will see you in the morning. Angus is due next Monday. Talk to him, please. It may come to nothing. But, it can't hurt."

She got up and let herself out. *Next Monday? Just how long am I expected to stay?*

CHAPTER SIX

At 8.30 am the next day, Tom focused his eyes on the ceiling for a good few seconds before he remembered where he was. Realising he was needed at 9 am, he quickly jumped in the shower to shock-start his body, put on his clothes and briefly checked his laptop. A message from Penny responding to his request for further information had come in but there was no time to consider it or respond. Perhaps after lunch he would have an opportunity to come back to the room and do so. He raced downstairs for breakfast hoping he wasn't too late.

Breakfast was served in the living room and when he slowed to a casual entry, he found Broden and Coira seated at the end of the long table.

"Good morning, Mr Greer."

"Good morning, Coira. Morning, Broden. How are you this morning?" he said, pulling out a chair to join them.

"Not *too* bad," Broden mumbled, as he placed an empty cup on a saucer, filling it again from a small personal teapot next to him, his hand shaking a fraction.

"Ellen," Coira said at volume. The maid soon appeared.

"May I take your order for breakfast, Sir?" *Such formality, but so quaint,* Tom thought, delighted he wouldn't have to trundle off on an empty stomach. "I can do almost anything you wish. Eggs in any style. There is cereal over there on the side table. Bacon, mushrooms …"

"Oh, thank you, Ellen. Eggs with some toast would be fine, if that would be alright, please."

"Of course, Sir. How would you like your eggs?"

"Poached, thank you."

"Very good. I will bring in a fresh pot of coffee in a moment. Tea on the table, in the middle there, Sir."

"Thank you," he said. "Have you already eaten, Coira?"

"Yes."

"I'm sorry I'm a little late for breakfast. I accidentally slept in. It's such a comfortable bed. I think you mentioned you wanted to leave at 9, Broden."

"No bother," Broden said, scratching his chin. "Listen, Tom, I have to admit. I'm a little nervous about visiting David this morning."

"Would you rather leave it, dear?" Coira said. "You've put off seeing him for so long now, it's probably not worth it, if it's worrying you. It's just that, Mr Greer is here now."

"No. I *do* want to go. I don't want to make a big deal of it. I think it neighbourly that we discuss what is happening in the neighbourhood. He's not being accused of anything, after all."

"I agree," Tom said. "There will be no accusations. Just a friendly visit to see if there is any information he can help us with."

"You mentioned saying something about being my nephew, Tom."

"Oh, I don't have to. It's just a bit of a ruse. A stratagem, as it were. I'm not recommending, I suppose, that we go over there and say, well, you've brought your private investigator, from London. It will shut him down. Cause him to clam up, even make things worse, given the police have already been there."

"I don't expect him to say a lot, anyway. He keeps things close to his chest."

"I'm happy to do quite a bit of the talking," Tom reassured him. "He's not likely to be our man, but he may know something or have seen something. It's certainly worth a visit. You can extend your courtesies and apologies at the same time about the police paying him a visit. It'll be fine."

They chatted about the weather. Quite heavy rain had been forecast for the late afternoon. After breakfast, Tom grabbed his jacket from his room and met Broden at the front door just after 9.45.

On the way to the garages, Broden said, "I think I'll take the utility. I don't know what the condition of his driveway is." Tom could tell how tense he was by the way he was rattling his keys.

There were a fleet of vehicles to choose from and Broden climbed into the Volkswagen 4 x 4 parked next to a deep-green Jaguar. "On the drive back, I'll show you the boundaries of the property, by road anyway. And where the other neighbours are," he said, gliding down the driveway, an anxious look on his face.

The road to David's was narrow. It twisted and turned around and descended down a hill for a good while before winding further up and around again. A couple of times, Broden had to pull over to let a car on the other side pass. Each time, he waved and the other driver waved back. It was a longer trip than Tom had expected, given they were to visit a neighbour, but eventually they turned into a driveway to the north and parked in front of a shed. There was no house in sight. Broden jumped out first.

"He's over there," Broden said, as if he knew exactly where David was going to be.

Tom was barely out of the car as Broden walked off at some pace.

They headed downhill and a house came into view with sheep in the distance. David appeared to be digging. He saw them approaching but looked up only once before returning to his digging. As Broden and Tom got closer, he stopped again and stared at them both.

Before they were within thirty feet of him, Broden shouted, "Good morning!" and waved in an overly friendly manner.

David extracted another shovelful of dirt.

When they were almost upon him, David stopped his work. A large frown creased his forehead. Tom could see that he was trying to remove a large rock but that he had a way to go to get it loose and on a tray. A tractor with a tray sat further down the hill.

David was a burly looking man. Solid and stoutly built, he had a thick, ginger beard which matched a full head of red wavy hair. "Hello,

Broden," he said. "To what do I owe the pleasure?" He held one hand up to shade his face from the sun that was causing him to squint.

"I'm sorry to interrupt. Perhaps you could do with a break. I'm sorry, this is …"

"Good morning, it's Tom. I'm Broden's nephew. Pleased to meet you," he said, stepping forward and holding out his hand. David looked at it for a moment, leaving it hanging in the air, wiped his hand on his trousers, then on his nose, before shaking it. He gripped his hand so hard, Tom felt like his eyeballs were about to protrude from their sockets. Relieved when David let go of his hand after longer than he expected, Tom placed it in his pocket and moved his fingers to redistribute the blood.

"You don't look like your uncle. You didn't get his lanky genes," David said, taking a step back to his original position, still holding the shovel.

"That's true," Tom said, laughing. There was a moment of awkward silence.

"What's your business, gentlemen?" David said, then pressed his boot onto the edge of the shovel, causing it to sink deep into the soil around the rock, and threw the contents onto the pile.

"Two things really," Broden replied, his voice quivering. "Firstly, I've been visiting each of our neighbours and thanking them for their patience regarding the police visits and all. You know, this ghastly thing with the beagles – the poisonings."

David took an almighty sniff and wiped his chin with the back of his hand. He buried the tip of the shovel into the dirt leaving it standing upright.

"I see. You told 'em to visit me, come and check me out, now you want to thank me?"

"No, no. It's not like that. And *that's* why I wanted to come over. They visited *each* of our neighbours as a matter of normal enquiry, procedure, that's all."

"You honestly think I might poison your fuckin' dogs?"

"No! And that's why I wanted to come and apologise. Once you place a report …" He paused, his legs feeling like jelly. "Coira and I had no option. The police … they take it upon themselves from there." Any ability he had to speak now had taken a serious hit. The morning's anxiety had reached its pinnacle.

"You said two things; what's the other fuckin' one?"

Broden's heart pounded and he regretted the whole damn visit. His mouth opened as though he was trying to speak but David's hostility had inflicted a momentary paralysis, and his mind went blank. There was no doubt about how he felt about David now; he hated the man.

"I'm thinking of buying some land in the area," Tom said, coming to his aid.

"And what's that got to do with me?"

"Nothing, of course. I was just wondering whether or not you knew of anyone who is selling. I've fallen in love with this area." Tom looked around as if he was admiring all of its beauty. "I'd like to see what might be available. If you know someone …"

"Have you just? Well, what area, the north or the south? Or are you talking about the valley?"

Tom looked at Broden but he was no help. "Anything is fine," he said. "It's all bloody beautiful."

"What do you want to do with it?"

"Sheep, perhaps beef cattle." He could see at least one sheep in the distance.

"You don't look like a farmer to me. Where are you from, anyway? You don't even sound Scottish."

"I was schooled in London. But I was born in Edinburgh."

"What part?"

"What part of London?" Tom cleared his throat, thinking, *I thought I was the one supposed to be asking the questions, not deflecting this barrage.* "The King's school. Near Westminster."

"I meant Edinburgh."

"Central."

David stared at him with his beady eyes and spat on the ground. "I can't help ya. There are real estate agents in town."

Tom knew that David could smell a rat. But equally, Tom could smell no rat poison.

"I gotta keep going with this," David said, and pulled the shovel out of the soil again.

Tom knew it was best if he and Broden left before they dug themselves further into another hole. He decided he needed to be careful if he wanted to avoid being hit over the back of the head with the shovel but he needed to try one last time.

"One last question, David. I don't want to buy into an area that has some rogue maniac on the loose, if you know what I mean. Have you ever had one of your dogs poisoned? Frankly, I can see what it has done to my uncle and aunt. Do you know they've had several prized champions taken from them? I'd appreciate if you could tell us anything – anything suspicious you may have noticed at all." Tom paused, looked at Broden, then back at David. "As a neighbour." He took a step backwards, well outside the swing circle of the shovel.

Broden looked on, eager to hear what his neighbour had to say and thankful that Tom was there to ask the question.

David sniffed again. "No. I keep to meself. And I expect others to respect that. I've seen nothin'. You gonna get a bad person anywhere. That's my view, laddy. Your uncle here. You think about it. He's getting targeted. No one else's dogs around here are being poisoned. There's gotta be a reason. Now, good day to you both."

As Broden walked back up the hill, relieved to be leaving, he said, "Well, that went well. I told you he wasn't a very pleasant fellow."

"He's alright. He just has a chip on his shoulder about something. And he's no fool, Broden. He could tell I was lying. More importantly, he didn't care."

"How do you mean?"

"He didn't care I was lying. Because, he has nothing to hide. I think, despite his attitude, he would have told us what he knew or suspected, if he had any information at all. But he doesn't have any. He's not your man. If he knew who was killing the dogs, well, you wouldn't want to be that person."

When they got back on the road, they drove towards the village. Along the way, Broden pointed out the entrances of all the immediate neighbours. "I suggest we have an early lunch in the pub," Broden said. "What do you think?"

"My thoughts exactly," Tom said. Both men had forgotten altogether about Fenella preparing lunch.

"The thing is, Tom, we've been so lucky for years. There has never been any trouble. It seems to have come out of the blue."

"It's a difficult one, that's clear to me. It must be a vendetta of sorts. You've won many awards. Perhaps it's jealousy? Someone is jealous."

"There is a show on Wednesday. It's south from here. About two hours. You can come and meet some people then. And tell me what you think."

"Well, I could. I was hoping to be back in London by then. I have some commitments. This whole thing is likely to take more time than we would like. It's going to be hard to make a lot of progress just at this point. It's probably the beginning of more work to come."

"Of course, I understand. I'm grateful you can be with us for however long you can. Just being able to talk frankly with someone about it, besides family, is a big relief. Thank you, Tom."

"It's all part of the job."

Broden drove with an ease now that wasn't evident before. "I'm glad we got that visit out of the way," he said. "And tomorrow is Sunday. None of us work on Sundays, as a rule. You should ask Fenella – or I will – to take you for a drive. You can have a think about the next step. It's been so intense, I think I need a break. This whole thing is getting to me."

"It was on my radar to get to the highlands, if possible. I suppose I'm there already though. I brought my camera. I'd love to take some photos if I could, just of your beautiful property."

"By all means. Go for your life."

On the way back to the estate after lunch, Broden remarked how tired he was. The visit with David had taken its toll and even though a glass of wine with lunch at his local had settled his nerves, he was exhausted. "I'm going to have a wee nap this afternoon. Coira will want to know what he said. I'll tell her you will talk to her tonight. You can tell her, if that would be alright. I'm far too tired for a conversation with her now. It's all extremely draining."

The opportunity to get Broden's view on Angus, the cleaner, would have to wait.

Broden vanished upstairs as soon as they arrived back. Tom got his camera and took a stroll around the property in a different direction to where Fenella had taken him. He stopped at various locations and snapped several photos. When some darker clouds rolled in, he decided to head back in the direction of the sheds. Rain started to fall as he let himself in to one of the large sheds. He flicked on a light, finding a separate part that housed a ride-on mower and tractor. Shelving was everywhere, built in to the side of the walls, meticulous in its order with items sorted by size. Garden tools, plumbing fittings, hoses, fertilisers and plant foods, screws, nails, hammers, axes, spades, fuel. But no poisons and no antifreeze.

The sound of the pouring rain that lashed the shed's iron roof became deafening so, tucking his camera under his jacket, he dashed to the house. He took his shoes off at the door and crept upstairs. In his room, he found a large thermos of sorts on the table near the window, accompanied by a slice of teacake, some cups and tea bags. *How thoughtful of Coira,* he thought. He made himself a cup of tea. He slipped his trousers off, ready to lie on the bed. Now it was time to check that attachment on Penny's email but there was a knock on the door. It was the same three light taps he'd heard last night.

He quickly pulled his trousers back on.

"May I come in?" Fenella said as he opened the door.

"Of course. I've just made a cup of tea. Would you like one?"

"Oh yes, please." She took one of the two seats near the window.

Tom made another cup of tea in silence before he said, "I expect you want to hear what David had to say?"

"Not especially. I will be more interested to hear what Angus has to say."

It was just before he sat down that she saw he had his fly undone. And when he sat, it opened wider.

"Well, anyway, he's not our man, I agree. He's bit of a blunt one. Knows what he knows and that's all."

"I expected as much," she said.

"You know your grandfather said I should take tomorrow off. Have a think about what our next move should be. But I haven't got into things enough. I really should be making more progress."

"What do you think you should get into?"

"I'm not quite sure yet. Perhaps I should sit down with Coira and ask her to tell me a little bit more about these ladies she competes with in the dog shows. I know she doesn't think it's one of them, but she might be willing to tell me more about them."

"Talk to her after Angus would be my advice."

They both sipped on their tea. Driving rain pelted against the window now and they fell silent again. Tom took a piece of cake and asked her if he could split it with her but she shook her head.

"That was delicious," he said, grabbing a napkin and wiping his lips. "Your grandfather took me to lunch at the pub, not far from here. The 'Beacon' or was it the—

"Stand up for a moment," she interrupted him.

"Sorry?" he said.

"I said, stand up."

He stood up.

"Your zipper is undone. Here, let me fix it."

She moved to the edge of her seat and expertly did it up for him with one swift lift.

Not knowing quite what to say, he paused. "Oh, sorry about that. That was tricky, doing it in reverse from your angle, ha!"

He sat back down and went to take the last part of the slice.

"Why did you sit down?"

"Shouldn't I? What have I done now?"

"Hop up."

He got up.

"I think you should take them off."

"What?"

"Your pants."

"Why? Is there mud on them?" He looked down, remembering he'd been over hill and dale.

Looking up to him from her chair, smiling now, it really wasn't something he was used to at all.

"What's wrong with you?" she said, no longer smiling.

"Wrong? I don't think anything is wrong with me."

"I'll be the judge of that."

She stood up and gently pressed her fingers against his chest, moving him back a tad. She took off her top. And then her bra. Then her jeans.

CHAPTER SEVEN

"Fenella, perhaps you should take Tom for a drive in the morning. Show him something he hasn't seen before," Broden said, as he handed her an apple juice. He passed Tom his pre-dinner sherry, then poured himself a glass. "Chat along the way about any ideas you have for his investigation. I'm ready for a little respite from it all. We can talk about it when you get back."

"Poppa, I've already agreed to show him some things tomorrow he hasn't seen," Fenella replied and smiled at Tom as he took a slow, careful sip of his sherry. "We're actually going to take a drive out to the edge of the loch. And pack a picnic. I've got some things left over, since you both plain forgot all about the lunch I'd arranged for today."

"Oh, yes. It completely slipped my mind. Sorry about that, love. I was in trouble from your grandmother."

Coira arrived in the living room just then and Broden passed a glass of sherry to her. "Thank you, dear," she said and took a seat.

Ellen entered the room carrying a cheese platter which she offered around. The rain had stopped, the late sun casting a warm glow right into the room through the tall windows. "It's such a shame the seats are wet outside. I'd love to be sitting out there," Coira said, peering across to the paved landing.

"Has Broden mentioned the visit to David's property?" Tom asked.

"Only briefly. He wasn't up to it, he said. What did you think? He's not a nice man, I'm sure you found out," she said.

"I've certainly met friendlier, but he's harmless I think. He's got no motive. I think we need to be looking at someone with a motive," he said.

"I've told you that, dear," Broden added.

"Let Mr Greer talk, please!" she snapped at him.

"Let me be to the point, Coira, if I may." Tom cleared his throat and sat up on the edge of the chair.

"Please do."

"If you could say you had one, just one main rival. A show rival, a competitor for awards, as it were, one person you don't particularly like. More importantly, who might not like you. Perhaps a person you consistently beat in competitions. Can you think of anyone?"

"Barbara," said Broden.

"Oh Broden. Would you please shut up! This is hard enough for me as it is. No, not Barbara at all. I like her, or at least I tolerate her. Let me think, please!"

"Short of catching people in the act, we need to be thinking outside the box," Tom said. "Has this sort of thing ever happened to any of your rivals?"

"Years ago, but it wasn't the same," Coira said.

"How do you mean?"

"Well, about ten years ago, Elsie MacDougal had to cancel her appearance because it was suspected that her dog had been baited. It died the night before. That's the only time I can think of something remotely similar." She downed her sherry in one gulp. "Broden, be a dear and get me another one, would you? I need to think."

"Surely the whole industry is rocked when this sort of thing happens. What has been the reaction?" Tom pressed.

"I said we should go to the press, make it well known," Fenella said.

"I didn't want that. Maybe it was a mistake. I made the decision not to a while ago. There have been more since then," Coira said. "Should we go the press now, Mr Greer?"

"What have the other breeders, the owners, said to you? I assume they are supportive?"

"Mostly, yes. They have taken extra precautions, I'm sure. Some have even called me and given their support. I think a lot of them are worried that it might happen to them. Naturally."

"What about this so-called anti puppy-farming brigade? The commercial breeders; I know *you* are not that, but could it be that someone, a deranged person, has confused you with them? I can see the wonderful way you look after the beagles, Coira, but people can be ignorant of course. Have you had any hate mail from extremists? Misguided people? Anything at all like that?"

"No. I thought it was that sort of thing at the beginning. Lumping us in with that lot. That disgusting bunch. Oh, they make me so angry. Please, Mr Greer, don't get me started on those 'puppy harmers', I call them. Because, *that's* what they are. They harm the dogs for their own gain, in my view. The things that people will do for money," she replied.

"They wouldn't exist if people didn't pay for their service, Nanna," Fenella said. "But people do pay."

"Don't defend them! I simply don't agree with it."

"If the protestors were going to target beagle owners, then they wouldn't come near us, Tom. There are plenty of puppy farms they can have a go at," Broden said, handing Coira another sherry.

"Do they have better security than you? I don't want you to take this the wrong way, but your security is minimal. Even the sheds aren't locked."

"I know. But I'm reluctant to change my lifestyle here, Tom," Broden replied. "It's never been a problem before now."

"Well dear, the dogs are losing their lives. We must change, for their sake," Coira said and swilled half her glass.

Soon the conversation turned away from the dogs but only after Coira clarified that the next dog show, 'a mini-show' was on Tuesday, not Wednesday. Broden mentioned it was important Tom come along and Tom casually mentioned that if it was alright, he'd book a return flight home for Wednesday.

After a late dinner, Tom walked upstairs with Fenella to her room on the first floor. Broden and Coira's bedroom was at the opposite end and they had already retired. Tom said goodnight but Fenella shook her head. "You're coming in here with me. They won't hear us. The walls are a foot thick and there's three walls between my room and theirs."

The walls may have been thick, but the stairs creaked when Tom slowly and carefully crept back to his room two hours later.

* * * *

They had decided upon an early start the next day. Fenella chose the green Jaguar and placed a rug and picnic basket in the boot. The morning had started out very cold and sunny, however by the time they'd reached Muir of Ord and were properly on the A833, the sky was blanketed with high, grey clouds.

Tom was looking forward to seeing Loch Ness for the first time. He sat in the passenger seat with his camera resting on his lap. He couldn't wait to snap dozens of photos. Along the way, he tried to discuss some of the technical points concerning photography but Fenella didn't seem interested. They stopped briefly at Drumnadrochit, then continued on to Invermoriston where they walked across the old bridge to get a view of the falls in the River Moriston. During the beautiful drive along the side of the Loch for a good few miles, he was eager to stop by the road and take a photo, but Fenella said they would come back that way and, when they were ready, take the picnic rug down to the grassy bank. He would have ample opportunity then, she assured him, to take photos and impress her.

At Invermoriston Falls, Tom was in photo heaven. A short walk by the river led them to a small structure called the 'Summer House'. He took some photos of it both inside and out and chatted to some locals who told them some of the history of the area. With an abundance of impressive views, he regretted not having his telephoto lens but after all, this wasn't meant to be a holiday. He swore to himself to pack it every time in the future, regardless if it was a business or pleasure trip.

When they got back to the car, Fenella suggested they may as well continue on to the village of Fort Augustus. Tom was happy to take all of her suggestions. She told him he would see some locks on the Caledonian

Canal. "You will see the boats transit the locks, if we are lucky." On the way he asked how 'a loch' could be on a canal. "You will see," she said, negotiating the winding road in the Jaguar with calm precision.

In the village, boats of various sizes were lined up in a narrow, walled, deep canal. They stood on the grass beside the canal watching the vessels pass through the narrow passage through a series of locks. Tom was amazed to see the swing bridge move the entire road near what looked like stairs of locks that lowered the canal down to Loch Ness. He marvelled at this feat of civil engineering and he said as much to Fenella.

"Now you can see the difference between a 'loch' and a 'lock'," she said and smiled. "I enjoy teaching you things," she said.

Strolling around the village, he spotted the pub. When he suggested they go in, she reminded him of her plans for a picnic and soon they were back in the car. They headed back in the direction they had come, in search of a good spot to lay a rug down by the water.

Eventually, she pulled over by the side of the road suggesting they make their way through a gap in the bushes and find their way down to the edge. The gap looked tiny and they had already driven by a few spots he was sure were better for photos, just along the edge of the road. Nevertheless, he carried the basket and the rug under his arm and followed. Besides, as he was now very hungry, the sooner they ate the better.

A small grassed knoll came into view. "Over there," she pointed. A mere few feet higher than the pebbly shore, the tiny waves rolled in and though it was secluded, with not much space, the view of the water was good.

Tom extended the rug out over the grass, broke off a small set of twigs that were in the way, and invited her to sit. "I'm starving. What've you got in that goody basket?" he said, sitting on the rug with his legs crossed like a kindergarten child ready for a story from the teacher.

"Would you like a beef, lettuce and relish sandwich or a ham, cheese and pickle sandwich?" she asked.

"May I have both? Is there enough?"

"Of course. I brought extra just in case. And there is some leftover apple and rhubarb pie."

"Brilliant. Loch Ness! What a fantastic sight," he said, looking out over the glassy surface of the water. "It's exactly how I imagined."

She handed him a bottle of water. "How did you imagine it?"

"Well, on a day like today, I reckon. The sky being grey and the water that deep olive colour and kind of flat-looking. Not a soul in sight, not even Nessy. Wow, what a marketing coup that was," he said and laughed. "Who ever dreamt that up. A total boon!" He took a swig of the water.

"How do you mean?" she said, passing him a sandwich.

"The monster," he said, unwrapping the sandwich and taking a huge bite. "Whoever decided to spread that nonsense way back when, they should've been knighted for services to tourism! Sir Sillyrot. Ha!"

"Oh, it's not nonsense," she said, unwrapping her sandwich.

"It's not?" he replied, taking a double bite.

"Oh, no. Not at all. I've seen her."

"What?"

"Several times, right here."

"You're pulling my leg! When?"

"I'm not. Last year. Then, a few years before that, twice. It was a little bit further on from here, then. Over in that direction." She pointed towards the right of where they were sitting.

He took another sip of his water and looked out across the water. "I thought it was all bullshit. There haven't been any sightings for years. The thing would be dead. Washed up on the shore."

"I haven't told anyone about it, until now. You're actually the first person I've told."

"Are you sure? Tell me what you saw. Did you get any photos?"

"No photos. Nessy will not come out when cameras are about. It's not her way. Her neck was visible for a good ten seconds."

"I'll keep my camera handy, just in case," he said. "Do you have that other sandwich?"

She reached into the picnic basket and gave it to him.

It was soon gone and he moved to the water's edge to wash his hands. "I just wanted to touch it," he said, looking back at her with a smile. He sat back down. "You wouldn't have that pie handy, by any chance? Sorry, I'm just very hungry for some reason. This air is making me—"

"I have something else in mind, first," she said.

"Really? What else have you brought? Some of that teacake? I loved that—"

"No. I'm in the mood again."

"The mood?" Shaking his head, he checked himself. *Had she really said that?* "You're what?"

"Yes. I'm. I um, want … I want you to do it. To do it from behind."

"What! What are you talking about, Fenella? From behind? Behind where?" He looked around and almost coughed up the sandwich.

"On this rug. Now. Take off your pants."

"Are *you* out of your mind?"

"Are you *out* of your league? Or just out of practice?"

"Fenella. Good God! It's … it's freezing, haven't you noticed? And … well … we're out in the open. I'll get arrested!"

"Nobody can see us. Relax, would you? I need it. I need *you*."

"Can't it wait until we get back?" he asked desperately. "We can go now, if you like. That would be best, wouldn't it? Wouldn't it … surely …?"

"Tom!" A stern look and then a pause. "I don't want us to argue. It's just naturism. Calm down. Open your mind. It's what's meant to happen. Now hop up."

With Fenella starting to take off her pants, he looked down the shoreline and across the water, blinking quickly. "Shouldn't we talk about the dogs? I mean, I need to tell Coira … something. Your grandfather is in a state. Can't you tell?"

"I told you what to do. Talk to Angus, the weirdo. Now, you will have to stand up," she said. "Your legs are too short to be kneeling. Up you get."

Complying, but with one eye on her and one eye on the lookout for any 'normal' people, he eventually fell on the rug exhausted, ready for a sleep.

"Thank you," she said. "We can go now."

* * * *

It was quite late when they got back. Too late for a pre-dinner sherry. They had stopped at Inverness where he had two pints at a pub, seeking inspiration in silence to solve the beagle deaths. He had finished the first before she was a third of the way through her non-alcoholic cider.

At dinner, Coira and Broden wanted to know all about their trip. Tom was ready to mention everything, bar one small detail.

"I'm glad Fenella showed you some of the sights, Tom. Anyway, what are your plans for tomorrow? Did you come up with your next move?" Broden asked, as Ellen delivered a roast duck to the table and proceeded to carve it.

"I've had one thing in mind; I mean I *have* one thing in mind. Can I suggest that we have a family meeting, perhaps at pre-dinner drinks tomorrow, to assess where I'm at with the whole investigation?" He was hoping that Angus would simply admit the whole damn thing and that it could be done with.

"Absolutely. Fine idea," replied Broden.

There was no knock at his door that night and he was thankful for the break. If anyone needed a respite, it was him.

* * * *

"Get focused on the bloody dogs," he mumbled under his breath as he showered the next morning. It was already 8.30 am when he pulled on his trousers and glanced out the window. Angus was already there! Rushing downstairs, he almost knocked over Ellen at the bottom bringing some trays back into the kitchen after serving breakfast. "Oh, I'm sorry, Ellen," he said, carefully stepping around her and headed straight out the front door, knowing he couldn't lose the opportunity to see Angus.

He crossed the grass to the kennels, but slowed to a swagger as he approached the perimeter fence. The ruse with David had backfired somewhat, so he'd decided honesty was the best approach this time. Get straight to the point.

"Can I interrupt you for a minute?" Tom said.

Angus was pressure cleaning the wooden deck. Tom doubted he'd heard him. He gesticulated at Angus to turn the pressure cleaner's motor off.

"What did you say?" he asked.

"I said, if I could interrupt you, just for a minute?"

Angus dropped the water gun and stood there. He was a large man with a thick beard and arms that looked like tree trunks. Bulging muscles shaped his masculine physique. "What can I do for you?" he said.

"My name is Tom Greer. I'm an investigator and friend of the Paterson's. I've been here for a few days looking into this awful thing with the dogs."

"The poisonings you mean?"

"Yeah. That's right. I've been asking people what they know."

"What they know, hey?" He moved closer to the edge of the fence.

"Yes. Can I ask you a few questions?"

"Fire away," he said. Even though it was cold and early in the morning, he could see Angus was perspiring.

"Well, do you have any theories, for one? You can speak to me confidentially."

"Not really. It's baffled us all. I've never seen anything like it."

"How often do you clean the kennels?"

"Every ten or so days. Today is a six-monthly clean."

"Have you come across anything suspicious?"

"No."

"You do this for a living?"

"I don't do it as a hobby."

"I mean, you do this for a job. You clean others?"

"I'm a jack of all trades. I don't just clean."

"Right. What about people? Have you seen any odd people around? On the street, near the property? Anything that's caught your attention. Strange people?"

"I can't say I have, except … except for the lass who lives here. She's an odd one, if you don't mind me saying."

"What lass?"

"That Fenella. A bit of a psycho, but you didn't hear that from me."

"What do you mean?"

"Just what I said." He paused.

Tom shook his head. "Why do you say that?"

"Look. What did you say your name was?"

"Greer, Tom Greer. I'm a private investigator from London."

"Look, Mr Greer." He picked something out of his teeth and looked back in the direction of the house. "I'm a married man. I got kids. She … she came onto me one day when I was in the shed. I told her as much. She wouldn't let me say no. I've heard some things about her."

"Like what?"

"Like, she has been in a home or something. A facility, I believe, they call it. In Glasgow."

Tom closed his eyes for a moment and his stomach turned – and not because he hadn't had breakfast.

Angus seemed to notice that this was all news to Tom. He took a step forward, right up against the fence and lowered his voice. "I had to threaten her, Mr Greer, that I'd give her a slapping one day, if she ever did that to me again. If you catch my drift."

Tom stared at Angus in shock. He realised no one would want a slapping from this large man.

Angus began to speak more freely now. "Look, I'm not saying nothing, about nothing. I don't know anything, but … I'm also not sure what she's capable of. I'm not saying she done it, that it's an inside job. Nothing like that. But, put it this way," he looked at the house again and then back at Tom, "you're wasting your time, Mr Greer, if you think it was me. I think the cops know who it was."

Tom gaped at him, speechless.

"*That's* why they don't care."

Tom felt an immediate need to get back to the house. He found his voice. "Thanks. Thanks Angus. I'll ah … will ah … let you get on with what you're doing."

He turned away but looked over his shoulder as Angus said, "And Mr Greer. You said it was confidential. I don't want you to be telling my wife or nothing. I certainly don't want to come looking for you, if you know what I mean."

"No, no, no! Of course not," Tom said, then headed back to the house.

Once in his room, he tried to gather his thoughts. *Think*, he said to himself. But he couldn't think. He never could on an empty stomach. With his head spinning from Angus' unexpected information about Fenella, he went downstairs and peered into the dining areas. No one was about so he went into the kitchen to quickly fix himself something to eat. He was even more eager now to decide on his next move.

Tom hadn't noticed that Ellen was washing dishes until she spoke. "Good morning, Mr Greer."

"Oh, good morning Ellen. How are you this morning? I expect I've missed breakfast."

"Yes, but I can fix you something, Sir. What would you like?"

"Thank you. But, you don't have to do that. I can grab a bowl and have some cereal, if that would be—"

"It's no bother at all, Sir. I'm about done here. You can take a seat at the bench, if you like. I can make you some eggs and coffee."

"That would be brilliant, Ellen. Thank you so much." He sat down and after a moment of watching her cook his eggs, he said, "Ellen, do you mind if I ask … have you been with the Patersons long?"

"Almost twenty years, Sir."

Soon she placed a plateful of scrambled eggs and toast in front of him. They chatted about the weather and Loch Ness, as he slowly processed the information from Angus on Fenella.

"Ellen, you know why I'm here?" he said, just before he finished the last of his toast.

"Yes, Mr Greer." She collected his plate and went to place it in the sink.

"Thank you again. That was delicious. Can I ask you some things, Ellen? I mean, would you mind?" he said, tapping the napkin against his lips.

"What sort of things, Sir?" she said with her back to him as she turned the tap over the sink on.

Tom paused for a minute and waited to see if she was going to turn around. When she didn't and began washing the dishes, he said, "About Fenella."

"What about Fenella, Sir?"

He got up from his chair and walked over to the sink. "Do you mind if we sit down, just for a minute, Ellen. Just so I can ask a few more questions, that's all. I will try and not take up too much of your time."

"I really must be getting on with my chores, Mr Greer. I have a list …"

"Please, just a minute of your time. It won't take long."

She sighed. Tom pulled out another stool from the bench so she could sit opposite him. As he resumed his seat, Tom realised she was younger than Coira but her wrinkled face indicated she was possibly nearing sixty. She looked at Tom with concern.

"Has Fenella been unwell?" he asked.

"She has had … she was unwell earlier in the year, Mr Greer."

"How so?"

Ellen paused, began to say something and then stopped.

"I understand the need for diplomacy, Ellen. And loyalty. I do." He held her gaze directly. "But, it's important I am aware of her condition. Quite important, given what I've been asked to investigate."

"She was in a clinic for a time. In Glasgow, Sir. Then … then she came and stayed with Mr and Mrs Paterson."

"To rest?"

"You could say that, yes."

"What type of clinic was it, do you know?"

"Oh, Mr Greer, I would rather—"

"Ellen, it's important."

"It was a psychiatric facility, of sorts. I don't know the details. Just that, just that …"

"Yes?"

"Just that her parents, her mother, had done all she could, ever since she was a child, and …"

"She has a history of mental illness?"

"I shouldn't be telling you this, Sir." She started to rise but Tom grasped her arm gently.

"Telling me what, Ellen? What?"

She lowered her lids and started to cry. "I can't say it."

"Why are you upset?"

She didn't answer but, remained in her seat, crying softly.

"What shouldn't you be telling me? That she has been unwell? Or is there something else?"

"I can't say, Mr Greer. It wouldn't be right."

"Is it about the dogs? I'm sorry this is upsetting. I truly am, Ellen. Please don't cry." He paused and looked behind him. "Is it?"

Looking back at him now, she said nothing, but held his gaze.

"You know something, don't you?" he said. "Don't you, Ellen? What is it? It's very, very important, that you tell me. Perhaps it's time … time you told someone."

"I can't, Mr Greer," she replied, now sobbing.

"Why?" He looked around at the door again, hoping that Fenella was not about to walk in. He needed to seize the moment.

"Because, I can't," she said, tears rolling down her face.

Now was not the time for sympathy. "Ellen, I'm dreadfully sorry to put you in this position. I really am. But, I have to say it. You have a *duty*. A duty to Broden and Coira to tell me anything you know."

"I saw her do it!" she said, loudly.

"Shhh…!" he said, shaking his head. "Ellen, just calm down. Please. Just … take a minute. Tell me what you saw," he said quietly, leaning in closer. "Tell me exactly what you saw."

"She threw something over the fence, Mr Greer, into the yard. I was outside hanging up the washing. She saw me. She knows I saw her do it!"

"And?"

"And a dog was dead the next day, Mr Greer!"

Shaking his head, he leant back on the stool, running his hand over his mouth.

"She came and saw me. In the kitchen, the day after."

"What? The day after the dog died?"

"Yes. She grabbed that big knife there," she said, pointing to the knife rack. "She said … she said, if I mentioned it to a soul, she'd use it to split me from ear to ear. She said that! I'm so scared Mr Greer." Shaking now, she added, "I've been living in fear for months!"

"Threatened you, here?"

"Yes, Mr Greer."

He paused to comprehend the enormity of it all. "Right," he said eventually, digesting this confirmation of Angus' suspicions. He felt such a fool; duped, almost. But despite feeling deflated and devastated, he also felt an uneasy relief that at least he'd got to the bottom of it quickly. Especially as he had thought he never would. He looked at the clock on the wall, running his hands over his mouth. The family meeting he had convened for that afternoon now needed to be brought forward.

"Ellen," he said, placing his hand on hers. "You've done the right thing. I can assure you of that. I want you to get in your car and I want you to go home."

"This is my home."

"Do you have another place you can go to?"

"My sister has a flat in Inverness."

"Do you have a car?"

"I do, but it's being serviced."

"Well, I'm going to drive you now to your sister's place. Let's go. I don't think it's wise that you be here, just at the moment."

"I can't leave the work, it's …"

"You have no choice. I'm going to go and get my keys. Stay here, please. I will be back in less than a minute."

Grabbing his wallet and keys from his room, he returned to the kitchen and they were out the side door and into his car within a matter of seconds. On the way to Inverness, Ellen started to cry again and kept crying softly for the rest of the way.

"This will all be okay, don't worry. It will all be okay. Trust me," he said. "Do you have a phone on you?"

"Yes."

"You may want to call your sister. Will she be at home?"

"I think so. I'll try. She may be at work. I have a key to her flat, I can use that."

"Good. Good thinking."

When they got to her sister's place she hadn't made the call to her sister. "Just go inside and rest, and let me look after it from here. It might be alright to come to work tomorrow, but we shall see. I think I need to get back quickly now."

"Oh, Mr Greer, I'm so upset. But what are you going to do about it? What?"

"Don't you worry, Ellen. I have all that under control."

As he headed back to the property, he knew he had no plan about what to do next at all. Worried that Fenella might have seen them leave, he put his foot down, not caring that he broke the speed limit.

When Tom arrived back at the house, he was relieved to see Broden with the dogs. He jumped out of the car and rushed over to him. "Have you seen Coira, Broden?"

"She was out here a minute ago looking for Ellen. I think she went back into the house. Why?"

"No reason. I was thinking of bringing the meeting forward, that's all."

"You were?"

"Yes."

"To when?"

"Now, actually."

"Right. Well, I'll be in, in just a minute. I need to finish up here. It won't take me long."

The minute he went inside, Tom heard Fenella call to him from the living room. "Where have *you* been?"

He found Fenella and Coira sitting together on a lounge. "Something came up with Ellen. Um, I was, um, in the kitchen having a late breakfast when she got a call."

"From who?" asked Coira. "I've been trying to find her everywhere."

"Her sister. In Inverness. She's apparently been taken ill and needed to let Ellen know. It sounded a tad serious so Ellen wanted to go and see her straight away. I offered to drive her. She said her car was being serviced."

"Oh, that's awful," Coira said.

"Yes. It seemed a bit urgent. I couldn't find you but thought it would be best to just take her myself."

"Oh, I should call her. I'll get the phone." She rose from her seat.

"I wouldn't do that. I mean, she had to go to the hospital straight away. So, she is probably in the ward with her, right now. Just at this very moment. She said she would let you know as soon as she knew more. She's going to call *you* and tell you all about it. She said it would be best if she called you later today once she knew more."

"Oh, dear. It never rains but it pours. It's probably her heart. Meredith is not one for looking after herself," Coira said in a worried tone and sat back down.

"I'm going to get a glass of water from the kitchen. Can I get you ladies anything?"

"No, thank you," Fenella said, almost pompously. He wondered if everything she was to say now would annoy him. He looked at Coira, waiting for a response.

"I'll make a cup of tea when Broden comes in, I'm fine."

In the kitchen, downing the water, he thought that all his white lies would be cleared up and explained later. There were far more important things to worry about.

He returned to the living room with a full glass of water and avoided looking at either of the women, as he tossed over in his mind exactly what he should say.

"It's getting close to lunch time," Fenella said, breaking the silence.

"Well, before we eat, I'd like to bring our meeting forward. I've already mentioned it to Broden," Tom said.

"That's fine with me," Coira said. "What do you think, Fenella? It will free you up for this afternoon."

At that moment, Tom couldn't help but think it was going to have the exact opposite effect.

"Whatever," she said. "I'm interested to know what Angus had to say for himself."

"What about Angus?" asked Coira.

"Let's leave it until Broden can join us, shall we?" Tom said. "I'll discuss it then."

"Yes. Is he finished yet?" Coira got up and opened the large glass timber framed doors that led outside onto the patio. "Broden! We're all waiting for you," she yelled, in the direction of the kennels.

He finished his water and went back to the kitchen to fill up, avoiding sitting with Fenella. By the time he got back, Broden was in the room and had taken a seat.

"You know, those dogs," Broden began. "The very minute after Angus cleans, they seem to go on a shitting spree, just to get back to the smell, I guess. It never fails to amaze me. I had to clean it up."

"Wash your hands before lunch, dear," Coira said.

"Sorry. I should have done it before I sat down. Speaking of which, when is lunch? Did you find Ellen?" asked Broden, looking at Coira, then Tom.

"Yes. Well no, she had to go to Inverness. Her sister, Meredith, is unwell," replied Coira.

"Again?" said Broden. "That's a spanner in lunch, then."

"Tom has something he wants to discuss with us, dear. And I'm very eager to hear. So, please stop thinking of doggy do and your belly for a moment," Coira said. "It's still early yet for lunch."

"Well, thank you Coira," Tom said. "I don't mean to take too much time. I had a small chat with Angus this morning. Fenella thought it was a good idea."

Fenella stared at him and sat back in her seat, arms crossed. She had already noticed he was refusing to look at her.

"You did?" Coira said, turning to Fenella.

"Nanna, Tom needs to talk to everyone, you know. Not just the neighbours and your friends or competitors and what not," she said.

"And what did he say, Tom?" asked Broden.

"He said it might possibly be an inside job." He turned to look at Fenella for the first time.

"What do you mean, 'an inside job'?" asked Coira.

"He would say that; he's a pig of a man," said Fenella. "What would he know!"

"Of course, I doubted it at first. But then, I remembered something. I remembered that I had not spoken to Ellen. Ellen, who has been with you for what, twenty years? Your faithful housemaid. Really, your dear friend, dare I say it? Someone you trust," Tom said.

"Oh my God! You're not going to tell me it's Ellen! How could she ... I ..." Coira rocked in her chair.

"No, no," Tom said, holding up one hand. He paused and looked again at Fenella. "Are *you* going to tell your grandparents or do I have to?"

"Tell them what?" Fenella said abruptly.

"Fenella, please," he said. "It's ..."

"Please *what*?" she fired back, sharply.

"Fenella, I spoke to Ellen this morning." He paused and looked at Broden, before looking back at Fenella. "As well as speaking to Angus. And, well, she told me everything. What you did. And what you told her."

"What did you do?" Broden asked Fenella.

"Nothing, Poppa! I don't know what the hell he's talking about!"

"Don't lie, Fenella. It's really not necessary now. We can help you," Tom said.

"What did Ellen tell you?" Fenella said, frowning and shaking her head, sitting on the edge of her seat now. "WHAT?"

"Yes. What did she say?" asked Coira, utterly confused.

"She told me that she had seen you toss a bait into the yard. And that a dog died the next day. And, well, that she basically sprung you doing it. And you threatened her. Threatened to cut her from ear to ear, if she told anyone."

"She's lying Poppa! I swear!"

"Fenella," Tom paused, attempting to slow things down. "You've been unwell. I know that, now. Angus even said it."

"I have told you what I think of him! That pig! Yes, I've been unwell! I'm getting better. Much better! I thought you were different, but you're no God damn fucking different from the rest of them," Fenella said.

"Fenella!" Coira said. "That's enough. I will not have that language in this house!"

"Fenella, dear," Broden said, calmly. "I want you to level with me. We have told your mother we would look after you. It's been a very, very stressful time. I want you to look me in the eyes. I want you to tell me the truth. I don't care what it is, love. I truly don't. You're family. We can get whatever help you need."

"I *am* telling the truth, Poppa!"

Tom shook his head. "Fenella, it's …"

And just then, the home phone rang. Everyone stopped talking and let it ring and ring.

Coira sighed, got up and shuffled into the hallway to answer it.

"Yes, speaking. Who?" She paused. "Oh, dear. When? Oh …" They could all hear her as they sat in silence.

Fenella scowled at Tom, her eyes fierce with anger.

Tom caught a glimpse, enough to divert his own eyes away to examine the pictures of the beagles on the wall.

They waited for Coira to get off the phone but her conversation went on and on.

"I can't believe you're doing this!" Fenella eventually said to Tom.

Tom shook his head while Broden remained motionless.

They heard Coira hang up. She returned to the room as white as a ghost.

"That was Meredith, Ellen's sister. She … she's on her way to the hospital. It's Ellen who's there. Ellen … she … tried to kill herself. She threw herself in front of a train! It was just coming to a stop. Her injuries are severe. Meredith arrived home and must have just missed her by a minute. She found a suicide note Ellen had left in her apartment, apologising for everything." Coira lifted a shaking hand to her face and her arms wobbled. "For killing … the dogs. I can't believe …"

Coira's knees buckled beneath her and she fell hard onto the floor.

CHAPTER EIGHT

It was 5 pm in the Paterson household when Dr Stirling slowly descended the stairs with Broden.

"She'll rest mostly now. Just pop in and check on her every hour or so, but most likely she'll sleep until morning, I expect," the doctor said.

"Thank you so much, John, I will," Broden said, as they reached the bottom. As the family physician for more than thirty years and old friends, Broden trusted him.

"I've only given Coira the one tablet. But I'll hazard a guess that's all she'll need. Dreadful circumstances. My heart goes out to you, Broden. I just hope all this passes now, but I suspect it will take some time." Stirling placed his bag down beside him. "You know, when I was at university – it seems a whole lifetime ago now – they didn't have much knowledge about these disorders that people can develop." He was a short man and had to peer up to see Broden's face. "I really don't know whether it's this thing they call Zoosadism, but unfortunately we're seeing more of it. It's very odd and extremely worrying."

"I had no idea she would be so cruel – so hideously cruel to our beautiful beagles."

"Well, Zoosadism is a very odd disorder, so the studies have shown. Taking pleasure in harming our fellow creatures, whilst abhorrent to the rest of us, can be a very powerful mental illness indeed. In fact, in some cases it has led to a crossover into harming people. In any event, we may never know if it was that at all."

Broden crossed his arms and nodded, still in some disbelief. "You spend your whole damn life thinking you know someone, John. Thinking you're a good judge of character. I certainly did. How wrong can a man be? I obviously didn't know her at all."

"You mustn't be too hard on yourself. Coira will need you to be strong." He picked up his bag, held his hand out and Broden shook it firmly.

"Thank you, again, John," he said. "Let me walk you out."

"Call me in the morning, if need be. But I'm sure she'll be fine. Perhaps a little bruised around her hip from the fall, but that's all."

* * * *

In his room, Tom was on his back on the bed, one hand on his brow, thinking yet trying not to think. There would certainly be no pre-dinner sherry for him that evening. There was a knock at the door. Different from the knock he was used to; a knock he knew he would never, ever hear again. "I'm going to go into Ellen's quarters," Tom heard Broden say. "I want you to come with me please, as my witness."

He remained silent as he followed Broden downstairs. The servants' quarters were tucked in behind the kitchen, down a short, narrow hallway. The door to Ellen's section was locked. Broden reached into his pocket and put the key in. At first, he put the wrong key in. "I haven't been in here for twenty bloody years," he said, fumbling with the keys before opening the door. Bending down to fit under the door frame, he went in, followed by Tom.

Inside was a single bed, bedside table, wardrobe, small table and chair, tiny bathroom, and windows with curtains pulled across them. A laptop on the floor caught Tom's eye. He pulled the curtains aside to let some light in, picked it up and placed it on the table.

Tom turned to see that Broden hadn't moved. He then watched Broden go to the bedside table and pull out the little drawer. He took out a small booklet and sat on the bed to open it.

"What is it?" Tom said. He received no answer as Broden flicked through the pages before stopping at one. "Here," Broden said, handing the diary to him with the pages opened.

'*It has been two weeks since Agador's mother passed and they are still none the wiser. Do they not know the hurt they continue to inflict on themselves by yet again, as each day passes, treating me the way they do? Worse than their own pets. Worse than a mere dog. Worse ... again, yet again. They think I don't notice, but I do.*'

Tom handed the diary back and opened the heavy old laptop. He switched it on. The laptop wasn't locked and he checked the browser history. It did not take long to see that more than six months ago, someone had searched for information relating to antifreeze. He closed the laptop down.

They sat without speaking for a moment, both lost in their thoughts.

"Did you find anything on that?" Broden asked, nodding towards the laptop.

"She researched poisons. There's no doubt."

"It's horrendous. Simply horrendous! I need to get the hell out of here," Broden said, throwing the diary on the bed and walking out the door.

Following him out, Tom heard the sound of the gargoyle nose ring being beaten twice against the front door.

Broden answered it to find two police officers standing outside.

"This is PC Hammond and I'm PC Tallison. I made the phone call earlier this afternoon, Sir, when I confirmed the passing, earlier today, of Ellen Fabia MacNeacaill."

"Yes," Broden said. "I took the call."

"It's incumbent upon us to pay this visit in the circumstances," PC Tallison said, "as the last known place of abode of the deceased."

"Of course, I understand. Come in." He stepped aside and they moved into the hallway. They followed Broden into Ellen's quarters.

PC Hammond took some notes in Ellen's room and collected the laptop and the diary. "These will be returned to the next of kin as soon as possible," PC Tallison said. Broden thanked them for attending.

Tom was waiting for Broden in the living room.

"I'm going to have a whisky, Tom. Would you have one with me? It's been a very, very long and terribly unpleasant day. I suspect Fenella will not be joining us."

"I feel awful," Tom said. "Dreadful. I owe her an apology."

Broden took two glasses and the bottle from the cabinet. "Ellen lied to you, Tom. I can see why you fell for it. As for Fenella ..." He paused and placed the bottle and glasses on the table. "She confuses me and a lot of people. It's been the same way since she was a child." He gave a glass with a double shot to Tom and filled his own glass to the top.

"It really wasn't good enough. I didn't look into it properly. I stupidly jumped to conclusions without giving her a chance."

"Hindsight is a wonderful thing. It's totally useless, though. If anyone should feel bad, it's me. I took that woman for granted, in her eyes, it would seem. Whether I did or not, I don't know. I certainly didn't do it intentionally. That's no excuse for what she did, of course. But this is not something we know. I don't know. I grow older and I know less and bloody less."

Sitting in the silence of their own company, sipping slowly, it seemed unnecessary to talk further. Tom looked out through the windows and across the lawn as Broden poured them both another drink, took out his pipe and slowly packed it.

All light eventually faded and the room and the house fell into a soft darkness. As Broden puffed away on his pipe, he said, "I don't feel like eating tonight. You're welcome to fix yourself something from the kitchen. I may come down later and eat."

"Thank you, Broden."

"I expect you will be flying out tomorrow?"

"Yes. I'll book the 10 am to Gatwick."

"I'm going to go upstairs to check on Coira. You can help yourself to the rest of the bottle. I will see you in the morning."

Tom watched as Broden put down his pipe, refill his glass, take it with him, and slowly ascend the first steps. His usual efficiency and urgency seemed to have left his old bones. Tom felt sorry for him and Coira and Fenella. And, he admitted, for himself. It was too soon to process how he felt about Ellen. And the dogs; he was glad he had never got to know them.

He poured himself another glass and sat back down alone in the darkness. He thought about knocking on Fenella's door to apologise.

Was it too early? But time was running out. He thought about Alister and wondered what he would do. But then he felt sorry for himself again. He could have done without this whole thing. If only Alister had not asked him.

Alister was one for mottos and little sayings, and Tom remembered one now: *Sometimes you feel compelled to do something you know is right, my boy, yet it is still unwise to do it.* It was a conundrum of sorts and it seemed so apt now.

Resolving that right was going to trump unwise, and aware of the significant risk involved, he left his whisky and walked up to the first floor, slowly, shamefully. It was his turn to knock on her door. Like it was a code now, he gave three light taps.

When she opened it just enough to see, he said immediately, "I'm sorry …"

But the door never opened wider.

"Just leave," she said.

"We had …"

"Just get *out* of this house!"

The loud sound of the slamming door followed by the clicking of the lock signified she didn't care anymore if anyone heard at the other end of the hallway.

CHAPTER NINE

Out of courtesy to Coira and Broden, Tom would have to wait until morning to obey Fenella's wishes. He felt he deserved her punishment. When he awoke, he wanted to leave straight away and simply be done with it all, but he would have to wait. He splashed water on his face and looked at himself in the mirror. Tears had been shed the day before, yet none had fallen from his eyes. A woman was dead – someone who had made him breakfast only the day before. Unable to look at himself further, he ran the shower and stood under the water in despair.

Downstairs, Tom found Broden in the living room sipping a cup of tea.

"Good morning, Tom," he said.

"Good morning, Broden."

"Not sure Coira will be down just yet to help with breakfast. Please, help yourself. She may very well sleep all morning."

"I think I'll be heading off soon," he said. There now seemed to be little point in waiting for Coira.

"What time did you say your flight was?"

"10."

"Well, you will be there in good time."

"I'll be down in a minute with my bag."

He went up to his room and tidied it, pulling the sheets and the cover over the bed and placed the pillows in their original positions. Some light rain had started to fall outside and he took one last look out the window. The dogs were up and about, looking hungry and eager to be fed their morning treats. At least they would be safe now.

Tom brought the car around to the front. He just needed to go back inside for a last goodbye to Broden, ask that he pass on to Coira his warm regards and to collect his bag and jacket that he'd left in the hallway. As he was slipping on his jacket, Coira came down the stairs in her dressing gown and slippers with Broden following behind.

"I wanted to thank you before you left," she said, and stretched her arms around him, holding him for a long time. At that moment, she reminded him of his mother – someone who gave love unconditionally, no matter what. She stepped back and tidied her hair with her hand.

"I can't say that I deserve it, Coira. I feel, in some ways, I failed every single person in this house," he said, tears unexpectedly starting to surface like she had somehow squeezed them out. He found it odd that he couldn't control them.

"We all feel bad. I don't know if I will ever come to terms with it. But, if you hadn't come, then it would have gone on and on and we don't know what would have happened then. I don't want to think about it. But I wanted you to know how much we appreciated your help," she said.

Tom wiped a tear away from his left eye and nodded. "Thank you, Coira." He picked his bag up and Broden opened the door. Tom popped the boot of the car, placed the bag inside, then turned to shake Broden's hand for the last time. The rain fell gently on them, and Tom knew he would never see the Patersons again. He kissed Coira on the cheek and she grabbed his hand and squeezed it.

He started the car and let the window down, then with a nod in their direction, he drove slowly away. He glanced up to the far window on the first floor and saw Fenella, standing like a statue and looking down on him, just as she had done that first day. Their eyes met one more time and as he took the driveway, Tom wondered if the image of her looking down would forever be etched in his memory, like a scar, reminding him where he had been, and exactly, what he had done.

* * * *

It was never going to be easy to go back into the office the next day, so he didn't. Nor the next day. He called Cathy saying he was not well and that wasn't a lie, resolving that he would not go back to work until the following Monday. Told he wasn't in the office, Alister called him on his mobile at home.

"I hear you got a result for the Patersons. That you flushed her out. Well done!" he said.

"Is *that* what I did?"

"Tom, you should be pleased."

"Alister, she committed suicide. It's a little hard to feel pleased."

"She was obviously sick, Tom. If she was that sick, you never know where it may have led. Broden told me what the doctor said. And, they've already paid your bill. They were happy with your service."

"What? I never sent a bill." He couldn't bring himself to even open his laptop.

"Your office did, apparently."

"Did they just? Jason can't help himself. How bloody efficient and eager of them. A bit disgusting, if you want to know what I think."

"Listen, Tom. These things are going to happen. You're going to have to come to grips with the simple fact that in this line of work, which is a business like any other business, you might see some dreadful things. Most people don't see that."

"Lucky they don't."

"When are you going back to work?"

"Monday. If I feel like it."

"I'll drop by and see you then, my boy. And I'll take you out for a pint to thank you next week. I'll call you."

* * * *

Deep in a slumber, Tom was awoken by the sound of the television. Marzena had arrived home from work. Looking up at her in a daze, he could see her sitting on the other couch with a glass of wine next to her.

"Have you been asleep there all day?" she said. She wasn't expecting an answer and continued watching the screen as she munched on an apple.

His body felt like a lead weight, sunken deeply into the couch, held down by some overwhelming force beyond his control. He got up and stumbled into the kitchen, wearing only underpants and socks, to get a glass of tap water.

"We're going to that new Chinese restaurant around the corner tonight," Marzena said, still looking at the TV. "Then we're going to the pub. Want to come?"

The last thing he needed was more drinking. "Thanks. But no. I might have an alcohol-free night."

Marzena laughed. "Good luck!"

Tom took his glass to his bedroom where he called Paddo who answered almost straight away.

"That was quick. What are you doing – sitting there waiting, and hoping for me to call you?" Tom said.

"That's it. I've been in the same chair waiting for you to call since we last spoke," Paddo replied.

"I believe it. Hey, how are you going, son? What are you up to tonight? I was wondering if I could come and see you?"

"Tonight?"

"Yeah."

"We're not up to much, I don't think. I haven't seen Bessy all day. She'll be home soon. We'll probably just slip out for a bite later," replied Paddo.

"Right, well, if you could stand some company, I could be over to yours soon."

"Okay. Sounds good."

Tom decided to drive to Paddo and Bessy's flat in Ealing to guarantee that he wouldn't drink. Besides, he wanted to show them his new car. Helena arrived home as he walked out the door. He told her he was off to see Paddo and Bessy. It was Tom's rule that everyone in the house let the others know where they were going, even if was just down to the shops. But not everyone followed it.

When Tom walked into his friend's flat without his usual pack of beer, Paddo was surprised.

"What? No beer! You're expecting to drink mine?" he said.

"No. I'm not drinking."

"Uh-oh, something's wrong." Paddo laughed. "*That's* why the unexpected visit."

"Good to see you, stranger! What've you been up to?" Bessy asked him, with a simultaneous hug as he entered the kitchen. Paddo reached into the fridge and opened a can of beer for himself. He poured Bessy a glass of wine.

"Sure you don't want one?"

"One. But that's it," he said, back in familiar territory where old habits die hard. "I've been working, well, except the last part of this week when I'd had enough."

"That's good, isn't it?" asked Bessy.

"Yes and no. Mainly no."

"What's the no bit about?" asked Paddo.

"If I told you, it's …"

"Just tell us in general terms. You've told us all about confidentiality obligations."

Tom shook his head. "I'm not really enjoying it, not like I thought I would, for one," Tom said. "Frankly, it's pissing me off."

"Why?" asked Bessy.

"You know, it's just coming down to the fact that I don't think I'm very good at it. And it's hard to enjoy something, I guess, if you're no good at it."

"I thought you would be a natural, Tom. You get on well with people and you seem to be a good judge of character. Plus, you can be sneaky, not to mention cheeky," Bessy said and laughed. "It's not like you to take things too seriously. Something must have happened."

"I don't know about a good judge of character. I've just come away from a job where I was anything but."

"So? No one's perfect," said Paddo. "Why are you placing so much pressure on yourself? Anyway, sit down, would you?"

They transferred their drinks to a raised bench and sat around it on stools. Darren, the cat, wandered in from one of the bedrooms and brushed his side up against the stool Tom was sitting on.

Paddo was not particularly fond of cats, mainly because he thought they were environmentally destructive, but Bessy had managed to convince him that a house cat would be a good idea whilst they were city dwellers. Paddo liked Darren even less after he completed a unit in his environmental management course that dealt with domestic animals and their impact. But he understood Bessy's point and with responsible cat 'parenting', he tolerated him.

"Yeah, I know, but it's just a struggle sometimes," Tom said as the cat jumped up on the bench and he gave him a scratch under the chin.

"I don't know why you are being so impatient," Bessy said. "Take a look at my situation, for example. I'm doing two days a week at St Mary's as a trainee nurse and there is not a moment that I feel I really have a proper clue. Of course, I actually do if I stop to think, but I'm still learning."

"That's different," Tom said.

"Not really," she said. "And I'm dealing with people's lives. I mean, not a lot is expected of me just yet, but a time is coming soon that I'm going to get thrown in the deep end."

"Isn't there some saying – I don't know exactly – about the 'ten thousand hour rule' where you can't consider you've mastered something until you've done it for that amount of time?" Paddo said.

"I suppose, but ..."

"You can't expect miracles, Tom – to be really, really good at something, straight away. You're just starting out. What's it been, twelve months? It's the same for everyone, no matter what you do," Bessy reassured him.

"What about the people you work with? How are they?" asked Paddo.

"Do you mean do I get on with them?"

"Yeah."

"Sort of. I mean, Stephanie's fine, mostly. We don't cross paths that often. I like her. Jason is the office supervisor. He's pretty business-like, very serious. Bit of a tosser in some ways. Not much of a sense of humour. Not the type to go and have an ale with. I don't hold that against him.

One of the other guys works a lot from the Canterbury office. I might have had two conversations with him. Robert seems cool. But I haven't got to know him well."

"Do you socialise with any of them?" asked Bessy.

"No, not really."

"Comradery in that line of work would be important, wouldn't it? Like cops?" asked Paddo.

"Probably. My mentor, Alister, has been pretty good. A great old guy, actually. He calls me 'my boy' all the time. I don't think he has any kids of his own. He's the one who gave me the last job in Inverness. It nearly did my head in. I feel ... I don't know exactly. I feel like, sometimes I want to run away to Australia again. How about we all leave in the morning? I'd rather not go by myself." He took a sip of his beer. "What do you say, Bess? Don't you miss Jeparit? We never did go to the pub there. And I want to go."

"Sorry, Tom. I have a date for breakfast with *this* bloke in the morning. Are you still coming?" she looked at Paddo.

"Of course, darling. I wouldn't miss it for the world, and Australia can wait," he replied, smiling at her.

"Are you guys seeing each other during the week or are you ships passing in the night?"

"It's fine, actually. Late nights on Tuesdays and Wednesdays with the course after work but other than that, we're both home by a little after 6, usually," Paddo said.

"And how's the job? It's the Department of Environment something?"

"Yeah. It's a cumbersomely long name that will change to something else soon, probably. It's fine for an office job. My ultimate aim is to get out into the parks and work my way up from a field officer to some sort of management role for the park. But I have to do the hard yards and deal with the bureaucratic side of things first, I think."

"Sounds like a plan," Tom said.

"I'm hoping so. We don't want to be living in London forever. This flat is ridiculously expensive for what it is. But that's London."

"And what about you, Bess? Am I the only one pissed off? Looks like it."

"It's been great, actually. I don't mind this part of London. I prefer it to where we were for the first few months. It's very different for me. It's been exciting. I can see why Paddo prefers Norwich and maybe one day we'll go back there. At the moment, London is serving our purposes. I love nursing and it wouldn't bother me working in a hospital the size of St Mary's or even in a tiny little surgery somewhere."

"Well, that's very cool to hear. Where are you going to take me for dinner?" Tom asked.

"Do you ever, at any stage, stop thinking about your belly, in one form or other? Be it food or liquid?" asked Paddo.

"I suppose so, but I couldn't say I'm consciously aware of it." He drained the last of the beer and placed the can on the counter, looking at them both with his usual cheeky grin.

It was a short stroll to one of their local pubs. Over dinner, Tom mentioned that he'd gone back to Norwich a couple of weeks ago on a new job and had visited Miriam, Paddo's mother.

"You did?" Paddo said, as he cut into his steak. "You old softy, you."

"I didn't stay very long. I was in Norwich just for a few nights. Your mum seems to be going well."

"Bessy and I try to get there once a month. And, of course Roger and Henry are there every second or third weekend," Paddo said. "They're very good to her. I've grown to like Henry, now that he's kind of loosened up a bit."

"I agree," Tom said. "He's a cool guy."

"What sort of work would you be getting in Norwich?" asked Bessy, tucking into her steamed monkfish with lemon and herbed butter, and salad. "Oh, sorry you probably can't tell me."

"It's a missing person's case. Paddo, do you remember a second-hand record shop in Norwich by the name of 'Anti-Vale Vinyl?'"

"Yeah, why?"

"It's related to the case. I'll leave out the details. I couldn't place it at all. I was curious to know if you could."

"I went there a few times. It closed down, all of sudden like," Paddo said.

"Do you remember when it closed?"

"Not exactly. It had been well and truly closed by the time we went to Australia. That guy I knew that I told you about – Dennis Whitcombe – he used to work there for a little while," Paddo said.

"Dennis Whitcombe? You told me about him? I don't remember you telling me," Tom said.

"Yeah, he was the guy I ran into when I was on my bike, the same day I ran into you. Not literally, but it was that day, years ago, when I saw you taking photos of the market stalls and we went and had an ale and got well and truly hammered. You hatched your evil plan for Henry, then you told me you were going to Australia. I told you I was totally shocked to see Dennis – he was a beggar!"

"I don't remember that."

"Maybe I didn't tell you. Anyway, he worked there well before it shut down and then next minute, well maybe a year or two later, he was out on the street begging, with teeth missing! My parents knew his parents. Wealthy types, so I was surprised. It was gob smacking and so weird that he fell that low."

"Where would this Dennis be now, would you know?"

"I would have absolutely no idea. If he's still alive, somewhere in Norwich, probably. Not with his parents I'd say. He hated them."

On the way back from dinner, Tom took them up the street, a little further past their flat and showed them his car.

"Just a little different to the Troopy," Bessy observed. "Nice choice, Tom. More your size."

"Yeah, I don't have trouble reaching the pedals in this one."

CHAPTER TEN

On Monday, Tom walked his usual route to the office but the spring in his step was not so evident as the last time. The night before, he had read in full the information the Morrows had sent to him. Now, as he took the stairs leading to the office, he decided he would call Penny and tell her he was back in London, ready to take the next step in the case, whatever that was. The alcohol-free days and Paddo and Bessy's words of wisdom had helped and he hoped that his feelings of doubt would be banished as he kicked into gear working for Penny.

Jason appeared in Tom's office before he'd had a chance to consider what was on his desk. "We've had quite an influx of work, some urgent, while you've been recovering from your little trip. I need you to kick in, pretty much straight away."

"I was hoping to move ahead with the Morrow case this morning – the missing brother," Tom said, not at all enamoured with Jason's abrupt tone. "I put it off, as you know, to go to Inverness."

"It's going to have to wait. I need these people off my back."

"Aren't you even going to ask me about the Paterson case? Why don't you take a seat for a moment?"

"What's there to know now? It's over, culprit found, we've been paid."

"There was a little bit more to it than that."

"You can tell me all about it when we get some breathing space. Right now, none of us have any. And I need you to do something this morning." Jason threw a file on his desk. Tom pulled it towards him and opened the folder.

"Our client, the insurer, is making the payout on Wednesday to the solicitor's trust account. The matter settled out of court but it's not over, as they say, until the fat man spills the cash into the coffers. All along, the insurer has maintained the fellow has been having a lend of them. They need the dirt on him by close of business tomorrow or they'll have to pay. They've come to us too late, as usual, but they're sure the guy is bunging his injury on. You need to bust him. We'll be heroes if you do and we'll get lots more work from them."

"What? In twenty-four bloody hours?"

"Also there's the claim to serve in the Drew-Darlington case. Cathy has it. The guy is dodging us. It's a difficult one. That needs to be done by close of business today. And here," Jason said, putting a bundle of documents on his desk. "Moira Barnes, long standing client of mine. Worth a fortune, has been for years. She's into cosmetics and works for a number of big modelling agencies. It's also urgent. On Friday, she's going into a joint venture with a guy called Maurice Knoah Ballington. She's only known him for two weeks, likes to work quickly on gut instincts but wants us to look into him. She likes him, not romantically, but who knows? We don't care. But, we do care about whether he's going to rip her off. Check him out and get back to me on Thursday, my office, 10 am, on that. Got all that?"

Before Tom could answer, Jason's phone rang. "Gotta take this. Keep me informed," he said, as he left.

Tom felt like going down the street for a cup of coffee, or driving somewhere, anywhere, so long as it was a long way away from his office. Instead, he shook his head and pulled the insurer's folder closer to examine it.

Cathy's characteristic summary was on top. A payment in excess of £50,000 was to be made – the exact figure wasn't specified – for injuries sustained when falling on stairs that someone had failed to clean up in an office complex. The irony was that the claimant, Ira Cranmore Dunting, was on his cleaning shift and was the one actually responsible for cleaning that part of the building after hours, together with several offices serviced by the stairs.

Apparently, a five-year-old child had been told by his mother to wait for ten minutes in the reception area of her accountant's office while she signed some papers. He secretly escaped into the stairwell and down several floors then relieved himself on the steps. He never told a soul, and despite several office workers noticing the steps were wet that day, neither did they. There were a whole bunch of people who could be blamed, except for the child of course, but ultimately, it was the owners of the building who took the blame as a result of Ira's alleged fall. According to him, he had slipped in the dark and injured his back.

His solicitor argued it was reasonably foreseeable that such an accident would occur in the inadequately lit stairwell. An important light had blown, and even though his client was a cleaner, he didn't see the puddle or expect it. Therefore, it was negligence because the little boy's accident had been left there for more than five hours. It was not in dispute that Ira had fallen, just whether his back injury was as bad as he claimed.

Boring, was Tom's first thought and he tossed the file aside.

He grabbed the other documents and lifted a photograph of Moira, Jason's long-term client. It looked like a commissioned glamour shot but Tom thought it was overexposed and way too glossy. The file said she was aged 43 and single. There was a list of property investments and business successes as long as her arm. *Also boring,* he thought.

Figuring it would be easiest to start with Drew-Darlington, he slipped into reception to obtain the file from Cathy.

Bobby Drew-Darlington owned several pubs, all on the verge of financial collapse, spread out over a wide area of greater London. He had to be personally served with some sort of court document. Examining it, Tom noticed it was stamped with formal court stamps and was clearly a large claim – £49,623. Bobby was known to be infrequently at his place of residence and would in any event never answer the door to anyone, not even his mother, it seemed. He could likely be found in one of the pubs, but not in the general bar area, and possibly somewhere else in the pub that the public could not access, or in the pub's office, from which he could easily slip away when tipped off that someone was looking for him. Another firm had unsuccessfully tried to serve Bobby last week and got the sack after several failed attempts. The plaintiff did not want to get a court order to allow service of the document merely at a known address, irrespective of whether Bobby was there, and wanted him to suffer the indignity of being personally served.

Tom picked up his phone and called one of the pubs on the list. "Johnno Topling from Keeping It Fresh Bakeries, here," he said. "Got a special offer. Would Bobby be available? I'm sure he'll be interested." After three calls to different pubs, Tom had still been unable to speak to Bobby. The next call offered a glimmer of hope. A fellow who sounded quite young and maybe a little on the slow side, answered the phone.

"Ah, I don't know. He was here a minute ago … I think. Hey, Pete, is Bob still out the back?"

There was now no time to wait. "Sorry, got to take this other incoming call. But thank you, I'll call back later. Thanks again," Tom said and hung up.

He grabbed his coat and issued some instructions to Cathy as he prepared to go out the door, "Be parked somewhere outside this pub, in exactly forty-five minutes. Here's the address. Here's the claim. Bring it with you and I'll see you there, outside the pub." He rushed down the stairs and onto the street. In two minutes, he was at his favourite bakery asking for his friend, Al.

"Al, could you do me a favour? It's worth a baker's dozen of your favourite pints. If it works, that is. If not, half a dozen, delivered either way."

"What is it now?" Al said. "Explain to another woman you really are a top catch when you're sober?"

"No, no, that's next week. You and I are going out on the turps soon. Listen, if you could, I just need to borrow a dusty white baker's shirt and apron, or something like that. And, like a tray of goodies. Like a small tray. Here's twenty-five quid," Tom said, handing him some notes across the counter.

"What do you want on the tray?" Al asked, folding the money into his trouser pocket.

"I don't care. Something that looks fancy and has a good profit margin for you. May as well make some money out of this as well."

A minute later, Tom darted out wearing the baker's shirt and apron, with a fresh dusting of icing sugar on the front. He carried his work shirt in one hand, the tray in his other and went and got his car that was parked not far from his flat.

The traffic held him up so he called Cathy and said he was running a little late. "I'm there already," she said.

"Don't go into the pub yet. When I get there, I'll go in first, then I'll send you a text but it may be gibberish. Don't respond. I'm not going to pull my phone out all the way. That will be your key to just come inside and serve Bobby immediately. Just walk casually to the bar or wherever I'm sitting and say, "Robert ... etc., and serve him. Got it?"

"Okay," she said as she sat in her car.

He knew he needed a bit of luck to pull this off and was due for it. When he arrived at the pub, he saw Cathy's car outside and he strolled past, giving her a wink. Then he rested the tray between his hand and hip, as he opened the pub door and walked in.

"Hello, hello!" he said loudly when he was halfway to the bar, breaking the silence. It was early and there were only a handful of old male regulars inside, some quietly mumbling to themselves as they sipped the day's first pint. At the bar, Tom was greeted by the young fellow he thought may have answered the phone.

"Is the big man about. Bobby? My name is Johnno Topling, from Keeping It Fresh Bakeries. I rang a little earlier."

"Um, I dunno. Who did you say you are?"

"Johnno. We got a bakery at Chelsea; it's just opened. You should come down some time after work. Before, even! Whenever you want. Listen, given we've just opened, we're on the lookout for new customers. Got some samples here. We can supply all your fresh bakery needs for the kitchen. Breads, cakes, desserts, you name it. I was hoping to see the owner and leave these samples." Smiling, he placed the tray on the bar.

"Just wait a minute," the bar attendant said.

He was gone for more than a few minutes. Tom thought that was a good sign; he could imagine the bar attendant being questioned carefully.

He glanced straight into the CCTV camera, hoping Bobby might see the tray. Eager to give the impression he was keen to impress, Tom re-arranged the various pastries, pies, buns and cakes neatly on the tray.

The barman returned to serve a customer, followed by Bobby. He walked slowly with a sway of his shoulders and an outstretched belly like he owned the joint, which of course he did, but perhaps not for too much longer. He approached Tom, sniffed, and grabbed his nostrils, then wiped his hands on the bottom of his shirt before taking a close look at the tray. "Where did you say you were from?" he asked.

"Keeping it Fresh Bakeries."

"Samples, is that right?"

"Yep. I can bring more back. Got some very special deals at the moment. If you could leave me with one of your menus – lunch and dinner – I could come back with some prices," he said excitedly.

Bobby grabbed a cream bun and inserted it into his enormous mouth like a torpedo into a compartment of a submarine. It was gone in two mouthfuls. He grabbed a napkin from near the till and wiped his mouth. "Got a card?" he asked.

"Yes, I do." He reached into his pocket and then the other. Giving a sigh of frustration, he said, "Oh, where are they? Bloody hell. I left them in the car."

While Bobby helped himself to a pork bun, Tom grabbed his phone and pressed Cathy, followed by a couple of letters, then slipped it back in his pocket. He didn't think Bobby had noticed as he was too busy devouring the bun, but when Tom heard the text go through, he regretted not turning the phone to silent. It didn't seem to matter. Bobby was now licking his fingers.

"We can do pretty much all your pastry needs. Beef pies, pork buns, all the desserts, special order pies …"

"You got a price list on yer?"

"Yep. But, we would prefer to specially cater it, once we know what you have in mind."

As Bobby went to lift another pork bun, Cathy stepped inside the door and approached the bar.

Bobby was meaner and looked bigger than he did in his photo on the file, so Tom thought they'd better be quick.

"Aren't you Robert Drew-Darlington?" Cathy said with a big smile, as she got to the bar. "Do you remember me?" She had pulled her top down a little, showing a bit of cleavage and hidden the claim in her bag draped over her shoulder.

Bobby looked at her as if she had two heads while he picked the remnants of the pork bun out of his front teeth with a tooth pick. "Yeah. Who are you?"

"I'm Cathy from EAC and Co, Sir," she said, changing to a formal tone. She pulled the document out of her bag. "I formally serve you with this court document. The nature of it is a claim filed in court against you for an amount specified in the claim. Your attention is directed to the contents of the claim, including the time to file a defence." She then handed it to him.

"Fuck you, I'm not taking that!" he said, taking a step back from the bar.

She dropped it on the bar in front of him. "I'm bound to leave it with you, Sir. I make a note of the date," and she looked at her watch, "the time of personal service: 11.25 am."

Tom smiled, picked up the tray and said, "I'd best be going." He scurried to the door with Cathy close behind him.

"Great work, Cathy. 'Remember me!' That was bloody brilliant! Nice touch with the top too!" he said as they went out onto the street.

Soon, Tom was fighting his way through traffic again, but this time, he was munching on a cream bun on his way to the bakery with the beer for Al.

* * * *

Keeping it fresh meant keeping busy and that seemed to be the key, so after lunch he turned his attention to tomorrow's task. The insurer had given the firm a lot of work over the last few years and most of it was good paying work, albeit time consuming, boring old surveillance. He disliked surveillance immensely, but recognised it was part of the job.

He'd fallen asleep in a car on his last watch and eventually was awoken by a London Bobby on patrol.

The Ira Dunting file was not thick but it was filled with detailed information. Ira had only been a contract cleaner for about six months when the incident happened. As a result of his injury, he could no longer work in any physical type of capacity. His pastimes included snooker and golf. Whilst it was still possible to play snooker once or twice a week, 'with considerable pain and spasms', golf was now entirely out of the question. The injury was 'life changing' he claimed. There were two reports from specialist doctors both agreeing, stating the nature of his injury was inconsistent with an ability to be a cleaner and a golfer, although there were some prospects of improvement over time, perhaps a very long time. And at age 49, Ira was no longer a young man.

The two doctors for the insurer put the injury into a 'minor' category and said that he would 'periodically' need pain relief for 'intermittent' bouts of 'mild to moderate pain'. But that in any event, with the time off work already and rehab, the injury would 'not prevent working as a cleaner or playing golf'. Ira had taken up working from home, selling carpet cleaning products and a range of other household cleaning items. But his income was a fraction of what it had been. Ira was still a regular at the Barbican and Foley Snooker Club of London, a male-only, below-street venue with a liquor licence and situated east of the business district.

Delivering beer to Al had made Tom keen for a pint himself, so a visit to the snooker club just might be in order. He told Cathy he would not be back until tomorrow. "The things I have to do!" he said with a smile as he headed out.

As he sat on the train, he thought about some strategies. Gut instincts told him that Ira was lying and greatly exaggerating his pain. It was not surprising how many greedy but dumb claimants over the years had forfeited their compensation by getting caught doing the very thing they said they couldn't. The PI course was filled with many such examples. Ira had cancelled his membership at his local golf club. A copy of an affidavit on file from the president of the snooker club said that there were times when Ira would simply 'yelp' in pain while playing snooker, 'So while he could bend down and play, he had to stand higher and it was evident to all of us in the club it was always a tremendous struggle for him'.

The file also had some words from Ronald, Ira's brother, who happened to be a very good golfer. He'd given evidence that he used to play golf regularly with Ira but that was all finished now.

The sign at the door said a complimentary half pint for visitors or the guest of a member would be served on arrival. Tom descended the stairs knowing it was now his turn for something complimentary.

He was surprised to find a lady behind the bar in this all-male club. Taking a seat, he admired the four, full-size snooker tables and the fine, soft lighting over each. Two of the snooker tables were occupied but no other patrons were about.

"First time in, Sir?" the bartender asked.

"Yes, I've been meaning to come in for ages."

"Can I get you something?"

"Um, the half pint, the complimentary, if that would be alright. I'm happy to pay for another."

"The stout or the IPA?"

"The IPA, thanks. Sorry, did I have to sign in to the club, or anything?"

"It's fine," she said as she pulled the tap.

Tom thanked her and took the glass with him as he strolled slowly around the club. The noticeboard advertised an upcoming general meeting. There was a display of past club champions and a print-out of what looked like a tournament roster. Ira was due to play at 7 pm that night against a Joe Brierly.

After ordering another pint of the IPA, Tom sat down at the bar to think. If he had more time, he could come up with a plan. Some insurers had lots of experience with exposing false claims, *after* the claimants had received their compensation, but many had spent all the money by the time they got busted.

Tom noticed a plaque hanging on the wall behind the bar. It was a commemorative plaque of past presidents of the club.

"That list goes back a few years," he said to the bartender.

"Yeah. Sure does. 1956, I believe," she said.

One entry was for a 'Broderick B Allsopp,' listed as president from 1958 to 1967. "What a history! Like that fellow Allsopp, president for what, ten years in a row!" he said.

"He was a bit of a legend. Only died a few years back," she said as she unloaded a dishwasher.

"I bet he was a legendary snooker player, too."

"He was apparently a legend of all sports. Some of the older members often tell stories about him. Tennis, cricket, golf, he could apparently play them all and win too, so the story goes. Wish I was like that," she said.

After he'd finished the beer, he said, "Thank you very much. I'd like to come back. Do you have a membership application form?"

She handed him one.

"Brilliant. Thanks again."

By the time he got up the stairs and onto the street, his next move was now clear. He would take the train to Ira's house but first, he needed to buy a couple of items – a small, quality writing pad or similar, and a small envelope. In a matter of fifteen minutes he had them, found a bench and sat down. With his best handwriting he wrote:

'Ira,

Sorry for the awfully short notice. I don't know whether you remember me but I was at Pop's (Broderick Allsopp) funeral some years back. I'm his grandson. I'm sure I met you there. In any event, I got your address from one of the boys down at the Barbican. I'm having a commemorative game of golf with a few others from the club (exclusive few!?) tomorrow morning, teeing off at 8.30 am at the Finchley course. One of the chaps has pulled out. Hoping you could join us, as I remember someone said you are a very good player. A day to remember Pop, with a few pints afterwards! Hope to see you there.

Kind regards,

Steve

P.S. Apologies again for the short notice. Better late than never …'

Tom placed his note under Ira's front door at 8 pm under the cover of darkness. Knowing Ira would be playing snooker and would see it as soon as he got back in, perhaps late, he felt he had a 50/50 chance of the entrapment working. Ira wouldn't have much time to properly consider the invitation which was a good thing. And if it didn't work, no one would know Tom had been behind it.

Unfortunately for Ira, the words 'exclusive few' caused his ego to cloud his caution. Not only did he turn up, despite the fact he couldn't remember 'Steve', but whilst waiting for the non-existent others to show, he took a number of practice swings without flinching, looking like he was ready to belt golf balls down the fairways. He even took a session on a putting green, all of which was captured on Tom's trusty telephoto lens.

Ira's lawyers made an urgent application for the evidence to be set aside on the grounds of entrapment; or some such similar dirty play. Failing that, they argued Ira was misled and 'fraudulently coerced' to make a special effort despite his injury, merely making it 'out of obligation and respect for the late Mr Allsopp' and 'notwithstanding it would come at substantial personal cost to his health'. But the judge allowed it and that was the end of Ira's claim.

Tom was busy the rest of the day in meetings with the insurer and taking various phone calls, including some very angry ones from Ira and his solicitor. He could not get task three started, that of Moira Barnes, until Wednesday morning. On further consideration of the file, he decided he would not have to leave the office for this case. He took Cathy out to lunch and they had a good time laughing about the look on Bobby's face when she told him who she was.

"He thought you were going to say you were an old school friend or something! He had no idea," Tom said. "I loved it!"

They shared a bottle of wine and returned to the office at 3 pm. Tom put the finishing touches on his work for Moira, then went home early and got the best night's sleep he'd had for a good while. With things improving again with his work situation, he was in a slightly better state of mind.

* * * *

At 10 am the next morning Tom was sitting in Jason's office. "Moira's was the easiest of the three you gave me, by far," he began, watching Jason sip a coffee. "You wanted me to check out this guy she proposes to go into business with. Mr Ballington – 'Maurie' to his friends – is an ex-bankrupt. He self-filed seven years ago. Clean slate since then, except for the little matter of the insolvency of one of his companies. It went under after losing an appeal from a judgement of a lower court two years ago, when the company was ordered to pay two creditors something in the order of £250,000. He was divorced ten years ago. He's currently a director of four other companies, one of which is being sued by a competitor for false and misleading conduct and infringement of intellectual property rights. One of his other companies has a receiver appointed. His house has two mortgages and …"

"That's enough. So you think she can do better?" Jason said.

"Just give her the facts. That's all. She's an experienced business woman. She can make up her own mind. Armed with my report, she should ask a few clever questions, I think. There's more in the report." He handed Jason the folder.

"Right. Thanks for that, Tom. Good work. I will get it to her before lunch."

"I need to get back to Penny Morrow now," he said.

"Look, Tom, something has come up about you," Jason said. "Just wait a minute."

"What?"

"The Morrow matter. They called me late yesterday."

"Who called you?"

"The husband. What's his name? Edgar."

"And?"

"And they've complained about you. They're upset you haven't got back to them and, apparently you said you would, even if there was nothing to report."

"Are *you* bloody kidding? I haven't had a chance! Every time I was about to, I was given a new case and it was always urgent!"

"I know, I know. But, anyway, I said I would take over the case."

"You what?"

"Something like this happens every so often, so don't take it personally; it's for the best. You shouldn't take it badly."

"That's not right, Jason. It's my case! I don't want you to take it over!"

"Well, that's what I'm going to do. I told them – him – that I would. Look, he's a whinger. They both are. We don't need matters like that, anyway."

"What do mean *matters like that?*"

"Look, if the cops have hit a dead end after four years, so will we. It's inevitable. And they won't pay our bills when we do. I can see it coming now. People like them have unrealistic expectations. I'm not planning on doing much; a couple of routine things. That's all. I've already diarised when I'm going to send them a final bill and ditch them." He flicked to the page of a diary sitting on his desk. "Terminate the retainer. Two weeks max. So, forget it and move on."

"Listen, Jason." He paused to choose his words, infuriated now. "*If* you do that … Christ, I can't believe you're doing this to me! If you don't put me back on it, frankly, I don't think I can hang around here any longer."

"Tom, I think you're blowing it way out of all proportion. You've done some bloody good work of late. But, we all know you've been under a lot of stress."

"No, Jason. Screw that! There's a right and wrong here. It's got nothing to do with stress. I'm not stressed!" Stomping out and straight past Cathy he went into his own office and slammed the door behind him. The diploma in the red cedar frame crashed down, cracking the museum glass in two. *That's it. I'm done.* In a flash he was down the stairs.

CHAPTER ELEVEN

Marzena and Helena, both not long out of bed, sat in the kitchen having breakfast and discussing last night's shifts. They did not expect to see Tom barge into the kitchen and grab a beer straight from the fridge without saying a word.

"Aren't you supposed to be at work today?" Helena said, scooping a spoonful of yoghurt into her mouth.

"I've already been to work! Where's the bloody opener?" He rifled through a kitchen drawer and before they could respond, he found it and knocked the top off the bottle.

"But it's only eleven o'clock," Helena said.

"Ha, that *is* a short shift! Where can I get a job like that?" added Marzena with a giggle and poured coffee into her cup.

"You can have *my* job. Take *my* office! They'll be looking for someone this afternoon. Go right in and ask for Jason. You can't miss him. He looks like an arsehole!" He took an almighty swig and the bottle was already half empty. "And ..." he belched, "tell him I'll give you a reference!"

"Sounds like you don't want to work for *him*," Helena said, raising her eyebrows. "I'd stick to your current job, Marzena."

"Why not? He is a perfect, ah ..., you don't need to hear it." Tom lifted the bottle again to his mouth, tilted his head back and let the liquid free fall. Helena started to laugh.

"I thought you were trying to cut down on your alcohol consumption?" Marzena quipped.

"I don't know what you mean … where's that flavoured Polish vodka? Can you get it? It's been lying around here for weeks," he said, placing the empty on the bench, holding his hand over his eyes and shaking his head.

"Whoa, it's not even lunchtime dude, slow down. Pretty bad morning hey?" Helena said.

"Just average. Typical, actually."

"I don't know if we should give it to him," Helena said to Marzena.

"That's fine. I'm going to clear the hell out anyway." His phone was sitting on the counter and it rang. He ignored it.

"That'd be your phone, Tom," Marzena said.

"Greer!" he said, picking it up.

After a minute of listening, he raised his eyebrows, shook his head and blinked. "Well, you might put up with him because *you* have to, he's *your* partner. But he isn't mine Steph, and I can tell you now, he never will be! I'm sorry for you and the others, but I can't work with the prick. Sorry for the language but …"

He listened some more. After a moment he added, "Actually, no. I'm not going to be back today. I'll be there in the morning to pick my stuff up. Sorry but …"

Then, "I can see your point of view, but it's not acceptable that he does what he does. He heard what went down in Inverness. I'm not after a shoulder but he's rude. It's always all about the money and it's not fun, Stephanie. It's just not. He fobs me off, unloads work he's too bloody lazy to do himself, stresses Cathy out, and then it all becomes urgent. Then, steals my best case! So, no. Sorry. Screw him."

Marzena, who could not help but hear all of this, went and got the vodka.

"It's not about the stress. I can handle stress! It's more … thank you for your concern. I'm not burning bridges … not with you, anyway. I don't care about him. I might be only twenty-six Steph but … yes, I know, but …"

Eventually, he thanked her and hung up. Three filled shot glasses awaited him and the girls.

"I've quit!" he said. *"Na zdrowie!"* he exclaimed, toasting in Polish, pronouncing it not quite as well as the girls had taught him. The girls followed suit. Marzena filled the glasses again.

"I'm not having another," Helena said. "Tom, you have mine. I've got laundry and packing to do. I'm off to Rome this weekend."

"Good on you," he said. "Give my kind regards to the Romans. And when you're there, do what they do, whatever it is." He was well and truly on his way now; he just didn't know where.

The second shot had weakened Marzena's resolve to go shopping that morning and before she thought too carefully, she had changed clothes and was ready to head out the door with him.

"Let's slip in and see Al, my baker lad, and see if he can join us," Tom said as they headed down the street. "Have you met Al before? He's a top Scouser, really good fun."

"Is he the guy who vomited in our kitchen at the last party?"

"Yep, that's him. He's unbeatable," he replied, pounding the pavement now as if there was nothing more important in the world than seeing Al.

When they got to the bakery, Al was just finishing up his shift.

"I've been working since 3 this mornin', so yeah, I'd love a pint or two. I gotta be here for the next twenty minutes, but I'll go home and meet ya for lunch. Where you gonna be?"

"I don't know. One of the boozers over near Camden, I reckon. I'll call you. That's near you, isn't it?"

"Yeah, that'd be sweet, cheers."

Back out on the street, Tom hailed a cab. "Good. I'm in no mood for the bloody train," he said as he pulled on his seat belt. "I'll get the fare."

When the cab approached the corner of Parkway and Arlington Road, he said to the driver, "This is fine. You can let us out here anywhere." Turning to Marzena, he said, "You happy with walking now?" It didn't appear she had any choice.

"Yeah, sure. I'm happy to go with the flow. You know your way around here better than me."

Marzena, in her high lace-up boots strapped tightly around blue-denim jeans, hit the footpath first. With her white shirt and old leather jacket, one she'd purchased the last time she visited Camden Markets, she looked in complete contrast to Tom. He was wearing his favourite beige trousers that looked too big and too wide for him, making him look shorter than he was; a white business shirt; dark, checked, woollen vest; and brown jacket. He thought he looked good. He felt better than good. But a trusty second opinion was in order.

"I'm starved," he said, heading off. "I should've got something at Al's. They make top pork buns there. Had one the other day. You should try them."

"You're always starved. I don't know what a pork bun is."

"I'll take you there one time for a sit down. We can pop into that little Polish supermarket thing you like to go to, just around the corner. I want some of those Polish sausages. Why don't you bring those home more often? They're brilliant."

"Helena does that, not me. I'm trying to take some weight off. She's like you, she doesn't care."

"Hey, what are you saying, Marzena? Don't you think I care how I look?"

"Not really."

"Oh. Well I do."

"I don't think anyone else does, Tom. So, don't worry about it."

"Ha! Get a bit of vodka into you and you're a comedian, hey?"

"I wasn't trying to be funny, Tom. We need another drink, if you want me to be funny."

He wholeheartedly agreed and before long, they had chosen the first of the venues that took their fancy. It sold Polish beer and it wasn't crowded. They took a seat near a window. "Are all Polish beers over 5% alcohol content?" he asked, twirling the bottle to examine it. "This packs a punch. It's 7.2%! I'm not complaining, mind you."

"No, although a lot are." Her perfectly spoken English always took on a stronger, more lively accent when she drank and she added, "I like this beer the best."

"Do all Polish girls drink beer?"

"Of course not, but a lot do. Some drink wine, vodka …"

"Sorry, that was a pretty stupid question. Maybe even sexist. Words are coming out before I'm thinking. My head is still spinning a bit from this morning's events."

"I've noticed!"

"It's pretty cold for beer, over there, isn't it?"

"Yes, it's cold, but it's cold here too. You can drink vodka to stay warm, sometimes with the beer."

"You like London better than Krakow?"

"No. It's just different. Krakow is a very good city. It's my favourite in Poland."

"Why?"

"It has a good feel. The nightlife is good. Restaurants and bars are cool. Modern, yet has history. Warsaw, I like less. Weren't you supposed to be ringing your friend?"

"Al, bloody hell, I forgot!"

After telling Al where they were, he said to Marzena, "I want to go to Poland." It was almost like he wanted to go there before he wanted to go home.

"Well, if you're quitting your job, you can go whenever you want."

"Would you come with me?"

"I'm not quitting my job. Someone has to pay our rent."

"Can't you get a week off?"

"Oh, I don't know."

"Have you *ever* had any time off from that grubby pub?"

"Grubby is it, now? You spend a lot of time there."

"Yes, but does that moron of a publican ever give you a break?"

"I get every second weekend off, every second Friday and Saturday. You know that, Tom."

"I mean a week or two holiday?"

"No. I'm not full-time. I'd have to take unpaid time."

"Well, maybe you could just take a week off. What do you think? I could shout your airfare."

"Maybe. I would have to check with the boss. She's a bit of a bitch. I wasn't planning on going back to Poland for a while."

"You could tell work that something has come up. Tell the boss you have to go home to see your mum."

"That's true, actually. And my father. They want me to come home regularly. I've been a bit slack over the last year."

"And they live in Krakow?"

"Yeah."

Watching the stream of people wander down the road, they chatted some more about Poland.

"We should give it some more thought, over an English pint, this time. Are you happy to have an ale?"

Placing her hand over her stomach shaking her head, she said, "This beer is bloating me now. A white wine. The house special is fine. Whatever is cheap. Choose something."

As Tom went to the bar, he felt the spontaneity of the day really kick in, of the things that were now new in his mind and which were somehow uplifting and refreshing, like a breeze of fresh calming air had blown away some of his frustrations. His anger had dissipated a little although he knew it was really the alcohol flushing its temporary potion of relief through his veins. He watched the bartender fill the pint glass and he wondered how long this feeling was going to last. Then he felt a pang of sorrow that he'd lost the Morrow case. *Did they really think I wasn't genuine? That I wasn't going to get back to them?*

"Cheers," Tom said and handed the glass of wine to Marzena.

Not long after, Al joined them, a pint of beer in hand. Tom said nothing to him about the details of the job done on Bobby. Al knew what Tom's job entailed and was not one to press for any information. Marzena thought Al was handsome and his Liverpool accent cute, and soon forgave him for his indiscretion that night of the party.

"It's all too easy for me to have a blow out with me shifts an' all. I'm sorry, again, about chundering in the sink," Al said to Marzena.

"It's fine. You weren't the only one who was ill that night."

"You come around to the bakery some time. I'll give you some treats to take home. Just like ya mum might make ya," he said.

"Get the pork buns," Tom added.

It was cheers again, and again, until a late lunch.

After two more pints, Al left, saying he was shattered after his shift and had another early start at 3 am. Marzena led Tom around the markets and the stalls in the town, up and around the various ins and outs and side detours. She bought a scarf and put it on. Tom was happy to browse and follow her, doing his best to remove from his mind the happenings of the morning. But as the alcohol started to wear off, things began to stick in his craw. He suggested they walk back to the train station. At a pub not far from Edgware Road, he switched to a spirit in an effort to lift his own while Marzena told him more about Poland. But a fade was now inevitable, and the earlier breeze that had gently blown through his mind had gone. There was no second wind. They wandered back to the flat slowly and both were asleep before dark.

Sometime shortly after the light faded, Tom turned his head back and forth on his pillow, dreaming and murmuring. "I'm sorry, so terribly sorry." But his apology wasn't being accepted. Agony, now. He could see her, standing alone and crying. He felt like crying too but he couldn't. Someone said from nowhere, "You fool. You let her down. How could you?" Suddenly a gunshot. *Have I been hit?* he thought. He looked at his leg. "It's in your back!" Nothing. His body started to move backwards. He couldn't control his legs. The floor started to move. But it wasn't the floor, it was him. The walls flew past. He held his arms out. She said, "Stop. Stop it now! Why did you do it? I trusted you." But he couldn't see her eyes. If he could just see her eyes. "Fenella, Fenella, don't let me fall!" Someone took his legs out from underneath him. He began to fall, waking suddenly, heart pounding, sighing out into the darkness.

CHAPTER TWELVE

Tom had already cleaned out the drawers of his desk and noticed the box the Morrows had left him had been moved to Jason's office. He emptied the broken glass from the framed diploma into a bin.

"It's Alister on the phone, Tom. Do you want to take it before you leave?" Cathy asked, standing in his office with her phone head-piece attached.

"Sure. I'll take it."

"What about a long lunch, my boy, can you get the afternoon off?" Alister asked.

"Absolutely, I have the afternoon off. In fact, I'm leaving in about five minutes, permanently, and I'll never set foot back in this place again."

"Right. I see. That doesn't sound good, then, does it?"

"What about if I meet you at the last place we went for lunch?" Tom said. "Unless you are over Middle Eastern food?"

"I'll see you there at 1 pm."

Tom rolled up the diploma and placed it in his bag with his little red cedar bowl. He grabbed the cedar frame, tucked his laptop under his arm, picked up his bag and stepped into Stephanie's office. "Give my goodbyes to Imran and Robert," he said.

"Will do. Good luck," she said. "What are you going to do?"

"Not sure. Take a break. I'll figure it out."

"Don't be a stranger," she said.

Cathy kissed him on the cheek, as he stepped into reception. "I'm going to miss you," she said.

"One day, Cathy, when I run into you in a pub somewhere on some Saturday night, in a few years, I'm going to come up to you and say, 'Remember me!' I'll never forget that!"

She smiled. "I can't even give you a hug, with your hands full! It's not going to be the same around here. You're leaving me, with *this*. Not fair, Tom."

"You'll be right."

When he got home, he dumped his gear onto the bed and had a quick cup of tea with Marzena before heading back down to the other end of Edgware Road. He found Alister sitting inside the restaurant at their usual table.

"You remember what I told you once about this job?" Alister said, as they waited for the food.

"Once? Try several. You're going to tell me again, no doubt."

"Sometimes you can feel compelled to do something you know is right yet it is still unwise to do."

"And quitting might have been unwise, right?"

Alister smiled. "Only time will tell. The job's not really a team sort of thing, in my view, anyway. On a day-to-day level, teamwork is less a factor. You're out there working by yourself. It can be a lonely sort of a thing. But, and this is something you might have lost sight of, bringing the actual money in as part of a team, is a team thing with a firm that size. I know you didn't get on with Jason. I agree he's hard work. I knew his father and he was the same."

Minted lamb with spiced chick peas, with a large side of baba ghanoush and flat bread arrived delivered by the owner who told them the eggplant, pistachio and tomato salad was not far away.

"Are you going to go out on your own?"

"I don't know. I don't know if I even want to do investigation anymore."

"What would you do instead?"

"I don't know. Maybe professional photography. Put my uni degree to some use."

"Don't you think you might get bored? Like, taking family shots and wedding photos?" Alister shook his head. "Word is you are a pretty good PI. Naturally talented, one might say. A little unusual with some of your methods, apparently, but good. Why walk away?"

"I'm going to think about it," he said as he took a gulp of water.

"Isn't there something about the job you're going to miss?"

"I was looking forward to doing my best to help the clients with that missing person case I told you about. I was enjoying that work, the little that I did. It was the case that kept me hanging in there. But Jason took it from me, and I can't do anything about it now. It frustrates me. And it caused me a lot of grief to lose it – knowing that poor lady was grieving her lost brother and Jason is just going to fob her off. I like helping people, if I can. I'll miss that."

"If you're going to stay in London, the rent is going to be expensive for a sole operator."

"Will I need an office?"

"It's not essential but for a number of reasons, highly advisable. You don't want people coming to your home. Better if they don't know where you live. You also can't conduct every meeting in a café or some park. Having an office gives a professional look, as well. I tried without an office for a couple of years in the eighties and it didn't work out."

"I want to clear my head," he said, shovelling in a mouthful of his meal. "I'm not sleeping that well anymore."

"By all means. You liked Scotland, I hear. Why not go back there for a holiday?"

"It's beautiful but I need to get away from somewhere I associate work with. It was pretty intense, that job. Have you heard how Coira is? Maybe I shouldn't ask." As much as he felt for the Patersons, and he dared not extend his mind to Fenella, he knew he needed to keep a distance now.

"She's doing fine. They've decided not to get a new maid for a little while. Downsizing will be the next step."

"Alister, I do appreciate all the support you've given me. I don't want you to think I'm not grateful. I just don't think it's worked out, how I thought the job would be."

"Look, since I've retired, it's a pleasure to be spending my time doing this. And really, since my wife died, well, I don't have much else to do, frankly. I don't miss the job but I like keeping in touch with my old students. I'll miss what we do."

"You're very good at it." Tom pushed his empty plate to the side.

Outside, after lunch, it was time to say goodbye. "I'm heading in the other direction to you," Alister said. They shook hands. "Please, keep me informed of your next moves. Where you land and all that stuff. Maybe just take some time away. Get some perspective."

"I will Alister. Thank you for everything."

CHAPTER THIRTEEN

Plac Nowy, Kazimierz, Krakow, Poland, two weeks later

The small, red-brick pavilion-like structure in the centre of the old market place had all of its windows closed but one. Tom was waiting for what Marzena said would be a treat, something very much to his liking – a foot-and-a-half long *zapiekanki*, or pizza bread. The old lady who had made it for him said something in Polish as she handed it through the window. When he said, "I don't know," she pointed to a bottle of sauce and he nodded. As he held it, she placed a splattering of the sauce over it and smiled, seeing his hungry eyes.

"You like?" asked Marzena.

Tom munched on his treat as he sat on an old iron chair with his elbows perched on a tiny table. "It's fantastic!"

They had arrived that morning and still had their bags with them, patiently waiting to check in to the accommodation Marzena had booked. The two-bedroom apartment around the corner on the first floor of a building had a kitchen, although he very much doubted he would be doing any cooking. It was only for two nights. After that, Marzena had arranged to stay with her parents for another two nights and to bring him along, if he wanted to come. If he wanted to go off exploring on his own, that would be just fine too.

"This district we are in – you can see from the signs over there – is Kazimierz. Historically, it's been a Jewish area. Has been for more than 500 years. You can imagine, maybe, what changes happened during the

Second World War. But, it has survived. You can see the buildings. Some have been here for a long time."

Tom looked on, blowing the pizza bread cool, as he did.

"There are quite a few synagogues and museums, just a short walk from here," she added.

People seemed relaxed to Tom. Many sat outside nearby cafes and eateries. Old men with big, heavy glasses of beer, smoked cigarettes and watched the passing parade.

"It's funny, but this little district, has become … I don't know, maybe just in the last twenty years, the centre of nightlife in Krakow. I wanted to show it to you," she said. "I used to come here as a teenager with my friends."

Tall young girls rode past them on old-fashioned bikes, like the type he was used to seeing in old photos. They didn't wear helmets and their long hair streaming behind them seemed to reflect a freedom that was so absent on the busy streets of London. These girls were in no rush to get to where they were going.

In his head, Tom tried to pronounce the names on the facades of the buildings. "How far are we from the main centre of the city?" he asked.

"The Old Town is not far down that way. Maybe, a twenty minute walk."

"What time did you say we can check in?" he asked, wiping his mouth with a napkin. "You sure you don't want some of this?"

"No, I'm not hungry. You enjoy it. She didn't say exactly. I think sometime around 2.30. She's going to call me. We have to go there and meet her to get the keys."

"What should we do until then? What about a beer? That man over there is making me thirsty."

"Sure," she said.

"You know, I haven't had any alcohol since we last had drinks that day in Camden."

"That must be a record for you. Don't you feel good?"

"I'm about to feel even better."

Soon they were sitting inside a tiny bar with very large glasses in front of them.

"I'm impressed with you Polish girls, you know. You're open-minded when it comes to beer."

"You're too easily impressed."

It started to rain quite heavily all of a sudden, like a cloud had burst, and a few more people rushed into the bar to find shelter.

"Should we go to a nightclub tonight? I think I saw what looked like one on the way, not far from here," he asked.

"I'm happy to give it a try. There are two down the street and I think there are a couple more around the corner. We should make sure you get some food before we go out. Most Polish beer is much stronger than the English beer and you know what happens when you haven't had enough to eat."

"Good thinking," he said. "What about a restaurant? Somewhere nice. Can you recommend any? My shout."

"I might ask the lady who is going to let us into the apartment. The locals usually know the best places. I think I've only been to a restaurant here once, when I finished school. Do you like Polish food?"

"I think so. I like most food. I'm eager to try it."

By the time they had finished their beer and ordered a second, the rain had gone and a faint hint of sunshine tried to shine through onto the market area. Women were now setting up long wooden tables near where they had been sitting.

"It seems like a bit of activity happening over there," he said.

"All around where we were sitting changes from day to day. One day it's full of fresh food stalls and eating places – if you like Polish sausage and pickles, there's no better place in the world on those days. Other days, it's full of second-hand clothes and shoes. Then, you come here the next day and it's full of flowers and plants and fruits that might be in season."

"It sounds like you miss living here."

"I like it. But I don't know if I'll ever move back."

"Is there Jewish heritage in your family?"

"On my mother's side. My great-grandmother was Polish Jewish."

After they finished their second beer, she suggested they take a walk around the corner to where she remembered quite a few restaurants were located. "I'll show you where we could go to eat tonight, yes?"

"Okay. What time is it?" He looked at his watch and it said 3.30 pm. "Wasn't that lady supposed to have called you by now? We lost track of the time."

"Yes. She is overdue. I'll call her," she said. The call went straight through to a message bank and Tom heard her leave a message in Polish.

"What did you say?"

"I said we're just wandering around with our bags and are eager to check in."

After about ten minutes more of wandering, Marzena told Tom to stop. She walked across to the other side of the street and he followed. Peering inside a window she said, "I think this is the restaurant I went to after I finished school."

"Was it good?"

"I think so. It's very traditional."

"Authentic, you mean?"

"Yes. But there are some more up here." She walked on.

Tom's bag was heavy and his back had begun to ache. He began to regret not having a bag with a handle and wheels like Marzena's.

After another short walk, she stopped in front of another restaurant. There were two more opposite it. "Maybe, one of these." She described what was on the menu in the window to him at one place. Light rain began to fall again.

"It's after 4 and she hasn't contacted us," Tom said. "Not even returned your call. Should we be getting concerned?"

"I'll try again," she said, pulling out her phone. She spoke in Polish again, longer than last time. Tom wasn't certain whether she was leaving a message or speaking to the lady but when he saw her hang up and shake her head, he knew their frustration would continue. "I don't know what's happening," she said. "I think we should just walk there. It's not a hotel. Maybe there's a buzzer or intercom thing out the front."

"Sure, let's go. It's a bit rude, I think. I'm going to let her know we're not happy."

When they reached the apartment, there were no doorbells or buzzers or the like. "Are you sure this is the place?" he said, peering in the glass wall. After a third unsuccessful call, he said, "Did you ever actually speak to her or did she just message you?"

"We spoke when we were at the airport. You saw me on the phone to her then."

Light rain was falling again and he was concerned there would be another one of those cloudbursts.

"It's almost 4.30, for Pete's sake! I mean, bloody hell! She's probably gone home and forgotten about it. I reckon we need to think about ditching this one and finding somewhere else to stay," he said, dropping his bag on the pavement.

Marzena's phone rang and she started to converse in Polish. He heard her say "yes" a few times in English.

When she hung up, he said, "Well?"

"She's coming to open the door now."

"Thank God for that! I'm tempted to give her an earful," he said, exasperated.

When ten minutes went by and she hadn't showed, he went over in his mind how he would succinctly but politely get his point across that all of this was just a little bit rude. Eventually, a lady opened the door. "Please, follow me," she said in English.

Marzena went first, following her up the stairs. The door closed behind her, locking Tom out. She went back and held the door open while he made his way through, shaking his head. Upstairs, the door to the apartment was open and the lady was waiting for them inside. "I am so sorry," she said in English but with a heavy Polish accent and smiled. "It was, I think, very late for you. You wait too long. I was worried. The room, I hope you like. I was cleaning good for you. I hope is okay. I have vacuumed and everything is washed. I cleaned dishwasher, very good, in case you use. It took me long time."

Tom was pleasantly surprised by her sincerity and concern, but most of all by her beauty. Her twinkling eyes seemed directed just at him. Marzena might as well have been invisible and this did him in.

He softened. "Of course! No, no, it's not a problem at all," he said. "We didn't mind waiting. Thank you so much!"

Marzena looked at him and raised her eyebrow.

"The kitchen is clean. I hope so, that it is, for you. You may like to eat down in town. Is very good restaurants and not expensive. But supermarket, I can show you where." She picked up a map from the coffee table and showed him. "Here, I show you where is."

When she pointed to a spot on the map, he said. "Ah yes, I see."

"Anyway, if you need anything, you just call me. I can be here very soon."

"That would be brilliant," he said. "And this apartment is just wonderful, thank you again."

"Are you going to Auschwitz?" she asked, just when they expected her to be making her way out.

Marzena looked at Tom. "I don't know; we haven't discussed it," Marzena said. He hadn't even considered it.

"It is one of the things that lots of people do when they come here. I always ask. We have special deal. We can pick you up in private bus, just downstairs at 8 am. All you need to do is call me and I book everything for you. You pay guide on bus. They drop you back about 4 pm, right out front here."

"Okay, good, thank you," Marzena said. "We'll talk about it."

"And if there is anything you need, please call me. Here are two sets of keys. You leave in room locked, when you go." She placed one set on the coffee table and the other in the palm of Tom's hand, cupping the back of it with her other hand.

"It's been lovely meeting you, thank you again for everything, you've been brilliant," he said.

"Okay, bye, bye. Enjoy your stay."

As the lady closed the door, Marzena smiled at him, shaking her head.

"What?" he said.

* * * *

Plac Nowy and the market area filled up with a Saturday night crowd. Marzena had taken a nap in her bedroom and when she arose, suggested venturing back. After a snack of pickles and sausage, they stepped into a bigger bar that had an outside area tucked in behind the street. They sat under the night sky on lounges next to a fireplace. Marzena enjoyed a glass of wine and Tom had a different Polish beer than earlier. She asked him where he wanted to have dinner.

"I'm totally in your hands," he said.

After one drink, they walked to the first restaurant she had shown him earlier.

"They have an English version, I'm sure," she said, seeing him struggle with the menu.

"No, that's fine. Why don't you read a few to me, please?"

"Well, we could start with Polish farmers' soup. It's a meal on its own. Then, maybe some pierogi." She looked further at the menu. "But then, there's borscht, another soup. There are cabbage rolls, and rolled slices of beef stuffed with vegetables, eggs and mushrooms. There is a stew with meat. We could share a plate of vegetable salad."

"What's pierogi?" he asked, somewhat overwhelmed.

"It's a Polish dumpling. Really delicious. Fried in some butter and onion. Let me see … they have potato and sauerkraut filling."

"Let's get that. You choose some others."

"My mother makes Polish farmers' soup. It's possible she will make that when we are there. So, let's leave that."

Everything was served at the same time. The table looked like a wondrous, colourful culinary delight.

"I don't think you can expect me to dance, Tom, after that massive meal," Marzena said an hour later.

"We may need to re-evaluate that, for sure. Wow, that was so good."

On the way back to their apartment, he picked up two bottles of beer from a corner store. Drinking them revived their desire to go to the night club and after a change of clothes, they ventured out again and danced until 3 am.

CHAPTER FOURTEEN

It was a late, slow start the next day. Marzena was the first up and by the time she was out of the shower, Tom was making a cup of tea. Once he had showered, they decided to walk into Rynek Glowny, the main square of Old Town. Their heads were heavy and Tom's stomach was empty, but their spirits were sky high.

They stepped out onto the street where the air was cool and fresh, the sky grey. Soon they found a café where they ordered a late breakfast and coffee, but didn't linger. Instead, they wandered around the square, occasionally stopping to take a photo. After venturing into the side streets and browsing in souvenir shops, they decided to walk through Planty Park, then up to Wawel Castle.

When they got to the castle, Marzena translated some information for him.

The rest of the day involved a slow stroll back to Kazimierz and trying to find a couple of synagogues. In the evening, they shared some flavoured vodkas in a small bar, chatting with some locals, then pizza bread, before getting an early night.

The next morning, they caught the train to Marzena's parents' house. Perched on a slight hill, it had a narrow, fenced yard that went quite a distance down until it reached the railway tracks. The old house was basic and small, and Marzena's parents could not speak a word of English. In the afternoon, Marzena's father took Tom into the yard, showing him his shed and his garden tools. He was a short man, about

146 | Carl Spence

Tom's height and in his mid-eighties. He talked the whole time, picking up tools and wandering around the vegetable garden as he spoke.

Tom nodded as if he understood; it didn't matter a bit that he didn't. He walked alongside him, listening and saying yes with an occasional smile. Marzena sat in the kitchen with her mother. She explained that Tom was not her boyfriend, just a friend.

That evening, when Polish farmers' soup was delivered to the table with crusty bread, Marzena smiled at Tom. He told her it was a treat and very 'moreish'. Her mother asked her what he said and Marzena translated.

Marzena and her mother conversed in Polish for some time. After a while, Marzena turned to Tom, "My mother wants to know what you do for work. Can you just put it in simple terms so I can relay it back to her?"

Looking at her mother he said, "I'm, or at least I was, working as an investigator. A person who someone hires to find out things that maybe the police can't do or don't want to do."

After Marzena had translated it, her mother said something else.

"She wants to know what type of things you investigate."

"Sometimes crime. Fraud, infidelity, missing people. That sort of thing. Unfortunately, things that people might be involved in that aren't very nice."

Marzena's mother nodded her head after hearing from Marzena. She looked carefully at him. And then she spoke at length.

"What did she say?" he asked.

"She said that you should go to Auschwitz tomorrow. Before we go back home. That ..." She paused, as if she was thinking the most accurate way to translate it. "That you should experience it. You would find it moving and learn something important, but be prepared to be sad. She wanted me to ask whether you would go there."

Tom thought for a moment. Marzena's father paused from eating his soup, spoon in hand, waiting for his answer.

Tom nodded. "Yes," he said.

After dinner, Marzena called the lady who had checked them into the apartment. She would arrange for them to be picked up from the front of the apartment the next morning. The next day they caught an early train back to Kazimierz.

Tom realised he had come to Poland with Marzena to look outside of himself. To, somehow, get out of his mindset and, as Alister had suggested, to get some perspective. On a day he would never forget, at a place he never imagined going to, he was deeply moved by the experience and realised how lucky he is.

CHAPTER FIFTEEN

Soon it would be Christmas. It had been more than a month since Tom had left London and returned to live in Norwich at his mother's house. Once he had decided he was leaving and would travel overseas, probably to Australia once more, Marzena and Helena decided not to take up a renewal of their lease on the flat. Helena returned to Poland. Marzena continued in her job at the pub and found share accommodation in Fulham at a large terrace. He had kept his car so he helped her move and they vowed to keep in touch. It was not as if he had no intention of returning to London someday but he wanted to save money before his trip, and living back in Norwich made the most sense.

The week before he returned, Paddo, Bessy and Al, together with some of Marzena's friends, had come to a farewell party at the flat. Paddo and Bessy had a long chat with him during the evening and tried to suggest that he wait a year or so before returning to Australia. They wanted to go with him so they could visit some of the places they hadn't been to last time. "We could do it style, Tom," Bessy said. "Now that we all have a little bit more money, we could even book tours to Uluru and Tasmania. Wouldn't that be fun?" But he'd already made up his mind to leave soon. He could always go again later.

Paddo expressed some disappointment that Tom was not returning to investigation work. His concern was echoed, of course, by Alister, at one final lunch before Tom moved. "I hope you've properly thought this through. You know what I think about your abilities, my boy, and what may ultimately make you happy."

Tom intended to book his flight no later than the week before Christmas. His mother had mixed feelings. Rosemary was very happy to have him back in her house and out of what she considered a dangerous job, but also disappointed he was leaving the UK again. Rosemary often expressed her concerns over dinner when she could have his undivided attention. Then he would say "Just think about me getting off the plane in the bright, warm sunshine, Mum and heading to Bondi for a swim, sipping a schooner of beer and planning a tropical holiday in the north." One night he asked her, "Why don't you fly over and meet me there? When was the last time *you* had a holiday?"

Although he regretted letting the car go, he had to sell it as he needed the cash. On an unusually milder day than any over the last month, he drove to the outskirts of Norwich to get it serviced. He left it at a garage, then walked into the heart of town to get some lunch and think about what he would say in an online advertisement.

When he found a café to his liking, he ordered a burger and chips and began reading the classifieds on his phone, merely to see if he could spot a car like his for sale and get some ideas for the wording of his own ad. Growing bored with cars, he flicked to the sport. Just at that moment, he looked up and glanced slightly to his left. Side on to him, some fifteen or so feet away, two people sitting opposite each other caught his eye.

At first, he thought nothing of it and read the football news. But something was niggling at his subconscious. After a minute, he looked at the couple again. The man's face was somehow familiar. He stared through the window for a minute, trying to place him. The man got up and walked to the counter. It was then Tom noticed his shoes – the same smart two-tone leather shoes Edgar Morrow had worn that day in his office. He now realised why the man was familiar; it was Edgar Morrow. But who was the woman he was with?

While Edgar stood at the counter paying the bill, it occurred to Tom that he hadn't thought about work, or the Morrows, for some time now. The last person he wanted to run into was Edgar, the man who had complained about him to Jason. And Jason, well, he was the last person that Tom wanted to be reminded of.

His meal arrived and he kept his head low as he tucked into the burger, taking the opportunity to examine Edgar's friend, albeit from the other side of the room. The lady was perhaps late thirties, possibly a little younger than Edgar, with wavy, golden-blonde hair and very well dressed – maybe over-dressed for the café. She was holding a little mirror to her face, fixing her makeup. He watched Edgar turn and smile at her, then collect his receipt and return to the table. Tom was relieved that Edgar hadn't seen him. Edgar grabbed the lady's hand and held it as they exited the café, their fingers intertwined.

This was a distraction he didn't need. By the time he had finished lunch, several thoughts had gone through his mind. He wondered whether Jason had ever carried out his strategy to 'ditch the Morrows' after two weeks. And just where did poor Benny Longmire go? It was coming up to five years now since he'd gone missing. But the shoe shops were in London, so what was Edgar doing in Norwich? And why was he with another woman? He pictured Penny's sad eyes and felt somehow he would like answers, just like she wanted about her missing brother.

After lunch, he placed an advert online for the sale of his car. No rush to sell he figured, so long as he was gone by the middle of January to catch the peak of the Australian summer, then all would be just fine.

Three days before Christmas, he still hadn't booked the flight. That afternoon, his mother took him to a department store and made him choose some gifts to put under the tree. He chose new swimming trunks and a small beach towel, all at his mother's suggestion. "You'll also need to get a rash shirt in Australia. Paddo mentioned you allowed yourself to get quite sunburnt far too many times last time. That's not good at all," she said.

"He's a tattletale and he got burnt himself a few times."

"But he's got lovely brown skin. You're much paler. They say sun damage mightn't show for years, so just be vigilant about it, will you?"

"Of course, Mum." But shopping with his mother was not his favourite thing – he felt it was more like what Purgatory might have in store for men like him.

As they wandered back to the car he realised he hadn't got a present yet for her. "Is there anything you need? Now's a good time, since we're in town." He hoped she wasn't going to suggest returning to the department store. And when she said she needed a new pair of shoes, he regretted that he hadn't simply got her a gift voucher at the last store.

"Mum, when I was a kid, you took me shoe shopping for a whole day once. I don't know if I've ever recovered from that. The therapy you paid for helped for a while but frankly, I'm not sure I can do that again. Regression is a serious possibility."

"Oh, come on! It won't be that painful. Hop in the car. We'll only go to one place. It's late. I'm a bit over shopping myself. I know a place that's having a closing down sale. We'll be in and out in a flash, I promise."

As they drove to the store, he knew what was about to unfold. It would not be the only store they would go to and she would never buy shoes at the first place she went. He would be dragged to another store and asked his opinion several times, only for each opinion to be ignored. Then after an hour or two, he would eventually say, 'Yes, they look great,' to every pair she tried on, whether he thought they did or not, just to have a merciful end to the torture.

He prepared to go into a semi tuned-out state.

As they approached the store, he said, "Oh, I've been here before."

"You have? With who? I thought you hated shoe shopping."

Thinking quickly, Tom said, "No, no. I mean, before it was a shoe store; when it was a second-hand record store, years ago." He didn't like lying to his mother but he had vowed to himself some time ago to get serious about confidentiality and be diligent about it. He only knew the shop from his visit months ago, shortly after Penny Morrow had come to see him. And he had never gone inside.

"Oh, good. They still have plenty of stock," she said, as they entered. "I want to see if they still have the pair I tried on last week. You can give me your opinion."

Tom studied the room and tried to imagine how it might have looked when it wasn't a shoe store. Vastly different, it seemed. It was busy and he was the only male inside. Several ladies sat on the leather couches trying on shoes while several more wandered around, brows-ing. It seemed it was understaffed. One young girl stood at the counter handing a bag to a lady who looked like she had just paid and two other ladies were lined up behind her.

"Here, I found them. Hold my bag, Tom, please."

"The only man in a ladies shoe store and now I'm holding a bag."

"Relax, would you?" she said. "Be patient for me. It's Christmas."

He looked for a space to sit but had no luck there. Waiting in the car was out of the question. Checking the classifieds on his phone was shaping up as the best option.

"I need to get a size seven-and-a-half," Rosemary said, now looking around for a member of staff to help her.

This – the waiting – was but one component of the whole process. He shook his head and also searched for someone to help them – prefer-ably quickly. If only he could whistle.

A lady emerged from the stock room with two boxes and handed one to a lady sitting behind them and the other to another lady behind her. "That's an eight," she said to the first lady. "If it's too small, I have the half size." She then smiled directly at Tom and said to his mother, "I shall be with you in a moment. I just need to serve this other lady who's been waiting."

He blinked a few times and realised he had seen the lady serving customers before. It was the lady he'd spotted having lunch with Edgar Morrow that day, a week or so ago. It was unmistakably her. *Does Penny know this woman? Are they friends, colleagues in the same game of selling shoes?* It seemed to him to have been a little odd to have seen Edgar in the first place. But now, it seemed even more strange that he had been with this lady. Looking at her more closely, he was now intrigued to be inside the store.

When she barked an order at the young girl to go and get a size seven, it seemed she was the owner, or at least the boss.

"Now, can I help you?" she said to Rosemary a few minutes later.

"Thank you. I tried a pair of these on the other day," she said, handing her one shoe. "Do you still have the seven-and-a-half?"

"Let me check. I think so," she said, and went out the back.

"Do you like them, Tom?"

"What?"

"I said, do you like them?"

"Oh, yes. They're fine."

The lady returned with a box. "There's a space here," she said, motioning to Rosemary to take a seat.

She tried both shoes on, stood up and turned. "I don't know," she said, biting her bottom lip, examining her reflection in the shop mirror.

"In truth, I think they are more suited to summer, but with stockings and a skirt, they can be practically worn all year," the lady said.

"Do they suit me, Tom?"

"Very much so, Mum." His mind was elsewhere now, in a heightened state of curiosity about this unexpected little connection with the Morrows.

After more deliberation and the inevitable trying on of two more pairs and another twenty minutes, and then returning to the original pair, which he observed were "the best" but "all of them are great", she decided to purchase the first pair she had tried. "Let me pay for it, Mum, since I'm giving them to you. But I'll let you wrap them up, since you're better at that."

"We can wrap them for you. Are they for Christmas?" the lady asked.

"Yeah. That'd be great," he said. She took the box and he followed her to the counter.

"You've got a busy store here but you're closing down? Are you setting up somewhere else?" he asked, figuring that it seemed a natural and polite question. Plus, he was curious.

"Yes, it's been busy. Not all days are as busy as today, I'm afraid. The old closing down sale sure helps. I might open a store in London if I can secure the right site." She grabbed a roll of Christmas wrapping paper and tore it.

"Bigger market?"

"Oh yes. Much bigger."

"I have some friends in London. A few ladies I'm always struggling to buy birthday presents and the like for," he said. By now, Rosemary had put on her old shoes and had joined him at the counter.

"Well," she said, as she wrapped the box, "you've bought a lovely pair of shoes for your mother. I hope she gets years of good use out of them. The quality is there, so I'm sure she will. Shoes are such a great gift. Women usually remember where they buy shoes." She smiled and took his bank card. She put the receipt in the bag and handed it to him.

"Thanks, Tom."

"Pleasure, Mum."

Spotting business cards on the counter, he decided to ask, "Do you mind if I take a card? If you're moving, it'll probably be a bit redundant soon, though, I suppose."

"Of course," and she picked one up and handed it to him. "The website will remain. I'm going to keep the name."

"Cheers," he said, with a smile.

"Thank you," she replied, also with a smile.

When they got into the car, it was Rosemary who was now curious. "I thought you weren't interested much in shoes. How come you asked her for her card?"

"I'm not. She just seems to know her products well, and they make a good present. That's all."

"A good present for all your girlfriends?" She laughed. "It's impossible to buy shoes for other people."

"Yep, that's it. All my girlfriends. Sometimes I don't have to guess where I got my cheeky streak from, do I?"

When he got back home he went straight into his room and turned his laptop on. The business card had the same business name displayed on the shop front: 'briskett and bafe shoes'. It was all in lower case and in the same distinctive style of writing as was displayed in fancy letters on the shop. He found the website but it had no pages of information other than 'moving soon'. When he clicked on contact details, it said, 'Amelia Briskett' and gave a mobile telephone number and showed a photo of her.

By dinner, Rosemary had noticed he hadn't said much since they'd arrived home. "You seem distracted, a bit quiet tonight. Are you feeling alright?"

"Yeah, I'm fine."

"Have you booked your flight yet?"

"No."

"Have you had any bites on your car sale?"

"One, but he was a time-waster."

"I thought you were going to book your flight before Christmas."

"It's expensive at the moment. I think I'll wait until after New Year, when the prices drop."

For the first time in months, that night he could not get to sleep.

CHAPTER SIXTEEN

Rosemary could see something in her son had changed. At breakfast, he sat staring at his coffee without speaking for ages. Then finally, he took a long swallow of his long black and said, "I think I'm going to drive to London tomorrow."

"But Tom, that's Christmas Eve! Why would you go then? The traffic will be madness. Why?"

"I want to deliver some gifts to Paddo and Bessy. I'd like to see Al and Marzena as well, and wish them happy Christmas."

"Do you have anything to give them?" When he didn't answer, she said, "What about after Christmas Day and before New Year? That'd give you more time. You *are* planning on being here for Christmas, aren't you?"

"Yes."

"I don't know," she said, now worried, as she cleared the table.

"I'm going to go for a walk," he said.

"Where?"

"By the river. I won't be long."

A stroll by the River Wensum had always been a favourite pastime for Tom, especially when he needed to think. He was deeply fond of its charm with its riverside walkway, and it had been part of his life since he was a child. He always felt good there.

It was bitterly cold now, with no prospect of any warmth for some time. Not in England. He walked fast, first out past New Mills Yard then doubled back, crossing up towards the lanes, along St Andrews Street, taking a shortcut through the walkway near The Halls and joining the path again on the other side of the river. He stopped and took a rest at Cow Tower, but he did not sit until further along, just before Bishops Bridge. The seat was wet. He brushed some water off it and sat, his long dark overcoat absorbing the remaining moisture. As he watched the ducks take their morning stroll around the base of the trees, he thought about calling Alister or Penny. Calling Penny was one of those right things to do but unwise. And in the end, he decided he didn't need to call Alister because he knew exactly what he would say: *And what's in it for you, my boy? And it's none of your business anyway. So what if he's having an affair. You have no retainer anymore.*

He continued his walk slowly, hands tucked firmly into the warm pockets of his coat. A lady walking her small dog passed him. She smiled and said hello and he nodded. He knew one thing. Before he could get back on track with his travel plans, somehow he needed to speak to Penny, even if only to wish her merry Christmas and perhaps say, by the way, I saw Edgar. That was risky and may very well be inappropriate. But as he walked, he pictured again her face in his mind – how pure and innocent and sad she had looked that first time she sat in his office. *This is not about your marriage? No.* He needed to know if she knew. If curiosity killed the cat, he was prepared to see how many lives he had and to die a little death, if for nothing more than to move on with his own plans.

* * * *

At 12.30 pm, he sat on the edge of his bed with the door closed. His heart pumped just a little harder than normal as he pressed her number.

"Hello," she said.

"Penny?"

"Yes."

"It's Tom. Tom Greer."

"Oh, hello Tom." She said it so casually, taking him by surprise, and he felt instant relief.

"I wanted to wish you happy Christmas. I hope I haven't called ... I know it's out of the blue ... at a bad time."

"Oh, thank you. No, its fine. I'm ... Merry Christmas to you." She paused.

"It's been very cold," he said.

"Yes, it has."

"Look, I hope you don't mind me calling, and I guess you didn't expect to hear from me again. I'm no longer at the firm. And I hope you don't mind me asking, but, did Jason ever get back to you and follow through with your case?"

"Yes. Yes, he did, in a way. We got a very large bill and he told us that he felt that it was unsuitable to continue investigating."

"Right."

"Where did you go? Are you with another firm?"

"No. I'm taking a break." She didn't respond immediately so he waited, then asked, "Have you engaged another investigator?"

"No. Edgar doesn't think it's worth it anymore."

He was tempted to say, 'Actually, I saw Edgar,' but he held back and instead said, "What do *you* think? I mean, about engaging another investigator?"

"I don't know what to think. It's been so long."

It was time to take a risk. "Well look, I'm going to be in London tomorrow. And, it's probably nothing, but I've kind of stumbled across something to do with the case. And, well, you might want to talk to me about it. I know I'm not working on the case anymore. I'm very aware of that. I just thought, that since I was going to be in London anyway, we could meet, perhaps discuss it, just briefly."

"What is it? What do you mean?"

"I'd rather discuss it in person, if we can. And just you and me. Just the two of us."

"Okay."

"It would be best not to tell anyone I called you. No one at all. I know Edgar was not happy with me. I got busy and I'm very sorry for that. I wanted to apologise. I should've called you and explained."

"Edgar was more upset than I was. I wanted to give you more time."

"Can we meet sometime in the morning? Say at a café?" he asked.

"It's a hugely busy day tomorrow. But yes, I suppose. Where?"

"What about the café next door to your store in Soho?"

"Alright."

"Say 11 am?"

"I can only leave the shop for half-an-hour."

"I shall see you then, Penny."

* * * *

"Mum," he said an hour later, "I'm going to make myself a sandwich and get on the road. I'm going to London and staying overnight. I'll be back late tomorrow afternoon."

"Where are you going to stay?"

"Probably with Paddo and Bessy. Or maybe Marzena. I don't know yet."

"Rebecca has asked Alan to come for dinner tomorrow night. Christmas Eve. You will be here, won't you?"

"Yes. Absolutely."

He woofed a sandwich down, threw an overnight bag in his car and set his phone in its holder. As he turned out of the street and looked at his watch, he pressed Paddo's number and increased the volume on the speaker.

"Hey, son, how are you? Merry Christmas!"

"Tom! Season's greetings to you too! I was going to call you today," Paddo replied.

"Well, I beat you to it. Listen, what are you doing this afternoon? Are you up for an ale, maybe dinner?"

"Sure. I was thinking of suggesting tomorrow, though."

"Yeah, I can't tomorrow. I have to be back in Norwich."

"Where are you now?"

"I'm heading to London. Just leaving now."

"We're in Norwich. Staying with Mum for Christmas."

"Of course, right. I'd forgotten you'd be doing that."

"What are you going to London for?"

"I wasn't planning on it but something has come up, workwise."

"I thought you weren't working."

"I'm not really. I have to see someone and I thought I would catch up with you and Bessy. But no drama, I'll be back tomorrow and maybe we can do it then, if I'm back in time."

"Alright, well that sounds cool. Give me a call either way."

"Right. Goodo then, say hi to Bess. I'm driving. I'll talk to you tomorrow."

"Will do, bye. Safe driving."

He turned the radio on and considered calling Al or Marzena. The problem with Al was that Tom knew he would drink too many ales with him and he wanted to be very clear headed the next day. With Marzena, he would have to sleep on the floor and he was a bit uncomfortable about asking her on such short notice anyway. Maybe she was in Poland for Christmas, anyway. By the time he got to London he decided to check in to a hotel where he could park his car nearby. He found one in Bayswater and got an early night.

The next morning, he took the Tube to Oxford Circus Station and walked to the café where he had arranged to meet Penny. Arriving well before 11 am, he took a seat and sent a message to her, confirming he was there. Ordering a cup of coffee straight away, he sat and waited.

A little after 11, Penny made her way through the crowded café, politely smiling at customers as they adjusted their chairs to let her squeeze through. She zigzagged her way to his table.

"Good morning." Tom smiled at her and got up, pulling the chair opposite him out for her.

"Good morning. Thank you," she said, the same polite smile on her face.

"Can I buy you a cup of something?"

"Yes. I'll have a pot of tea, please."

He placed the order straightaway. When he returned, she had her phone out, pressing the keys. She placed it back in her purse and sat looking at him. He noticed that her face was slightly flushed, but her beauty had always been so evident to him, and he held her gaze just for a brief moment.

"Thank you for making the effort, Tom, but I don't have a lot of time. I'm short staffed, and I feel stressed, quite frankly. So, I'm sorry. I don't want to be rude. But, you said something about finding out or stumbling upon something to do with Benny's case?" She scratched the side of her head, eyes intense as she stared at him. "What is it?"

"Thank you for meeting me." He sipped his coffee and put it down, without taking his eyes off her.

"I didn't expect to hear from you again."

"I understand. I hope you don't mind that I have contacted you."

"No. I don't mind. I've been living with this … well, you know how long. I would be more than grateful to hear anything. Something, whatever it is."

The waiter arrived with the tea and placed the pot in front of her. She turned over the cup on the table and poured a black tea. Taking a sachet of raw sugar, she tore off the top and emptied it, stirred it and then picked it up and leant back, gently blowing the top before taking a sip. She held the cup in both hands and looked at him. It was a cue to offload what he had found out.

"I'm back living in Norwich, at least for the moment. Do you do business in Norwich?" he asked. She placed the cup down.

"No, the shops are here."

"Never?"

"No. I told you, I've only ever been there once."

"What about Edgar? Does he?"

"What, do business there?"

"Yes."

"No. Not that I know of. Why? As in ordering stock, you mean?"

"Has he been to Norwich in the last month? The last two weeks?"

"No."

"You're sure?"

"Yes, I'm sure. He's been away once in the last month but that was to Peterborough." A frown had developed on her face and he could see she was becoming impatient, given he hadn't come out with the answer to her question.

"For business?"

"Yes. We're looking at setting up a shop there."

"Why there?"

"Its population is growing faster than most every other area. What's this got to do with anything? Why are you asking me this?" she said loudly, not rudely, but with the impatience he'd already perceived.

"You remember I told you Benny's old shop was now a shoe store?"

"Yes, I remember. You called me months ago."

"What if I told you … what if I said, that a few weeks ago, I saw your husband, Edgar, in Norwich?"

She shook her head dismissively with a look that indicated he was clearly saying something silly. "You must be mistaken, Tom. That's not possible."

"Well, I did. Is it wrong of me to tell you?"

"Wrong? It is, if you're making it up! Or confusing him with someone. You only met him once."

"It was him, Penny."

"What day was it?"

"It was the 15th. The 15th of December."

A moment passed and he watched her process the information as she stared at him. "That … that was when he went to Peterborough," she said.

"He was gone all day?"

"Yes. Most of it. He probably went on to Norwich and didn't think to tell me. It's not that much farther."

"Did he tell you where he had lunch?"

"No. Why would he?"

"I saw him having lunch in a café in Norwich … with a lady."

"What? I'm not following, Tom. What do mean? What are you talking about?" Her impatience had become more apparent.

"Penny." He leaned towards her speaking softly and slowly. "I was having lunch in a café while I was waiting for my car to be serviced. I saw him sitting with some lady I didn't recognise. I wasn't expecting to see him, of course. To be frank, given I'd been thrown off your case, I didn't want to run into him at all. So, I never let on that I saw him. And he didn't see me. When they finished eating they left … together. He was holding her hand."

Her face went white. Confused, she blinked repeatedly. "Are you telling me …" She stopped and remained totally still. *"Did you actually contact me …* to tell me … my husband is having an affair?"

"No. I don't know that. I'm just telling you what I saw."

Her gaze went glassy, her nostrils widened, and her mouth quivered a fraction. She tried to say something but her thoughts somehow prevented any words.

He allowed her a moment before he decided to continue. "And there's something else," he said. "I've since found out who the lady was. Who she is."

Not a finger, not an eyelash moved.

"I ended up meeting her. It was again, by accident."

"Who is she?" Penny said, calmly, coolly.

"I was shopping with my mother. We went to a shoe store. In Norwich. The lady who was with your husband owned the store. The shoe shop."

He steeled himself for what he was about to tell her next. He saw a different woman to the one who had walked in and sat down with him but a few minutes before. He cleared his throat. "The shop is called 'briskett and bafe'. Her name is Amelia Briskett. Do you know her?"

"No."

"It's the shop I told you about. The shop …" He paused. "It's on the same site as the old record store that your brother Benny had. It's closing down. She was having a closing down sale. But it's the same site."

Penny took a napkin and held it to her mouth. She sighed and shook her head.

"Are you alright?" he said, worried that she looked ill.

"No."

"I'm sorry, Penny."

Suddenly, her hand shook as she held the napkin to her chin, and then, she coughed and vomited into it, again and again.

"Please, bring some water and some towels!" he said to the nearby waiter, leaping out of his seat and rushing to her side. "I'm so sorry, Penny. The waiter is coming! Please ... I ..."

The waiter brought a glass of water and a wet cloth and gave it to her. Lifting her head she said, "I'm alright. Thank you. Oh ..." and collapsed back on her chair.

He pulled his chair around next to her and placed his hand gently on her back, as people began to stare.

"Ah ..." she said, tears now slowly dropping onto the white table cloth. He picked up the napkin and she held it over her eyes.

"Don't try and talk. It's ... fine, just ... take your time. It's all okay," he said, gently rubbing her back. But he knew it was far from okay.

"Ah ... I have to get back to work," she said, swallowing and sniffing.

"No, you don't."

"Yes ... I do," she said, still crying.

"Work can wait, Penny."

"You don't understand. It's Christmas Eve! It's not fair on my staff. I can't leave them!" she shouted.

The waiter returned. "Is everything alright, Sir?" He placed a towel over the little mess on the table.

"It's fine. Thank you," Tom said.

She blew her nose and said, "I'm sorry. How embarrassing for you."

"Penny, don't be silly. Let's just ... just sit for a while. You've had a big shock."

"I've got to go," she said. "Got to get out of here."

"Look, Penny, I'm going to pay the bill and we're going to go for a walk. Would you come for a walk? Please? Then you can go back to the store."

She nodded. "Let me go to the bathroom first." She vanished quickly into the rear of the café.

The waiter returned and Tom gave him a twenty-pound note, telling him to keep the change.

When Penny reappeared, there was more colour in her face. "Let's take a walk to Golden Square," Tom said. "It's not far."

She offered no resistance. They walked slowly and silently. He was reluctant to say much at all. They were soon at the square and there was the usual crowd of people even though it was icy cold. Tom spied an empty space on a bench. "Let's sit for a while. Let's just sit down," he said softly. She offered no resistance again.

Tom felt he'd been grossly insensitive. It was unbearable to see her pain. She just sat staring at the pigeons. Suddenly, she spoke. "I expect you need to get back to your family in Norwich. Did you drive?" she said, still looking at the birds.

"Yes. But there's no rush."

"The traffic is going to be very bad. It's always madness on Christmas Eve."

"I'm sorry, Penny. I really am."

"It's alright, Tom. Things haven't been great for a while. It's probably my fault."

"How could it be your fault?"

"Since everything that's happened with Benny, I suppose I haven't been the wife he needed."

"I'm sure that's not true, Penny. And that's his problem. Surely, he could understand what it does to a person to have a brother go missing like that."

"Ah, yes, but understanding can only go so far." Her eyes had started to dry but still, she would not meet his. "You know, we were so happy when we first got married. Then, well, everything changed. I changed, I suppose. Not many men could put up with it."

"I think a lot of men could. Good men, that is. You're not to be blamed here. He should have put up … they're not the right words. He should have understood, Penny. It's not your fault. Not at all."

"I'm just so over it. Over everything. Everything." She shook her head, looking at the people as they wandered around doing their last-minute Christmas shopping. It was clear to him that she was now in utter despair. Tears welled up in her eyes again and her face contorted in agony.

"I can look into it more for you. I'm happy to. I want to. I don't want to give up. I don't want *you* to give up." He spoke quietly, calmly, attempting to provide some hope. He wanted to hug her, to help ease her pain but he resisted and just sat with her. "Are you going to mention this to Edgar?" he said.

"Oh, I'll confront him. Christ, its Christmas Eve!" She sniffed. "Thank God we don't have children. I certainly won't be having any now."

"I have to say, Penny. It's an odd coincidence that this Amelia is in Benny's old shop."

"I can't believe it! I don't get it. Even if he's not having an affair, what the hell's he doing, knowing that?"

"Maybe he doesn't know she owns it. Would he have known that was Benny's old place?"

"Yes. He went there! We both did when it was closed but still the record shop."

"Will you talk to him tonight? Are you working together today?"

"Oh, yes. I'll have to. He's at Mayfair all day. We'll not see each other until we get home. We're booked into a bloody restaurant at 9! I'm cancelling that. Christ almighty!" She ran her hands over her face and then pulled a tissue out and wiped her nose.

"Penny, I—"

"I'm going to walk back to the shop now," she interrupted him. "I can't leave my staff alone any longer."

"Do you want me to walk back with you?"

"No. No, thank you. I need time alone; I'm not going to get it for the remainder of the day."

"Penny, I only came to see you today to see if I could help. No other reason. I'm sorry that I upset you."

"Tom, it's not you. It's not something you need to apologise for. My life is a bloody mess. It's not your fault. But, I want to thank you." She looked at him now for the first time since the café.

"Would you consider putting me back on the case? I would, you know, for you. Look, to be perfectly honest, I was ready to quit. I *did* quit. I was about to sell my car. But I would … I want to help you. I've never wanted to help anyone – a client – as much as I want to help you."

She smiled ever so slightly in appreciation and wiped a random remaining tear from her eye. "Yes. I would. But not just now. I have some things to do – to say – obviously." She stood up. "You enjoy your Christmas with your family. Call me in the new year. Will you do that for me?"

"Yes. Yes, I most certainly will."

"Goodbye, Tom."

He watched her walk away into the crowds until she was gone.

CHAPTER SEVENTEEN

On the return drive to Norwich, Tom called Paddo and suggested that they have an ale in town at around 4 pm. That would give him enough time to drop off his car at home and walk back into the laneways to meet them.

They met right on time at the top of Bedford Street. Bessy gave Tom a huge hug and they walked in the direction of Pottergate, stopping at their favourite little bar where they pulled up some stools.

Bessy was excited to hear about Tom's plans to travel to Australia. "I'm disappointed you're not going to wait until we can come with you, but tell me, where's the first place you think you'll go? I bet you're going to say after Sydney, it will be Uluru. I'm so jealous. I'm so over the grey and cold here at the moment."

"Boy, I didn't know Aussies were such whingers," Paddo said. "They're not used to real seasons. She started complaining about the weather in September!" He gave Bessy a nudge and then kissed her.

"Just remember, before you start cuddling and kissing too much, you're with me, and I don't have anyone to cuddle and kiss," Tom said. He took their orders and went to the bar, returning with a pint each for Paddo and himself, and a glass of red wine for Bessy.

"You look a little tired from the drive, Tom. How was it? Did you get what you wanted done? It seemed all a bit rushed," Bessy said.

"I'm a bit tired but it was fine. I didn't end up staying with Al or even seeing anyone, not even Marzena. I just checked into a hotel."

"The work went okay? Was it unfinished business?" Paddo asked.

"Yeah, sort of. How long are you staying with your mum?"

"We're thinking we'll go back a couple of days before New Year's," Paddo said, taking the froth off his beer.

"So, when do you fly out, Tom? We should have a going away party for you," Bessy said.

He did not respond immediately with the enthusiasm they were expecting. He took a sip, scratched his nose and said, "I don't know if I'm going."

"What?" Paddo said.

"I'm, well, I may have to work for a while."

"To save some more money?" asked Bessy.

"No, not really. I've enough to go. It's just that, something has come up."

"With work?" Paddo enquired.

"Yes."

"Something new?"

"Not really. It goes back to when I was working in London. I want to do it."

"Well, that's good, Tom. Do you feel good about it? You seemed a bit down about this whole investigation thing for a while," Bessy said.

"I don't know if I feel *good* about it, but I *want* to do this particular job. It's very important to the client and I like her."

"Her?" Paddo smiled. "How old is she?"

"34."

"She's way too old for you."

"That's ageist," Bessy said with a giggle, half joking.

"I'm sorry," Paddo said. "Actually, no I'm not." He frowned, pretending to look serious, but smirked again. "A relationship might keep you anchored here in the UK," he added.

"You'll be sorry in a minute," Tom said, looking at Bessy, smirking himself now. "Anyway, it's not like that. She's married. And I feel sorry for her."

"Because she's married?" Paddo said.

"Shut him up, Bess. Please!"

Bessy laughed. "Well, cheers Tom, anyway. We're glad you're hanging around!" She raised her glass and all three glasses met in the middle.

Paddo told Tom that he was continuing to bide his time with the department until he could find his desired job in the field. Exmoor National Park was the aim and he mentioned that he and Bessy were taking his mother there for a few days to stay in the family holiday house after New Year.

Bessy explained how she had met Tom's other sister in one of St Mary's intensive care wards where she had a placement. Tom said he would be seeing her after New Year when she was bringing her husband and kids to visit their mother and he and Rebecca would be able to catch up with her then. After another round, they promised to see each other again soon.

* * * *

Penny was sitting on the floor in her lounge room when she heard the key turn in the lock of the front door. Next to her, a small Christmas tree stood decorated, with just the star on the top yet to be placed. Two neatly wrapped gifts rested under it, a joint one for her brother and his wife, the other for her niece. She was in the middle of wrapping one for her mother, but she paused to take a sip from her glass of white wine. She heard Edgar put his bag down, take his coat off and hang it on the rack in the hallway. He came into the room just as she was tying the ribbon around the paper to her satisfaction.

"Hello darling," he said, and bent down to give her a kiss on her forehead. "I'm sorry I'm late." He removed his tie, threw it on the top of the couch, unbuttoned the top of his shirt and twisted his neck free of its tight collar.

She ignored him as she placed the gift under the tree next to the other two.

"I ended up taking the girls out for a quick drink after we closed, just to thank them for working their butts off all day. One turned into two. What a day! But it was so good. We sold completely out of the Feorellese and most of the Hot Caramel range. We needed it. So many people paid with cash today. I've got a stack in the safe." He turned and said, "I'm going to jump in the shower, I think."

First, he grabbed a glass from the kitchen and poured himself a white wine. "Did you take Annie and Donna out?" he called over his shoulder, his back to her.

"No," she said, as she stood up.

While Edgar was in the shower, Penny refilled her glass. She could hear him humming as he washed. In the bedroom, she bundled up his clothes he'd left lying on the bed, threw them in the laundry basket and placed a small bag at the foot of the bed.

When he got out of the shower, she was sitting in the corner of the room on the Victorian chair, their most cherished wedding present. She was holding a full glass of wine in her hand, legs crossed, looking straight at him.

"What time did you say we're booked in for dinner tonight? 9 wasn't it?" he said, walking naked into the walk-in-robe. He searched for the trousers he wanted while he waited for her to answer. She didn't provide one. Finding the pair he wanted, he slipped them on, and emerged with a shirt in his hand. "Darling, how much time do we have?"

"That's a good question, Edgar," she replied, smiling ever so slightly.

"Do we have to go soon?"

"No. But you do. I'm not going anywhere."

"What do you mean?"

"I've cancelled dinner. I called the restaurant this afternoon and cancelled our booking."

"What for? Why?"

"Edgar, I suggest you sit on the bed for a minute. I want to talk to you."

He looked at the bed. "Alright. What's my bag doing there?"

"Sit, please."

He threw the shirt on the bed and lifted the bag. "It has stuff in it," he said.

"Yes, it does."

He parked his backside on the bed, his hairy chest facing her, and shook his head. "What the hell is going on, Penny? Why are you ..." He stopped in confusion. "Why are you acting so strangely? Did something happen at the shop today? What's wrong?"

"You have no idea, do you?" she said, her voice rising in anger.

"No idea? No idea *about what*? Can I get my glass of wine?"

When he returned with his wine, Penny asked, "Edgar, when you told me you went to Peterborough two weeks ago, did you actually go there?"

"Yes. Of course I did. You know that. Why would you ask me that?"

"I don't want you to lie to me, Edgar. There's no time left for that."

"I don't understand. I told you I did. I brought back some real estate brochures from there. Don't you remember? I've still got them. I showed them to you."

"Did you go anywhere else?"

"No."

She paused, watching him carefully and noticed the look of disbelief on his face.

"Did you go to Norwich for lunch?"

He picked up his shirt, turned away from her, and put it on slowly. Then he disappeared inside the robe again, and returned, pulling a belt around his waist.

"How long has it been, Edgar? How long has it been going on?"

Picking up his glass of wine, he kept his back to her.

"Do I have to ask again? Or, has it been *that* long, that you can't *fucking* remember?"

"Penny … it's …" He stopped and turned to face her.

"You had lunch with her. I know you did. What are you doing? Why have you lied to me? You cheating bastard!"

"How … when did you find out I was in Norwich?"

"I'm asking the questions, Edgar. Have a go at the truth, if you can," she said. "How long has it been?"

Edgar sat on the edge of the bed. He breathed heavily out of his nose and ran his hand over his face. "Two years. Maybe a bit more," he said slowly, looking straight at her now.

"Two years of lying."

"It's not, not what you might think."

She stood up. "Oh, I see. And *what* do I think? You know what I think, do you?"

"Look. I never meant to hurt you. It was … I made a huge mistake."

"Bullshit! You don't make a mistake every day for two years."

"Calm down. I hardly saw her. It wasn't every day."

"No? How did you meet her?"

"Does it matter?"

"Screw you! It matters to me. For Christ sake! How can you possibly say that?"

"I met her at a trade show. Look, she was the one who came on to me! I've been weak, okay, I guess. I don't … I don't love her. I don't, Penny. I love you."

"Oh, that's good to hear! You just want something else from her, is that it? Something, something I can't give you? Is that all it is? Sex?"

"No, Penny. We were going through a rough patch. Look, I'm sorry." He jumped up from the bed and took a step closer to her. "It … I wanted to end it, I absolutely did, more than once. I've been concerned about us. I've wanted to make things right with our marriage. That day in Norwich is the *only* time I have seen her in months. That's the truth, Penny. The absolute truth. Months. I'm sorry. I haven't … we haven't been … not for months."

"Sorry is not going to cut it, Edgar."

"Darling, please, I …" Reaching out, he tried to embrace her.

"Don't touch me! I want you out of here, out of here tonight! Your bag's packed. Take it and get the hell out! I don't want you back here."

"Darling! Please …"

She dodged his outstretched arms. "Don't you dare! NOW GET OUT! Actually, no," she said, calming herself for a moment and raising a finger. "You wait a minute. I want to know something more. I've been told that this woman, Amelia, oh yes, I know her name! That she's in Benny's old place … that she has the shoe shop. What the fuck, Edgar? You tell me. You tell me about that, you lying bastard!"

"For God's sake, Penny. Calm down. Stop shouting, would you? Look, I arranged it for her. She wanted to go into the business and, look, it was just the fact that I knew the place was vacant and would be good for what she wanted to do. That's it, simple as that. It was just a bloody vacant shop, Penny."

"What? You arranged for your mistress, your harlot, to take up residence in my brother's premises and you didn't think how that might affect me, how it might hurt me? Are you that callous or just plain bloody stupid?"

"I wasn't thinking about that. I should have, I guess. It was just an opportunity. The place was empty, Penny. I'm sorry about not telling you. It would be the last thing I would dream of telling you, obviously. I was trying not to see her."

"Oh, please, spare me!" Losing the train of her thoughts now, she asked again, "Where did you meet her?"

"I told you! At a trade fair in London. She wanted to set up in Norwich, where she was living. I was just helping her get started. I made a huge, huge blunder getting involved with her. You have no idea. None!"

Holding her brow in one hand now and ready to collapse on the carpet, Penny paused and took a breath. "Edgar, you're a liar. You were seen holding her hand when you were in Norwich. And now you expect me to believe what you're telling me? That you've made a mistake and have been trying to end it? Do you think I'm stupid?"

"Penny, I—"

"Get out. Just get out. Now! I'm going for a walk. Make sure you are gone when I get back!"

"Penny. Don't do this, please. I beg you! I can make it up to you. Please, we can work it out."

"Are you serious? No way, not a chance in hell!"

"So, you have … hang on just a minute. Just how did you come across all this, then, might I ask?"

"Oh, wouldn't you like to know?"

"I was about to end the thing, Penny. So yes, I would like to know. I made a bloody mistake and …"

"That fellow we hired. Who *I hired*, in fact, and who *you* complained about. Tom Greer."

"You put a fucking private investigator on me?"

"No, I didn't! But you must have forgotten he was from Norwich. Or didn't you know? Hmmm … you didn't think you would be noticed there! He saw you having lunch, didn't he! He then went with his mother to buy shoes. Bingo!"

She snatched her purse from the dresser and darted to the hallway. With her heart racing, she slammed the front door shut and was off into the cold darkness.

When she returned, he was gone. Where, she didn't care. Her mother was due to visit with her brother and his wife and their five-year-old child in the morning. A beautiful Christmas lunch had been planned for weeks. Sitting on the couch she cried until she could cry no more. She picked up her phone and braced herself to call her mother. Any potential for forgiveness that ran through her mind was expunged by the impossibility of forgiving Edgar for the hurt she was about to bestow upon her poor mother. She had already suffered enough with her missing son. And there was a young child now to consider on a special day of the year. Penny resolved she would have to be strong yet again. Her niece deserved a brave and happy face. In her shattered mind, there was no other choice.

CHAPTER EIGHTEEN

Tom slept better on Christmas Eve, thanks to the eggnog, but during the course of the next few days, he kept thinking about Penny and how she was coping with what he'd told her. It bothered him that he couldn't start back on the case immediately and anyway, he had no access to the box of information. He was certain Jason wouldn't have even opened it. Being in the company of family and friends, and having to hide what was really consuming him, wasn't helping either.

Rosemary was surprised but relieved that he had changed his mind about going to Australia, at least for the moment. She knew it was because of some important work-related reason and that concerned her too, but she kept her thoughts to herself.

The day after Boxing Day, Tom caught up with Paddo and Bessy at a play put on by some of Paddo's old theatre friends. This was a welcome distraction. Enjoying dinner before the show, they laughed and reminisced about the times they had experienced together in Australia. They all promised to make more effort to see each other in the coming year. Tom confirmed he was undecided about a move back to London but he certainly wasn't going to set up his own investigation company there in the near future. He had already asked his mother if he could extend his stay with her, at least until the end of January, and naturally, she said he didn't need to ask.

He called Al and Marzena and wished them the best for the season. As it turned out, Marzena had stayed in London and was planning a

New Year's Eve party. She was eager for him to come. He told her he might but he doubted he would.

The weather remained cold but not icy, although the longer-range forecast was for snow in the last two weeks of January. He didn't want to get snowed in. If he could get stuck into the case of the missing Benny Longmire now, he felt it would help. He reminded himself again to be patient as he waited for Penny's permission. She had said to contact her in the new year, so he planned to call on January 2nd to let her know he would be based in Norwich at least until the end of January. He would go to London to see her if need be. The sooner he started the better. He had the email the Morrows had sent him giving him a list of Benny's friends and some contacts, as well as the details of his employee, on his laptop. No harm in looking at that while he waited for the days to tick over.

On the morning of New Year's Eve, Marzena called and convinced him to drive to London for her party. She said it would be the best opportunity for a get together for some time and assured him he could crash on the floor of her bedroom if he wanted.

He packed a small bag, called out goodbye to his mother, and headed for his car, only to return five minutes later and inform his mother that he was going nowhere.

"What do you mean, nowhere? Have you changed your mind again?" she asked.

"No. It's been changed for me. Some bastard has slashed all four of my tyres. Come and see."

Seconds later, she stood beside his car. "Tom, who would do such a thing here? I mean, in such a quiet street? This is outrageous."

Tom bent down to examine the perpetrator's handiwork. He could see that whatever was used was very sharp and effective. He circled the car looking for any other damage but it appeared to be just the tyres.

"Who would do this to you, Tom?" Rosemary repeated, when he hadn't spoken.

Normally, he could keep this type of thing from her. He was angry that his work, apparently, had been brought to her doorstep. But he knew whoever the perpetrator was wanted exactly that – to get to him, more than to merely cause him inconvenience. He guessed that whoever it was, they had done so under instruction from the real perpetrator and would most likely have been paid to do the job.

It was impossible now for his mother to get her car out as he was parked behind her. "I better call Eric down at the garage. I'm going to see if he can bring some tyres over. It's important I get on to this today."

When Tom called the local garage, Eric told him they were closing up shop early but yes, he could come over with the tyres after 3 pm. "Sounds like someone wants to send you a message," he said. "Bastard!"

Marzena was next on his list to call. She was disappointed he wasn't coming. When she heard the reason, she said, "I thought you weren't working anymore, Tom!"

Eric arrived and they jacked up the car. By the time they had the old tyres off and all four new ones on, it was well and truly dark. Eric installed a portable light that allowed them to see. Naturally keen to allow Eric to get away and enjoy New Year's Eve, they worked as quickly as they could manage. Tom gave Eric some cash for his trouble and thanked him for his help. It wasn't enough to cover the full amount owing but he said he would come down at the garage as soon as they re-opened with the balance, and with some extra for his trouble.

"Have you reported it to the police yet?" Eric said, as he wiped his hands with a rag and put the last of the tools back into his truck.

"No."

"Maybe we should get them around now, before I take the tyres away."

"You go, Eric. You need to get home. I don't fancy getting a constable here on New Year's Eve. What are they going to be able to do, anyway? Prints are out of the question. I'll report it tomorrow. I've taken some photos."

"I've never seen all four slashed before. It takes a lot of effort to do that, and some knowhow. You'd have to work quickly, too. Sure are some bad bastards out there," he said, as he climbed into his truck. "You take care now."

"Thanks again, Eric. I'm sorry for getting you over here. I really appreciate it."

"Try and have a good evening."

When he went back inside his mother was waiting. "Do you have any suspicions about who could have done that?"

"Don't worry about it. In my job, you see it happen all the time," he reassured her. "I don't really know. It could be any number of disgruntled people I've dealt with in the last twelve months. There's been a few, believe me. I'm not bothered by it."

"This is what I mean, Tom. It worries me what you do. A lot."

"I know. And I'm sorry it was brought here. That makes me more angry than the tyres being slashed. But, whoever did it, wanted to get at me. I'm not going to let it. If I do, they win."

"When are you going to call the police?"

"I'm going to go and see them tomorrow. I've got photos. Please, don't worry. It's fine."

* * * *

Tom decided it was wise to stay home with his mother that night. At 7 pm, Steve Rubis called and invited him to come and see his band play, which was the last thing he felt like doing. He explained what had happened and Steve understood why he was in no mood to go out. "That's pretty sick shit, man," Steve said.

As a result of what had happened, Tom re-evaluated when he would call Penny. He decided he should call her earlier than he had first planned. The next morning, he waited until the civilised hour of 10 am and punched in her number on his phone.

"Hello, Penny. It's Tom Greer."

"Hello Tom."

"How are you?"

"I'm alright."

"Yes? You're okay? I've been worried."

"Yes. I'm alright. I'm staying at my mother's place for a few days while Edgar is in the flat. He's moving out."

"You've separated?"

"Yes."

"I'm very sorry to hear that, Penny."

"My marriage is over, Tom. I realised that after everything you told me. I thought I knew my husband, but I didn't. But I'm not the same person he married."

"Infidelity is not what you expected or deserved. No one deserves it."

"I … I need to get things in order, Tom. It's going to take me some time. I want to focus on my brother, not him."

"Okay, well, I'm still in Norwich. I think I will be here until at least the end of January. I have to go into the police station today about something else. I'd like to take the opportunity to speak with them about your brother, if I can. So I thought I would call you and see if you're ready for me to take the next steps."

"Yes please, Tom. I've discussed it with my mother and brother. We want you to go ahead."

"Okay, well that's good. This time I won't be doing anything else. I'll call you regularly."

"Thank you, Tom. The day after tomorrow, I'll be back in the flat and back at work."

"Who's looking after the shops?"

"We'll be in separate shops for the short term. But I'm not certain about any of that just yet. I might hire someone to manage my side of things, and I'll leave. I don't want to have to keep dealing with him."

"I'm sorry to hear that Penny. But perhaps that's wise."

"Yes. Well, I have support here."

"Alright, I'll call again tomorrow."

"Thanks."

* * * *

At 11.30 am, Tom was standing at the public enquiry counter at Norwich Police Station. It occurred to him that he'd never been inside the station before – undoubtedly a good thing.

"Good morning, Sir," said a young female constable.

"Good morning. I'd like to report a crime."

"Is it a hate crime, Sir?"

"No. Not really."

"What type is it, Sir?"

"It's against property. The tyres on my car were slashed yesterday. All four."

"There's a form you will need to fill in." She placed it in front of him. "You can fill it out here, or if you prefer, you can go online and do it. Was there anything else involved, Sir?"

"No. Just the car."

"Then it would be easiest if you fill out the form and leave it with me. One of our officers will then be in touch with you as soon as possible."

"Thank you," he said, as he took the paper. While he was filling it out, an elderly lady came in, complaining quite loudly about beggars in Norwich.

"Madam, we are diligently dealing with any persistent beggars that are reported to us. In certain cases, a CBO can be issued," the constable said.

"And what is that, missy?"

"A Criminal Behaviour Order. It forbids the person from entering parts of the city centre for a period of time."

"Oh, that. Well, he'll just be back. I can't walk safely to the shops without fear of being approached. It's just not right, I tell you!"

"Madam, when they are issued, they also prohibit the person to act in a way that causes nuisance, annoyance, alarm or distress to members of the public."

"I'm a member of the public and he causes me great distress."

The constable handed a police card to the lady and said for her to call the number on it if she encountered the beggar. "Do you have a phone?"

"At home."

"Okay then, you keep that card and that's the number you call," she said, pointing to it. The lady shook her head, moved away from the counter and made her way slowly to the exit, holding the card in a shaky hand.

Tom reappeared at the counter and handed the young constable the form.

"Do you have any questions about the form?" she asked.

"No, thank you. I've filled it out. There's no urgency with it."

"There's actually a space coming up on our website where you can appeal to the public for information. It's a regular service. Would you like to see if an appeal could be put out for your matter? Sometimes it helps. Someone may have seen something." The constable was not only very professional but patient and helpful as well.

Tom declined, not wanting to advertise where it had happened or have word get out that it had happened to him. Reporting the incident, just for the record, was sufficient.

"I'd prefer if it was just dealt with in the station. I'm happy with that."

A little surprised, she blinked and nodded her head. "Is there anything more I can help you with today?" she asked.

"Well, part of the reason I don't want a public appeal is because I'm a private investigator. My name is Tom Greer. I've been working in London but this incident actually occurred in front of my mother's place in Norwich, where I'm currently residing." He looked around to see if there was anyone else waiting to approach the counter. "While I'm here, I wondered if I could see Constable Donovan, to discuss a missing person case that I've been assigned by a client. It concerns my client's missing brother, Benjamin Longmire. The client has given me authority to discuss it with the constabulary here in Norwich. I'm sure you have procedures, but as I'm here …"

She glanced at her computer monitor and tapped something onto the keyboard.

"PC Donovan is now Sergeant Donovan. I can leave him a message. What did you say your name was?"

"Greer, Thomas Greer."

"Phone number?"

He took out a card and put it on the counter. "Hang on, that's an old card. I'm no longer with that firm." He took a pen and crossed out all references to his old office and circled his mobile number. He handed it to her and she looked at it, then typed some more information into her computer.

"Okay," she said. "Anything else?"

"He will contact me?"

"I've sent him a message."

He could see other people were now behind him. "Thank you. I appreciate your help." He turned and left, wondering how long it was going to take for Sergeant Donovan to contact him, or if he even would.

CHAPTER NINETEEN

There was no way Tom was going to do anything but keep Penny informed this time. Determined not to make the same mistake twice, he rang her the following morning to tell her he was waiting on a call from Sergeant Donovan. To his surprise, she said Donovan had already been in touch with her, asking questions about him.

"I told him he had my full permission, and the permission of Benny's entire family to talk to you and co-operate with you."

"And what did he say?"

"He said he needed to make some internal enquiries. That he would get in touch with you, if head office approved it. I really don't think they have much anyway, Tom. Otherwise, I assume we'd have heard more by now."

"Did he mention that I filed a report? That I had my tyres on my car slashed a couple of days ago?"

"No. What?"

"Yes. All four. Right outside my mother's place."

"By whom? I guess that's a silly question."

"No questions are silly, Penny. I don't know. I don't really care."

"Christ! I told Edgar how I found out he was having an affair."

"How did he take it when you confronted him?"

"At first, he kind of denied it. Then he acknowledged it, but down-played it. Said he'd made a mistake. Like, he should be forgiven, almost. I asked him to leave."

"You said he was moving out. And he has?"

"Yes. And I've changed the locks. I don't want him back here."

"What did he say when you told him I'd seen him with this Amelia lady?"

"He thought I'd engaged you to secretly check him out. I told him that wasn't the case and he'd slipped up, thinking no one would know him in Norwich."

"Right. Well if he's arranged the job on my car, then he knows that I'm in Norwich. If it's a one-off act of juvenile revenge, then so be it. I'm not concerned. But in my line of work, it could have been any number of people. One of the guys I worked with had his car rammed once by the ex of a client he'd busted. It's not unheard of. But whoever it was, they got some thug to do it for them, I have no doubt about that. What was his explanation about the woman? How did she come to be with him? Did he tell you?"

"He said he met her at a trade fair and she wanted to set up a store in Norwich. He just happened to know a vacant site. Didn't think it through. She set up shop and, well, it didn't make any difference. What I didn't know, wouldn't hurt me."

"You're kidding!"

"That's what he said."

"Until you *did* know! He gave you a double whammy. I mean, how low is that? I'm sorry, Penny. You probably don't need to hear it. But it's disgraceful, to say the least."

"You don't have to tell me. I know. Where do we go from here, Tom?"

"I want to hear from Donovan. If he hasn't called me by the morning, I'll contact him. I'll talk to you after that. By the way, did Jason give you back the box of Benny's things? I could use that; I never got a chance to look at it properly."

"Yes. I went in and collected it."

"Okay, well when we next talk, we can discuss that. Hopefully, I'll be speaking with you tomorrow."

After the call ended, he re-examined all the material he had on email. He remembered that Paddo had said something about a fellow called Dennis Whitcombe who had once worked at Anti-Vale Vinyl. But the only person listed who worked for Benny was an Alice McCrombie. By late afternoon, he had settled on tracking them both down to see what they had to say.

But at 4 pm Sergeant Donovan called. "I'm in the station until 6 tonight. I can see you after 5, if you want to come down," he said. "Bring ID with you, not just your driver's licence. I'm out of here right on 6, so don't be late."

Tom arrived at the station well before 5 pm, passport in his pocket, and his birth certificate in a plastic sleeve. Donovan kept him in the waiting room for a good twenty minutes before he made an appearance. He was a giant of a man with a wide frame, pot belly and what looked like a three-day growth around his jowls. "Come through," he said in the same brusque manner he had used earlier.

Tom followed Donovan down a hallway to a small office, noting the sergeant's slow swagger and massive shoulders that swayed from side to side as he walked.

"Take a seat," he said to Tom. It looked more like an interview room, with nothing in it other than a round table and two chairs. Donovan sniffed loudly through his large nostrils as he placed his backside down. "Where's your ID?"

I'm holding it, hadn't you noticed? Tom thought, as he knew it would be a tad unwise to say so. Best to leave judgement of the sergeant's observational skills for later.

Tom played the overkill card for his own entertainment. He handed him the birth certificate, then his passport, then his driver's licence and finally, his business card with 'EAC' scratched out. "Want any more?" he said with a smile. *Want to fingerprint me?*

"Stay here, while I copy them."

"Right."

Donovan's uniform seemed spotlessly fresh, perhaps on account of his recent promotion. The three stripes on his shirt looked brand new in fact. *No doubt awarded for his brilliant work in the case of the missing Benny Longmire!* Tom thought as he watched the sergeant leave the room. It struck him that, for a large man, he had a baby face – a strange combination when paired with the demeanour of a schoolyard bully.

Donovan returned and said, "Well, listen up. The thing is, Mr Greer, you may not be aware, I'm sure you're not, but some 275,000 people, give or take a few, go missing in the UK each year." Tom was aware, but before he could say so, Donovan took it up a pre-emptive notch. "And, *and,* there's about 16,000 currently missing, give or take a few, for more than a year."

"Yep, I'm aware of the stats," Tom said confidently, although they didn't quite match the statistics he'd come across in the investigator's course. But he understood the point the sergeant was making.

"Let me tell you this," Donovan continued. "Some 70 per cent of missing children are in fact girls between the ages of 13 and 17. A huge proportion, if not most, are simply runaways who eventually show up."

"I know."

"Now disappeared people, like Ben Longmire, that's a different category again. Seventy-five or so per cent that are over the age of 24, as he was, are male."

"Yep. I did a course in—"

"So, the thing is, you can imagine, the enormous amount of resources and time and energy and money that goes in to finding these people, each and every working day. Every day, in places like our constabulary. The forces across the UK can get up to a thousand calls a day!"

"I most certainly can imagine the work. It's overwhelming."

"No. I'll tell you what it is. It's bloody prohibitive."

"That too. But Benny Longmire—"

"Yeah, we know, he's been gone for a while. That's not a secret. It's public information. But, if you want to come down here and check our files, well, then you are gonna have to get a Freedom of Information application together. That's something you should know." He sniffed loudly again and sat back on his chair.

"I'm aware of that procedure, Sergeant, but what about just general information. You—"

"I just *gave* a bunch of it to you!"

Tom could see the sergeant was the interrupting type. And as he had already annoyed him, he knew if he was to get anywhere with him, he had to get to the point but remain polite.

"Look. I could understand if there was a detailed, specific, ongoing *criminal* investigation underway. That you don't want others, be they private investigators or the press or the public, knowing things that might compromise your position or your tactics or whatever. But—"

"That's right! What we do can't be prejudiced by giving information out. We just can't do it. Not in criminal investigations."

"But, if it's not at that stage, yet. In other words, if you've hit a dead end, my understanding is that it's not unheard of to work with private firms who might assist. Who could work with you. They are paid separately. I am paid separately."

"I wouldn't say we have hit a dead end."

"But, is there a criminal investigation?"

"I'm not at liberty to say."

"Okay. I accept that. But what about CCTV? Anything?" While he was going to press Donovan for some specifics, Tom knew he only had a slim chance of getting any and that he might not have another opportunity to do so. But he also knew that Donovan had to walk some sort of fine line. If the police hadn't turned up any clues in Benny's case in five years, and then refused to co-operate with someone like Tom, then the Morrow family would be doubly unhappy. Donovan would have to say something meaningful if he wanted to avoid a complaint.

"There are thirteen million CCTV cameras in Britain, give or take—"

"And is Benny on any, on that last day he was seen?" he asked, deciding to do some interrupting of his own.

"Well, he was seen leaving his shop but after that, there is nothing. Not in Norwich."

"Elsewhere?"

"I don't think we've had time to check the other twelve million and whatever, but you're welcome to try."

Tom took a long look at the newly promoted sergeant and smiled, then leaned in.

"Right. Listen, Sergeant. I don't want to keep you. But I also don't want to waste your time with an FOI application. I know what paperwork is like. I'm not expecting you to tell me confidential things. We all want the same result. There is a grieving family. Can you tell me *anything*? I can save you the time of that application."

"Look, Greer. We hold grave fears for him. I'll be honest with you. Most people turn up by now. Sometimes they hide under a rock while they wait to get out of the clutches of people they might owe money to or they simply don't get on with. He owed some money, but all those people are clean. Some are scummy but not scummy enough to bump him. We think there's a good chance of foul play. When we went to his flat, the feeling was he'd got up and left of his own accord. But when we got Forensics to go in a little later, it wasn't so clear. But based upon the information we have and the people we've spoken to, I can only tell you the same thing that we told the press. Though, they seemed to have lost interest."

"And what is that?"

"There's a gap between the time he got home and what happened then. We know he went home after work and some time after that, he went out or was taken out. We appealed to the public way before you even heard about the case. Nothing. We spoke to just about everyone in his street. No one saw anything. Or if they did, they're not saying. Some unconfirmed sightings here and there, as you always seem to get, but none have resulted in anything. It is, as I say, not a secret that it's a mystery."

"You still have his work computer, don't you?"

"Yeah. The family can have that back. We've made some copies and it's just a work computer, full of boring stuff unless you are into, I don't know, old albums and rare recordings. Nobody was out to kill him for some bloody record of someone who was a one-hit-wonder in the fifties."

"How long before the police give up on a case like this?"

"We never *give up*. It remains open. Some families choose to go down a different path in that period."

"What do you mean?"

"After a while, they get the Coroner or the government to formally declare the person dead. For a number of reasons. It's not straightforward, but it sometimes happens."

"I don't think my clients want that."

"The other thing is, we find bodies. There are more than a thousand unidentified bodies on our files at any one time. That's the UK, not Norwich."

"But if you found his body, with DNA you could identify him?"

"Most likely. But it's sometimes difficult. We've got his toothbrush and hairbrush as well as some other personal items taken from his flat. They're preserved in case something turns up."

"If someone is going to abscond, they're going to take their toothbrush, aren't they?"

"Not necessarily. You're assuming they're thinking clearly. People under stress don't always think to pack a bag, like they're going on a holiday."

Donovan sat back and seemed to have relaxed a little.

"Did you find out what sort of person he was?" Tom said. "Sorry, is?"

"You can work that out. Nothing unusual. A bit of a loner. Not a lot of friends. Eccentric maybe, but only mildly about the business he was in. I've known weirder types and have a few relatives who are stranger."

"Nothing suspicious in the car or in his house or the shop?" More relaxed himself, Tom was the one acting like a cop now.

The sergeant shook his head.

"Would you recommend I did an FOI? In your honest opinion? Just between you and I, although if you don't want to say, I understand."

"You should be aware that there are exemptions under the law for the police. It's up to you, but I think you will be disappointed. You might be better to use your clients' time, since they are paying you, on other things. It's up to twenty business days wait now to get any paperwork. I don't think you'll be happy with what you get sent, once we apply the exemptions."

Sergeant Donovan looked at his watch. Tom knew he was going to be given the line that it had been a long shift etcetera, but then, Donovan said, "Let me ask *you* something. Sounds to me like you haven't been working on the case long. But what have *you* come across?"

"I visited the couple who owned the building where the record shop was. Nothing there."

"We did that. Waste of time."

"I found out that Penny Morrow's husband, soon to be ex-husband, is having an affair with some woman who rents the shop now, the shoe shop that used to be the record shop Benny owned."

"Is that right?"

"Yes. I busted him by accident, having lunch with a woman. I'd stopped working on the case and was in Norwich. I told Penny and she put me back on it."

"Why the hell would he choose to have an affair with a woman in the same business as him and his missus? I mean, let alone with a woman working in his wife's missing brother's business premises? What a bloody …"

"Bastard?"

"Idiot."

The sergeant leant further back in his chair with a smile and shook his head.

"Oh, and it's probably unrelated. God knows, I've made a few enemies in the last twelve months, and embarrassed and upset a whole bunch of others, but my car tyres got slashed on New Year's Eve, all four."

"Really? Have you put in a report?"

"Yes. You can read it."

"Listen, Greer. I'm going to walk you out now. It's knock-off time. It's been a bloody long day and I started at 6. I'd like you to keep me informed. This case is very much open, despite what some people think. You tell Ms Morrow that and also, not to give up on the force. We're not as incompetent as she might think. Good luck to you. You'll need it." He stood up.

"I will. Thanks for your time. I appreciate it, Sergeant." Tom paused. "Before I go, you interviewed his only employee, an Alice McCrombie?"

"Early on, yeah."

"Can you tell me where she is?"

"You'll find her at the library. The big one in town."

* * * *

When he called Penny that night to give her a rundown, it was as she expected. "I told you they have nothing," she said.

Early next morning, Tom decided to track down Dennis Whitcombe and visit some random neighbours who lived in the same street as Benny. But his first priority was Alice McCrombie.

Alice could work in any section of the library. He realised it was a bigger task to find her than he had anticipated. There were people playing board games, some sitting at desks with earphones, and others just reading. It was easy to spot the staff members, working hard, helping numerous people at once. After a while, he noticed that some wore badges and it took him several goes to see what they said. He noticed one of the staff had a badge displaying her first name and then, in larger print: 'I can help – ASK ME!' All he needed to do now was find someone with a badge that said 'Alice' and ask her if indeed she could help him. But he couldn't find her and after half-an-hour, rather than asking for Alice, he decided to get a cup of tea and call Paddo.

"You said you knew Dennis Whitcombe," he said to Paddo as he sipped his tea. "The guy who used to work at Anti-Vale Vinyl. If I wanted to find him, where would you suggest I start?"

"His parents live out at Wells, I think. You could start there. But remember, he doesn't get along with them. He was a beggar, literally, the last time I saw him and he had some choice words for them. But they will likely know where he is. You may find him but he's not right in the head, so I don't think he'll be much help, whatever it is you want from him."

"What's the story with the parents?"

"I only know *of* them, rather than *knowing* them. I met them once as a kid because my parents knew them. A bit on the snobbish side. So, they may not even give you the time of day."

Upon finishing his tea, Tom went back into the library and asked for Alice. He told the staff member he was an old friend. She said he could find her in the next section. He set off, looking for a lady with a badge that said 'Alice' and which invited him to ask questions. He would seek to extend the privilege and ask about things that had nothing to do with books.

When he found her, she seemed to be in a rush and as she passed him, he said, "Excuse me, I wonder if you could help me."

"Yes. Just a minute," she replied, "I'm helping someone at the moment. If you wait, I will be with you in a second." She was gone again before he could say thanks.

While he waited, he opened a book and pretended to be engrossed in it, occasionally peering around to make sure she was still in sight. She returned after about five minutes and said, "Thank you for waiting. How can I assist?"

He produced one of his old business cards with the parts referring to his old firm blackened out and his phone number highlighted in yellow. He knew she was going to be shocked. She took the card and looked at it.

"First, let me apologise. This isn't related to the library. I'm sorry to interrupt but I'm a private investigator working for the family of Benjamin Longmire, looking into his disappearance."

She stepped back with a concerned look on her face. "What do you want?" she said.

"I know this must be a surprise after all these years. But as you would know, he hasn't been found. And well, I was wondering if you would agree to talk to me. The family – his sister especially – is in turmoil. She would be very grateful if you would spend ten minutes with me. Just ten minutes of your time, that's all."

"It's years ago. I've spoken to the police already. I don't have anything I can tell you. I only worked there six months."

"I know. And it's just routine."

"I don't know," she said, looking around as if to check who might be keeping an eye on her. "How did you know I was here?"

"Look, it's my job. It would be just so I could say to the family everyone has been contacted. It's very tragic but important. I'm sorry."

She scratched her eye. "What did you say – ten minutes?"

"Yes, max. That's all. It would be appreciated. And there would be no further contact. None."

She looked around again and looked at her watch. Tom watched her think it over. "I have a lunch break in half-an-hour," she said. "Come back then. Meet me out the front."

"Thank you, Alice. I shall be there." She went off in the same harried manner with which she had approached him, now with even more demands placed upon her.

As he stood waiting for her to appear, he thought how it was odd that he was back in his old home town actually working and that it felt good. He wondered if he should offer to buy Alice lunch so he could extend the ten minutes to get as much information as he could.

Alice McCrombie was thin with short red hair. She came out wearing sunglasses even though the sky was heavy and grey. She wore a smart, long coat and a bag over her shoulder.

"Can we go somewhere for lunch?" he said, as she stopped in front of him. "I'll pay."

"We can," she said. "I don't have a lot of time, so somewhere quick."

He suggested sandwiches and coffee at a nearby place he knew. On the way there, he attempted to make small talk about the weather but he was met with no response. They found a table inside and sat opposite each other. She chose a salad and a soft drink and he, sandwiches and coffee.

"What do you want to ask me?" she said, removing her sunglasses for the first time.

"What was he like?

"Benny?"

Tom nodded.

"To work for? Or in general?"

"Both."

"He was okay, I guess. We didn't fight. He was a little slow, maybe. Like, he knew his music. But wasn't the best business person."

"Did he owe money in the business?"

"A little. When the cops talked to me, that seemed to be all they were interested in."

"That he owed money?"

"Yeah. I think they thought he did a runner."

"But you don't think that?"

"Not really. Like, I've worked for people before who owed heaps of money. Much more than he did. You can see their devious little ways. But he wasn't like that. He was just, I don't know, slack."

"Like it wasn't worrying him?"

"No. Not that I could see. He knew I knew he owed rent. But he'd just put the letters aside and say he'd get to it, or something like that."

Tom bit into his sandwich, while she pushed some pieces of her salad around.

"What was he like with the customers? Someone I know told me he was arrogant."

"Not arrogant. He got a few offside, I suppose. He knew so much. Like people would come in and ask for something obscure, and he'd know more than they did. It was surprising, for his age. He was more interested in the music and its history, than the customers, I suppose. Wasn't the most tactful, at times."

"Did the police interview you more than once?"

"No. It was only once, not long after he went missing."

"The day before he went missing, that last time you were with him in the shop, what do you remember?"

"It was just like any other day. And then, I turn up for work the next day, and the shop was closed. It never re-opened after that. It was just like, he vanished or something, off the face of the Earth. It was totally weird."

"What about his behaviour that last day?"

"I don't remember a lot about that day. Nothing unusual, really. It was a Thursday, I remember that, because suddenly, I had a long weekend. That turned into a *very* long weekend," she said, raising her eyebrows and finally taking bites of her salad.

"How did you get the job?"

"Just an advert."

"Any other employees?"

"Nope."

"Did you ever socialise with him? Like, go for drinks after work?"

"No. Never."

"He never suggested it?"

"No. He wasn't really like that. I was always gone. I always went home before he closed up."

"Did he have any friends that you knew of? Any that might drop into the shop?"

"Not really. I think he was a bit of a loner. Not in a weird way. Just led a pretty quiet life, I thought. Though, I didn't know him that well, socially I mean. He was … he didn't … wasn't the kind of fella to, I don't know, attract attention."

"Female attention?"

"Any, really," she said, and gave a bit of a laugh.

"Enemies?"

"Not that I saw."

Tom finished his sandwich and was now sipping his coffee. Now, he could see she was willing to help if she could. "Thank you for doing this. I hope you don't mind me asking? It's clutching at straws stuff, now, after all these years."

"He's been gone a long time. What do the cops think?" she asked, taking a sip of her drink.

"They think he's been murdered. When the cops say 'grave fears', then they suspect he might be lying in one, somewhere."

"That's so freaking scary," she said, then took another sip from the straw. "It's not looking like much else now, I suppose. It freaks me out, God, when I think about it."

Tom was struggling now to think of what else to ask her. She seemed honest enough and he felt he could get a straight answer if she actually knew anything.

"Have you ever heard of a Dennis Whitcombe?"

"No, should I?"

"He used to work there before you, apparently. Before Benny took the business over."

"What does he look like?"

"I don't know. I'm going to try and track him down. Again, pie in the sky stuff, I just thought I'd ask."

"I'm sorry I can't help you much. I never went to the shop before Ben had it. I'm not that interested in old music."

"That's alright. I'm not either. I didn't think you'd be able to shed much light on all this. In that whole six months, that you were there, was there anything specific that you saw him annoyed about. Anything that sticks out, at all? Any incident with a customer, a supplier, anything like that?"

Thinking for a moment, she paused, ate some more of her salad and took another sip of her drink. "Actually, there was one fella who came in a few times. Benny got into an argument with him once. It was quite embarrassing as there were a few customers in the store. This guy said something about how he used to work in the store, or maybe it was some other store. I can't remember. He was complaining that the previous owner used to give him a discount. Benny wouldn't give it to him. Maybe he was that Dennis guy you were talking about. Anyway, he never said his name. He came in a few times after that and ticked Benny off."

"What do you mean 'ticked Benny off?'"

"Well, this fella used to come in, usually when it was crowded. He was a real pain. He seemed a bit like a loose cannon. Like something was missing from the picnic basket. He usually wreaked of alcohol. Benny politely refused to serve him at all. But then once, he came in and made a scene and Benny told him to leave."

"How many times did you say he came into the store?"

"Maybe three or four."

"Did he leave, when asked?"

"Ben threatened to call the cops on him, so he left after that. He just seemed like he wasn't the full quid."

"But otherwise harmless?"

"Not exactly harmless. He seemed like he had a bit of a temper."

"And did you tell the police at any stage?"

"No. We never gave it a second thought. Ben wasn't worried about it."

"Did you tell the police about it when they interviewed you?"

"No. I never thought about it, really. It was pretty minor. All shops get walk-in nutcases occasionally. You just get used to it. At the book store where I used to work, there was a guy who used to come in every week and expose himself. At Benny's store, we didn't get a lot of weirdos though. I guess that's why I remember *that* fella. Besides, all the cops wanted to ask me about was the money he owed, like the rent."

"What did this guy look like?"

"He looked like … I think he had a missing tooth. Unshaven, smelly. Skinny. That's about all I can remember."

"Seen him since, around town? Anywhere?"

"Nope."

Tom finished his coffee and Alice pushed her empty plastic plate to one side. "How long have you been at the library?"

"About eighteen months now."

"From Norwich originally? Sorry, I don't have anything else. I just appreciate your time."

"Yep."

"Me too. It's all a bit unusual for our neck of the woods," he said, raising his eyebrows.

"Very."

They left the café and he shook her hand. "Well, if I need to borrow a book, I'll know who to ask."

She smiled. "I'd best get back. I do hope something turns up. It must be very hard for that poor family. You said he has a sister?"

"Yes. And a mother and a brother."

She shook her head. "Dreadful. It really is so sad."

"Thank you, Alice. If you think of anything, call me. The number's on the card."

She smiled again, put her sunglasses on and walked away.

CHAPTER TWENTY

Wells-next-the-Sea on the beautiful North Norfolk coast would take Tom about an hour to reach by car from Norwich. He had to decide whether to drive out there that afternoon in the fast-fading light or make an early start the next morning. By 3 pm he had the address for Mr and Mrs Clive Whitcombe, business proprietors, but of course there would be no guarantee they would be home. With their wealthy lifestyle, he figured it was a strong possibility they might be in the south of France or staying in a chalet in the Swiss Alps at this time of the year. They could be anywhere. He had never been to this seaside town so he decided he would make the most of his visit regardless of whether the Whitcombes were there or not. He would head there first thing in the morning and leave calling Penny until tomorrow.

On his trip to Wells, Tom realised that while swimming was out of the question in these freezing conditions, sightseeing was not. But of course, he hoped to find Clive or his wife at home. The thought had occurred to him that it might be their summer house, possibly one of many homes, so he needed to be in luck – for Penny.

"They're a wee bit posh out there, so take your wallet," his mother had said at breakfast.

From Tom's research the night before, he understood that Wells was more down to earth than his mother believed, partly owing to the families who visited in summer and who loved the beaches, the casual homeliness of the town, and the fish and chips – said to be some of the best in England. Even if the Whitcombes weren't there, he could at least have a feed of fresh haddock smothered in salt and vinegar; walk along the seaside, imagining the town's summer personality; throw an occasional chip to the gulls; and think about his next move.

When he found the house, it looked like two – a Georgian façade on one, which was undoubtedly a Grade II listed property, and an exquisite annexed cottage. As he cruised past, he admired the house's period features and guessed it had at least six bedrooms. He thought it was highly unlikely that Dennis occupied one, and was now kicking back, enjoying a good book next to one of the three fireplaces, and chatting occasionally to his parents about today's stock market. He could almost picture the wall-papered living rooms with their artwork. Dennis, he was sure, would not fully appreciate any of it like his parents had wanted, and indeed, expected.

After finding a car park some distance away, he pushed the heavy wrought-iron gate open and walked up the beautifully tiled path. He pressed the doorbell, thinking how he had done a lot of doorbell pressing in the last year, and wondering how many more buttons he would have to push before he got to the bottom of the Benny Longmire case. After waiting for a minute, there was no answer; it did not look promising. But then, an older man carrying a garden hose appeared from the side path. Anyone would do; anyone he could talk to who might know something about the whereabouts of Dennis.

"Clive!" he said, rather loudly and presumptuously, a risk he considered worth taking, given the age and look of the man.

"Yes?" the man said.

Yes! His luck had changed.

"Lovely to see you again!" Tom said with a huge smile. *Gotta run with this now.* The man seemed taken aback and almost tripped over the hose that wasn't quite co-operating as he wanted. "Bit chilly for that this morning!" Tom added, trying to put him at ease.

"Just a minute," the man said, still struggling with the hose. It wasn't obvious what he was doing with it. Possibly about to spray mud off the tyres of the Bentley Tom could see parked out the front. Tom moved back down the path further.

"Do I know you?" the man said, as he bent down to deal with the hose, then rose with a pained look on his face.

"Clive, don't you remember me?"

"No. I don't."

"I'm a friend of Dennis'. We're old classmates. Oh, it's probably going back a few years now. It's not surprising you don't remember me. It's quite a way back, now that I think of it. We met several times, when Dennis and I were at school."

"Did we?"

"Oh, yes. Anyway, I was wondering if Dennis was about?"

Clive was indeed old, and the opportunity to take advantage of his age and perhaps fading memory, as unfair as it was, proved too much for Tom to resist.

"No, he's not." He appeared to be neither rude nor arrogant as Paddo had led Tom to believe. Rather, the open look on his face gave Tom the impression he might be willing to help.

"Oh, right. Will he be home later?" He knew very well he probably wasn't going to be home ever again.

"No."

"Right, well, it's just that I'm spending the whole day trying to track down some fellows from school. We're having a reunion. And I haven't seen Dennis in years. Where is he, perhaps close by?"

He could tell this question made Clive uncomfortable and possibly annoyed. He knew putting him unexpectedly on the spot was rather cruel, but he did it anyway.

"I don't remember you. What's your name?" Clive moved closer to examine him.

"Gabe. Gabriel Van Den Der Berg. My mother, she's Dutch. I'm sure you can remember her, with her accent. We were only little kids. She used to let me play with Dennis and drop me over at your house. Emma Van Den Der Berg. The blonde lady."

"I can't place her." He seemed totally confused, understandably, as he wiped his hands with a handkerchief. The bend in his back was still evident from dealing with the hose.

"Can you help with Dennis? The invitations are going out today. Or, we are trying to get them delivered, if we can. It's a very big and slow process with that many of us to organise."

"Look," Clive paused as if he needed to think about what he was going to say. "Dennis has been a little unwell."

"Oh, really … I didn't know that. I had no idea."

"It's … we haven't seen him for a little while. The last time we tried to reach him he was living in Norwich. I can't help you any further, I'm afraid."

"Do you know where?"

"No."

"Right." Tom stepped back and pretended to think for a moment. "Hmmm. You couldn't give me a postal address, by any chance?"

"No."

"Which area of Norwich was he in, do you know?"

"I don't know. Norwich, somewhere. He was in Sprowston, then Costessey for a while." Tom knew both suburbs well. "I don't know where he currently is, to be honest, as dreadful as that might sound."

Tom wanted to press him for more details, like whether Dennis was living on the street – a strong possibility given what Paddo had told him. But he was not going to touch upon it. He had a feeling Clive knew a little more than he was letting on, but could see it caused him pain to be speaking of his wayward son. At least he hadn't said he was dead. "Thanks Clive. Well, good day to you, Sir. Give my regards to Mrs Whitcombe. Perhaps she will remember me," he said as he began to walk out the gate.

"She passed away last year."

He had said too much. Wincing and feeling deep regret, and worse, a fool for speaking those words, he turned back. "Oh, I'm very sorry to hear that." This time he was genuine. It was always a fine line between saying too little and too much when it came to deception. He knew he'd just crossed the line.

Clive shook his head and Tom could tell somehow that he had once been a formidable man; a man of business and rules and class and privilege, but no longer quite to the same extent. No doubt he'd had his fair share of suffering and perhaps he'd mellowed. The money was perhaps the only thing left, besides the memories. Planting false ones wasn't fair. Tom stood closer to him now.

"Anyone who knew her knows that she is sadly missed," Clive said.

"I would have come to the funeral, if I'd known. I've been travelling. That's very sad. My sincere condolences."

"She had suffered enough, Gabe. Everyone who knew her, knew that."

Perhaps he meant more than physical suffering and could very well have been referencing the pain associated with Dennis. But he had to leave, just when he could have said more – something, anything – to make up for his visit of lies. He needed to walk away quickly. He could deceive this man no longer.

"If I'm going to get these invitations out, I must be going. I appreciate your time. Best regards for the new year. Goodbye, Clive."

"Goodbye, Gabe."

Tom sat on a bench eating his fish and chips. He felt cold as he looked out across the sand and the flat ocean in the far-off distance. A thin layer of grey clouds slowly moved above him and the wind whipped around his ears. He wanted to go back and say something nice to Dennis' father, but he knew he could never go back. He had to get in the car and keep moving; keep busy.

* * * *

By the time Tom got back to Norwich, there was still time to stop by Benny's street. It may very well be a waste of time, but he would never know unless he tried. The flats in that area looked pretty much the same and were all in a row. First, he visited the flats either side of Benny's old place. He had decided honesty was going to be the order of the afternoon. At each house, he rattled off the same speech:

"Hello, my name is Tom Greer. I'm a private investigator, working for the family of Benjamin Longmire who disappeared from his flat in this street approximately five years ago. Here is my card. Could I ask you for a

minute of your time and ask whether you may have seen anything suspicious or unusual at the time or just prior to it?"

One neighbour had only moved to the area in the last three months, and another two said they knew nothing and saw nothing, and they had already told the police that at the time.

After getting the same 'saw nothing know nothing' responses from several more neighbours, he knocked on one more door. A middle-aged lady answered it. After his introduction she said, "I did see something that day that I hadn't seen before or since."

"You did? What was it?"

"Well, I was in the front garden here." She stepped by him onto her little pathway. Her garden was one of the nicer ones in the street, comprising little pebbles and stones in a rockery, with a mixture of small and larger mature shrubs. Even in winter, he could tell it was well looked after, if not manicured to a degree. In the spring and the summer no doubt, it would be filled with colour. He followed her out, along the patterned tiles that divided it.

"I was in the garden here and I heard them before I saw them. There were two men who came around the corner there and then walked right past here. They were walking with a dog, and fairly quickly, so I recall."

"Yes."

"Anyway, people *do* walk their dogs, but I am usually familiar with those people. Sometimes I say hello if I'm outside. But I had never seen these two men before. They seemed a little out of place."

"How do you mean?"

"The way they were dressed. The one walking the dog, in particular."

"And how were they dressed?"

"In leather, lots of leather. Sort of …" She paused to think and perhaps choose her words accurately. "Not bikies, as in a gang or something, just a bit rough looking, if you know what I mean."

"What did they look like? How old?"

"Young. Maybe twenties. Not teenagers. They weren't kids."

"What sort of a dog, do you remember?"

"Yes. It was one of those little aggressive things. Like a pit bull. We never see those around here. That's mainly what caught my eye."

"Right. That's quite a memory. You said they were talking? Did you get a look at their faces?"

"Not really. I couldn't hear exactly what they were talking about but they were kind of focused. It wasn't the normal relaxed stroll of people walking their dogs, like you often see around here. People walk their dogs and stop and chat. They're not in a hurry. These boys weren't from around here."

"And they kept going up the street?"

"Yes. I went out to the edge there and saw them stop halfway up for a minute or two. Then they kept going."

"So, halfway up?" Tom asked, looking up the street. "Halfway up would be where Benny lived?"

"Well, I didn't know that at the time, but yes, I suppose. When the news came out that he went missing, I recognised him from his photo in the paper and in the posters and things they put around town."

"You knew him?"

"No. I had seen him maybe a couple of times. I said hello to him once or twice when he walked past here. But I didn't know him. I figured he lived up there somewhere. I didn't know which one, which place."

"Sorry, do you mind if I ask your name?"

"My name is Mavis Willington."

"And does anyone else live with you, Mrs Willington?"

"No."

"Did the police come and talk to you, at any stage?"

"Surprisingly, no. I know they talked to the fellow opposite and some other people up the street. But not me."

"Hmmm. That's a bit disappointing," he said, taking another look up the street.

"I told them about it though."

"You did?"

"Yes. And that's why I remember it – the boys walking and the dog. I suppose I would never have normally, but when they put out a public appeal for anyone who might have some information, I called the number up. The appeal made me think about seeing people I hadn't seen in the street before."

"And what happened?"

"I was put through to an officer on the phone and I told her what I told you."

"And?"

"I never heard anything. They never called back. I assumed they just checked it out."

"How long ago was that?"

"Probably four years ago."

"And have you ever seen these two men since?"

"No."

"Could you possibly identify the men from a photo?"

"I don't know. I doubt it."

It was starting to get dark and as he'd run out of cards, he wrote his number on his notepad and gave it to her. "Thank you for your time," he said.

"I hope I have been of some help. Those men probably had nothing to do with it. But I—"

"No, you've been very helpful. All information is just that, and it certainly falls into the category of something, well, not in the everyday ordinary, as you said. So, I think you were right to tell the police and me."

"I hope they find the poor man safe and well, somewhere."

"Me too. Thank you, Mrs Willington. I have to go. Please call me, if you remember anything else. Anything."

"Thank you, Mr Greer. I will," she said, and went back inside and closed the door.

As soon as he got home, Tom called Penny, asking if tomorrow was a good day to come and see her. She agreed, and told him to come to her flat after 7.

CHAPTER TWENTY-ONE

Tom arrived shortly after 7. Penny led him through the hallway and into the living area, showing him to a leather couch. The shoebox full of photos and paperwork she had given him last year sat on a large glass coffee table. "Thank you for coming, Tom, please take a seat. Can I offer you some tea or coffee?"

"I'm fine, thank you, unless you are having some," he said, as he sat down.

"I'll put the kettle on."

He watched her as she walked to the kitchen. He thought she looked a lot better than the last time he'd seen her. Her beauty and grace never ceased to exist for him; he could somehow sense her strength and courage whenever he was in her presence. He gazed at her while she arranged a plate of biscuits on a plate on the kitchen counter, then pulled the shoebox closer to him and lifted the lid.

"I don't even know whether that Jason fellow even opened it," she said from the kitchen, her back to him.

"It wouldn't surprise me." He withheld adding what he really wanted to say about Jason. He removed a couple of photos and examined them.

When the tea was ready, Penny brought everything over to the coffee table and sat down next to him.

"You have a lovely place," Tom said.

"Thank you." Moving to the edge of the couch, she poured the tea. "It'll probably have to be sold. Unless I can pay Edgar out."

"Have you seen him?"

"No. And I don't want to. I had to talk to him about the keys today. I'll have to see him next week about the shops." For a moment, they didn't speak while they sipped their tea. "I don't want to talk about Edgar, Tom. There are more important things now," she said.

Tom nodded. "I'm glad I've come to see you. There isn't a massive amount to report, but there is some."

"Some is better than nothing. I'm over hearing nothing."

"I told you about Donovan. He's a sergeant now."

"Yes."

"Well, after him, I saw Alice McCrombie, who Benny employed. She now works at a library."

"In Norwich?"

"Yes."

"She seemed a bit standoffish at the beginning, but then she relaxed. We went to lunch. I found her quite frank and helpful, really. She doesn't know much and is freaked out by the whole thing, understandably."

"Was she of any help at all?"

"She said one thing. Well, she said a few things, actually. She said your brother didn't worry about the money – the rent he owed or anything like that. So, the cops really went down the wrong path there. Their first reaction was that he ran away because of debt. You were right about that. They know that now. They also don't think someone was out to get him because he owed them money. They've checked out the people he was in debt to and there's nothing. It also wasn't enough money to be that concerned, so they wasted time following up that angle. This is all consistent with what Alice had to say."

"He was never very good with money."

"I don't think it has anything at all to do with money. It's something else, whatever it is. Now, Alice got to know him a little bit, to the extent that she felt he kept to himself, largely, and was okay to work with. As far as she could tell, there really weren't any major issues going on in his life."

"That would be right, I think."

"Mind you, she never went for a drink with him, never socialised with him; nothing like that. Never went to his place. She never met any of his friends. She did tell me one thing that might be important. There was a fellow who sometimes came into the shop and caused a bit of trouble. He wanted a discount because he had worked there before or something like that. Benny gave him a polite what for, but he came back, possibly up to four times and caused a scene, enough to cause Benny to threaten calling the beat bobbies on him. They didn't think anything more of it. As Alice said, all shops get a nutter from time to time."

"But you think there is more to it?"

"Not exactly. But this loony sounds like someone by the name of Dennis Whitcombe. I might be wrong about that, but my gut tells me differently. Sometimes you can trust gut feelings. He and his family are from Norwich. The family are well-established business people. I don't know him, but a good friend of mine does and he told me about him. My friend said Dennis used to work there when he was maybe twenty years old. Before Benny owned the record shop."

"So, you want to talk to him?"

"Well, yes. If I can find him. I found out a bit about the family background – mega rich posh types. Dennis is the black sheep. Very black, and totally estranged from his parents. I think they basically disowned him. Certainly, there has been some friction there. My friend saw him begging in the street some years ago. Needless to say, he didn't go into the family business. Sad story. I went to see his father, who lives in Wells in the north of Norfolk, to see if he knew where his son was living. I didn't tell him my real name or what I was doing, of course, just that I needed to track Dennis down for a school reunion."

She raised her eyebrows and gave the slightest hint of a smile.

"I felt sorry for him in a way. He told me his wife had died. But he didn't know where Dennis was. Last seen in Norwich, somewhere. He didn't tell me how recently."

"But this Dennis fellow is worth talking to?"

"We don't have much else to go on, so I think so, while I figure out the next steps."

"Is he going to be hard to find?"

"I don't know. He's the type who might hang around pubs a lot. He's probably an alcoholic and drug user. He's been cut off from his family and will have money issues. He could be into petty crime. Most likely he will have mental health issues. I've had a look on social media. He's got no presence. He has some brothers. I could try and speak with them, I suppose."

"So, you could check some pubs?"

"It's a big project if I did." He grabbed a biscuit. "There was an urban myth when I was growing up, probably exaggerated, yet with an element of truth, that Norwich, or its greater area, had 365 pubs. So, you could get drunk every day of the year and then, each week, ask for forgiveness in one of the fifty-two churches."

She smiled; a much broader grin this time. It was the first genuine smile he'd seen from her. And making her smile made him smile. Alister had warned him to stay clear of emotional attachment on all jobs, regardless of the client. However, Tom thought it was motivating him in this case. *Use whatever motivation that keeps you going,* Alister had also counselled him. *But be wary of emotions, as they can bring you undone if you don't keep your distance.*

"I have a few other avenues for tracking him down. If I do find him, it's likely to be a waste of time, but there's not much else I can do unless I find more information."

Tom helped himself to more biscuits, dropping crumbs on the couch without noticing. He told Penny about Mavis Willington next.

"Did the police tell you about one of Benny's neighbours, Mavis Willington, reporting seeing strangers outside his flat the day he went missing?"

"No, that's the first I've heard of it."

"I'd like to ask this Dennis fellow where he was that day. There are three things connecting him to Benny now. One, he worked at Anti-Vale Vinyl before he went off the rails. Two, he looks like he went back to the shop and caused a bit of trouble after he lost the plot, and three, he possibly fits the description of one of the rough-looking guys who Mavis saw walking a dog down Benny's street earlier that day."

"Tom, that's more than I've had from the police in five years."

"Well, I'm not confident at all it's anything. This Dennis character sounds like he's a bit of a fool, a no-hoper, not the capable type." As soon as he said 'capable' Tom looked away, worried about his choice of word.

"You mean … not *capable* of killing my brother?"

He turned back to her, relieved that she seemed to know the import of his comment. But she was now looking at the floor, blinking slowly.

"I didn't mean that, exactly, but possibly that's right," he said. "He's a lowlife but whoever is behind Benny's disappearance has been very clever about it. Dennis doesn't sound like he's in the clever category to me. His mental health alone might prohibit me from finding out anything."

Penny rose from the couch and walked slowly into the kitchen, running her hands through her hair. She'd allowed it to grow longer and it was shining in the light. He got up and walked over to her.

"I know this is hard, Penny." He felt it was hard for him too. He wanted to stay with her, to comfort her. Hold her. "But, that's where I'm at with my enquiries so far. I'm going to go back to Norwich tomorrow," he said.

She still seemed to be digesting everything and didn't respond at first. Then, she took a deep breath before saying, "Let me ask you, Tom. Do you think we are ever going to find out what happened to him?"

He couldn't see pain or anguish in her eyes this time. What was it? *Defeat, perhaps? The beginning of the path to acceptance?* "I don't know, Penny. I think we'll find out some more, but I don't know how *much* more. I would give it at least until the end of January, if not a little longer, before you ask me to stop. Not that I'm doing this for the money, it's not—"

"I know," she said and paused. "I trust you, Tom. You can't put a price on trust. I don't … I don't know how much longer I can do this. It's not the money, it's me."

"I understand." He moved back into the living room to collect the box. She followed him. "I should go," he said.

"Okay."

In those few seconds, the sadness in her eyes had returned. He felt an overwhelming urge to say he could stay longer if she wanted – just be with her, so she wasn't alone.

She moved into the hallway and he followed.

"I'll call you," he said.

"Thank you. Goodnight, Tom."

"Goodnight, Penny."

* * * *

A week later, the weather started to slow Tom's investigation down. It had been threatening to snow in Norwich for a few days and then suddenly, everything started to turn white, earlier than predicted. Further research had revealed Dennis Whitcombe's brothers, who had all gone into the family business, were overseas on their annual holidays, so he couldn't visit them in the hope they would know the whereabouts of their favourite sibling. Tom had been to more than two dozen pubs in and around Norwich. He'd mostly abstained from drinking, except on a couple of occasions when he could walk home. In each pub, he had tried sitting near the bar and dropping hints about Dennis Whitcombe being an old friend or a work colleague or a cousin. He told anyone who'd listen that he was originally from Cheshire and was trying to track Dennis down, but his storytelling had amounted to nothing. He enquired at the local hostels and even the hospital to see if anyone knew his whereabouts. He even visited homeless shelters and halfway houses, and rang transitional housing organisations, and drug and alcohol rehabilitation centres far and wide. It was all very frustrating. He started to think Dennis was harder to find than Benny.

It had snowed for two days, and when Tom's sister said how pretty it was, he snapped at her. "Rebecca, the only damn thing that's pretty is that it's pretty bloody cold." He wouldn't be going to any more pubs, especially in this weather, and potentially risk becoming known as the chap who keeps asking about Dennis Whitcombe – the skinny lad who used to work in the old record shop and who went bad. Besides, being from Norwich himself, this ruse could only extend so far before he himself was recognised. Eventually, he tried calling publicans with some cock-and-bull story about being the half-brother of good old Dennis, and how he hadn't seen him since, "well, since my mother divorced his father, but you don't need me to go into that." Then he'd try, "Has he been in, squire, that you know of?" but he soon grew tired of that as well.

Prompted by a memory of his own father telling him years ago what a great old publican Don Arneld was, he rang Don's pub and asked to speak to Don, only to be told, "Bloody hell, cripes, no he's not 'ere. He's been dead for ten years!"

Tom couldn't help himself and said, "Well, I guess there's no point in leaving a message for him then, is there?" But his sense of humour was evaporating as one unproductive day turned into another.

When he needed a break from trying to find Dennis, he turned to the list of Benny's friends that Penny had emailed to him. All of them said they hadn't had any contact with Benny for some time before he went missing. Only one had visited him at the shop and that was not long after it opened. She told Tom she'd had a brief relationship with Benny years ago when they were at university together. They had remained friends but didn't keep in contact much.

Tom called Penny several times to tell her he was still working on the case. He could sense her disappointment across the line. She gave him polite answers to his enquiries about how she was holding up, but he knew how she must be feeling. Not only did she have to deal with her marriage ending, her business winding up, and her mother's failing health, but now it seemed she would have to let her missing brother go too – to let that part of her soul die. Frustrated and annoyed, he realised he may have hit the dead end that Donovan had hit in this case a long time ago.

The shoebox of information gave up no clues to anything more. He had sat in his bedroom going through it with a fine-tooth comb, picking up photos time and again to stare at them until he could look at them no more.

CHAPTER TWENTY-TWO

In late January, Steve Rubis called again and invited Tom to his band's gig that night, but he was in no mood to go. Hardly a fan of the band's music, he was starting to regret ever reconnecting with Steve. It wasn't that he didn't like him, but he'd gone down a different path now, and the path of letting the good times roll had a detour sign in front.

"I'm sorry, son, I'm not feeling well tonight. Let me know when you're playing next and I'll definitely come to that gig." If his frame of mind improved, what he had said wasn't impossible. It just seemed unforeseeable.

"Sure, man."

But by 9.30 pm, as he was reading in bed, it suddenly dawned on him that he had forgotten all about the fact that Steve had been a collector of LP records and a customer of Anti-Vale Vinyl *before* Benny owned the shop. He may very well have known Dennis, even if he'd only worked there for a short while. And, in the circles that Steve mixed in, it was just possible he knew where Dennis had ended up. Norwich wasn't that big a place for it to be out of the question. He jumped out of bed, put on some clothes and headed to the front door.

Rosemary, just about to go to bed herself, said, "I thought you were tired. Where are you going?"

"Out Mum, I might be late. Change of plans. I'll see you in the morning."

He jumped in the car and headed straight to the gig. As he walked in, he was hoping to see Steve immediately and somehow get right to the point so he didn't have to hang around all night. But the band was just into its first set and he knew it was going to be a long night. *It had better be worthwhile,* he thought. He was tired and he hated the music. It didn't help that to his unappreciative ears, it was almost prohibitively loud.

Tom bought a drink and found a seat, trying desperately hard to enjoy himself. Understanding any of the lyrics seemed impossible, buried as they were, beneath Kino's screeching, distorted guitar playing. Others seemed to get it, but he just kept looking at his watch, estimating how long the first set was going to last. He nodded and said hello to a few people he knew. Trying to have a conversation was out of the question and mostly amounted to a shouting, "Yeah, just back in Norwich for a while. What about you?" They would say something in return up close to his ear, and he would nod and smile, only able to guess at what they had said.

Just after 10.30 pm, the first set came to a glorious end with an ear-splitting guitar solo from Kino. The crowd clapped and whistled and Tom joined in, secretly applauding the break. He watched Steve put his guitar on its stand and come into the crowd, high fiving someone on his way, before detouring to two girls in the corner of the room who were eagerly waiting for him. Pretty certain that Steve hadn't seen him, he went over and offered his hand to shake.

Steve grabbed it and pulled Tom close, almost yanking his shoulder out of its socket. Then, he enfolded Tom in his signature bear hug, burying Tom's face under his sweaty armpit and holding him there for a few seconds more punishment. "Sweet as! I didn't think you were coming!"

"I changed my mind. I haven't been out in ages."

"Beautiful. What did you think of 'Bringing Back the Barbarian?'"

"What?"

"The last song in the set. It's the single off our album."

"Oh, great. Brilliant, actually. Kino's guitar work is pretty cool. Hey, can I get you a drink?"

"Yeah. Get me a bourbon and cola," Steve said, as he and another guy clenched fingers and hands and their knuckles met before Steve returned his attention to the girls. He was pumped and in demand.

Tom scurried off to the bar knowing there would be strong competition for Steve's company. When he returned with the drink, a tight circle had enclosed Steve, and when he pushed through to hand it to him, there was no thank you. Tom was merely one of the fans now, and that continued until the beginning of the next set. He decided he had no choice but to hang around.

It was fifteen minutes to midnight when the gig came to an end, and by the end of one torturous encore, Tom had settled on his strategy. First, he'd get hold of Steve and make some small talk, then he'd be honest and tell him he was working as an investigator again. Oh, and by the way, did he know of a Dennis Whitcombe, given he had worked at the old record shop, as Tom needed to track him down. But his plan was foiled when he saw Steve leave the stage and go through a black curtain at the back. Tom wondered if he'd gone to the bathroom, given the gigantic glass of something Steve had consumed in the last set between songs. But when the crowd started to leave and the roadies started to pack up the equipment, and Steve hadn't reappeared, he realised he might have gone. He searched the venue, eventually returning to the front of the stage, where he saw Kino packing away his guitar. "Hey Kino, where did Steve go?"

"He's gone."

"Yeah, already?"

"He went back with Jen."

"Oh, right."

"You can come back if you want," he said, rolling up a cord.

"Where?"

"To Steve's place. We usually have a few drinks afterwards."

"Okay, thanks. I might see you there, then."

He parked in front of Steve's place and as before, Jen answered the door. "Steve, it's your friend, Tom," she yelled, leaving him at the door, just like she had last time. With his patience at breaking point, he walked in anyway.

"Hey, take a seat, Tom!" Delighted to see him, Steve sat nestled between two girls sitting on a couch, a massive joint in his hand.

"Hope you don't mind me coming back. Kino said it was cool. Just wanted to let you know what an absolutely sensational gig that was, old son."

"Yeah, thanks man. Do you want a smoke?"

"Ah, no. I'm good."

"It will make you better." Steve took a drag, with his other arm extended over the back of the couch, and went into a spluttering, coughing fit.

Tom took a seat on the other couch next to a girl he had never met. Kino arrived and several other people walked in and soon there was a crowd and a small party underway. Grabbing a bottle of beer from the fridge at Steve's suggestion, he thought again how difficult it was going to be to get one-on-one access to him. Waiting until he saw Steve get up and go to the bathroom, he went into the kitchenette so he could ambush him on his return.

Steve emerged from the bathroom and was doing up his fly when Tom took his chance. "Steve, I wanted to let you know something," he said.

"Yeah, what?"

"Well, I'm back working in private investigation."

"Really? Cool."

"Yeah, anyway, I thought you might be able to help me. I'm trying to track down someone for a client. I thought you might know him from the old days."

"Who?" he said, as he grabbed another beer from the fridge, knocked the top off it with a spoon and let the lid drop to the floor.

"A guy called Dennis Whitcombe. I only ask, because apparently, he used to work at Anti-Vale Vinyl."

"Fucking Dennis Whitcombe! That loser."

"You know him?"

"Do I know him! He's a tripper."

"Yeah?"

"He's a pisspot, too," he said with a smile, taking a huge swig of the beer.

"You know him from the LP shop?"

"I knew he worked there; that's where I met him. That's when he had his shit together. Man, he ended up on the street! Fuck, I used to buy records off him, but then he got all weird."

"What do you mean?"

"He's just a loser. A rich, spoilt loser. He'd try to get into our shows, then he'd freak the girls out. I banned him after a while."

"Do you know where I can find him?"

"Last time I saw him, he was living with Kino's fuckin' cousin or something ... Hey Kino!" The kitchenette had filled up and Kino had his back to them on the other side, talking to someone else. "Where does old matey, Dennis Whitcombe, live now?"

"Who?"

"Dennis Whitcombe."

"He's over in Bowthorpe. Out that way."

"Bowthorpe?" Tom asked, pushing his way over to Kino.

"Out past the industrial estate. In some old lady's house."

"Do you know the street?"

"I can't remember the name. I just know how to get there. Why, do you want some pot? I can give you some pot."

"No, no. I'm good. Good for that."

"I get some from him occasionally but he's a total nightmare."

"What does the house look like, where he lives I mean?"

"It's brick. He lives in the front part. It's sort of been converted to a flat, I think."

"In the front?"

"Yeah."

"Does Dennis drive? Are there any cars parked out the front?"

"Whitcombe doesn't own a car. The old lady parks her car out the front, I think."

"Sorry Kino. But I *really* need to track this guy down. For a client. The car the lady drives, what is it? If I go over there, I can maybe work it out from the car."

"It's been a while. Um, it's a little silver thing. Japanese, I think. Maybe Korean. I don't know. I haven't scored from him for a couple of months."

"Do you have his phone number?"

"No."

"What's he look like?"

"Skinny. Skinny and ratty."

"Thanks, Kino."

Tom's watch showed 1.45 am and now he was really tired. Tired but relieved.

* * * *

When Tom awoke the next morning, he remembered something Steve had told him the day they had reconnected last year. All Steve's LP records had been stolen. He wondered if Steve had considered that Dennis might have been involved. Steve had banned Dennis from the gigs, and due to the Kino connection, Dennis knew where he lived. But that sort of speculation wasn't helpful. He wasn't working for Steve. And he didn't care about the records.

Straight after a late breakfast, he made the short drive via Dereham Road out to Bowthorpe. He went straight to the industrial area first, sizing up where he should make a turn into the residential areas. He went up and down the streets and in and out of cul de sacs, searching for the car that Kino had described to him. He spotted a small silver Kia hatchback parked in front of a brick house. He parked his car and knocked on the front door. A lady answered. She was elderly, just as Kino had said.

"I was wondering if Dennis Whitcombe lives here?" he said.

"No. He moved last week."

Tom felt like he'd been punched in the face. He'd been so confident that he had found Dennis at last. "Oh. Well, I'm an old friend. Do you know where he's gone?"

"I have a forwarding address for his mail. Wait a minute," she said and closed the door. She came back with a piece of paper. "Here it is, young man." Frail and kindly, she added, "Say hello to him for me."

"Thank you," he said. "Very nice of you. Good day."

It was an address in Hethersett, only a 15-minute drive away. When he spotted the address, he continued driving down the street. This time, he parked quite a distance away. He sat in the car and thought about his strategy. From the outside, the flat looked bigger than the other place and had a space for a car. His gut told him that Dennis was inside that flat.

Tom decided to go for the jugular but what he had in mind was risky. It was worth it though, especially as it would be quick and by now, he was at the end of his tether. His patience was at the lowest point it had been for as long as he could remember. He set off down the street and was soon at the house. He knocked on the door.

A minute went by before he thought he heard footsteps inside.

"Who is it?" a voice said.

"Electricity," he said, quickly. "I won't keep you. The metre service."

Several locks unclicked and the door opened.

"Mr Whitcombe?"

"Yeah."

Tom paused for a brief moment and looked him up and down carefully. Kino's description of Dennis being skinny and ratty fitted. "I'm investigating the disappearance of Benny Longmire." He waited for a reaction. "Do you know him?"

Dennis stood dumbfounded, like what Tom had said didn't register at first. His eyes widened and then he scowled, revealing a greasy mouth with the promised missing tooth.

"What?" he said, without perhaps even knowing he'd said it.

"I would like to ask you some questions. About Benny Longmire. I'm a private investigator, working for the family."

Dennis leant forward, like he needed to see Tom up close, just to focus. Then, all of a sudden, he stepped back and slammed the door shut. Whack! Locks clicked all the way up to the top.

Tom smiled. There was no doubt that Dennis' mind was frazzled, just as he'd been told. He walked back to the car still smiling. Dennis had been given a surprise electric shock by the bogus electricity man.

Best just wait now and see what happens, he thought as he resumed his seat in his car.

But the street was quiet and this wasn't London. It hardly leant itself to covert surveillance, even in a small car, but he had little choice. Pleased and relieved that finally he had made some progress to report to Penny, he called her and told her he was sitting about 100 yards from where Dennis lived. She sounded happy or as happy as she could be. When she asked what he'd do next, he said he didn't know exactly.

"I should get off the phone now. A car has just pulled up in front of his house."

He watched a lady get out of a small car and go inside. She was in a hurry, almost running. *A good sign,* he thought. Perhaps Dennis now had a girlfriend and that might explain how he could afford the move to this location and maybe even why he moved. Possibly, he had called her and told her about the visit that had just been sprung on him. Tom welcomed these possibilities to ponder, now that he'd finally found him. For the next three hours, he sat and watched but the woman's car remained parked out front, and no one came or went.

By now, Tom needed to find a toilet and to eat in equal priority. He did a u-turn and drove away. Less than an hour later, he was back with a large, empty plastic bottle that had contained apple juice. He figured he could use the empty container in the car, if desperate, so that he didn't have to move again. Dennis' visitor's car was still there.

Tom waited until just after dark, then decided he needed dinner, so he would call it a day and come back in the morning. He didn't know how long he could keep up this surveillance. It was time to move things along by making Dennis nervous. As he drove home he hatched a new plan. It would be tricky but he decided to do it anyway, just for fun.

When he got home, he found an envelope and a piece of paper. Altering his normal writing as much as he could, he wrote on the paper, *We know what you did.* He figured that Dennis had done a lot of dodgy things anyway, so it would play nicely into whatever drug-induced paranoia he possessed and maybe illicit some sort of response. He wanted to annoy him and see what happened, and if nothing else, to punish him for being so bloody hard to find.

At 1 am, Tom drove back to Dennis' place wearing dark clothes and a black scarf to carry out his plan. He slipped the note under his door.

The next day, he returned once more and parked at the opposite end of the street. The same car was still parked in front. It was now a waiting game. The trick was not to be noticed at all while keeping a close eye on the flat.

CHAPTER TWENTY-THREE

Sitting in a freezing cold car by choice made Tom start to wonder if he was crazier than Dennis. It soon became obvious that Dennis was going to stay inside the warm house. When he needed something, he would send the woman out to get it. In the course of the next two days, Tom watched her leave for up to an hour at a time, several times, returning with what looked like a small bag of groceries, alcohol and probably cigarettes. If the note under the door was playing into Dennis' paranoia, sitting in a car was equally playing into Tom's weaknesses – a lack of patience and an aversion to surveillance. Something had to give and for Tom, it was going to be him.

As the hours passed, the relief of having found Dennis quickly gave way to a realisation that it was, in all likelihood, a huge waste of time. But his rumbling stomach was not yet ready to let go of the gut feeling that somehow, Dennis was worth staking out.

At 10.22 am, well into his third and (he'd concluded) last day, he glanced at the empty plastic bottle on the floor of the passenger side. This morning, he couldn't face using it in the way he had intended. An elderly lady opposite had already peered out through the curtains of her front window twice that morning and it was conceivable she was going to call the police, if she hadn't already. He pictured the cops arriving just when he had his pants open which would take a hell of a lot of explaining. He was about to turn the key and drive off, when he saw Dennis emerge for the first time and get into the car, alone. The wait had been

| Carl Spence

worthwhile after all. Tom waited and watched as Dennis backed out and drove up the street, then he followed discreetly behind.

Soon Dennis was heading east. Mercifully, Tom noticed, he was not a fast driver.

During his investigator's course, his instructors had made it very clear to the students that good driving skills would be an important asset, as sometimes, they would have to follow someone in a car. Tom had learnt that it might be the one and only opportunity to get some useful information and students were encouraged to complete a course in advanced driving skills. But Tom's impatience had made him decide he would learn on the job. He had also been told that a good car would be an asset. Tom felt comfortable in the little Volkswagen Polo as he could manoeuvre it with ease and precision. It was also a car that didn't attract attention when sitting in a street for long periods. But he was no rally driver. Thankfully, neither was Dennis, who drove a very old small three-door vehicle.

After a few more turns in various directions, Dennis turned left onto Norwich Road and then right and followed the B1172 until the roundabout when he took the exit onto B1135. It was not at all clear to him where Dennis was heading. He was more focused on getting into the rhythm of following him from a distance, trying to stay no more than three cars away. But when he saw Dennis take the exit onto the A11 ramp to Thetford and pick up speed, he knew that this was potentially a long drive. It looked like he was going to London.

Following the car became easy now, but as the miles clicked over, Tom began to regret not using that empty apple juice container. Dennis merged onto the Newmarket Bypass and then continued to the M11. Signs for London/Stansted Airport eventually started to appear. As Tom drove, he began eyeing off the apple juice container with each passing mile. He extended his arm and finger tips, but it was just out of reach, somewhat perilously now. He begged Dennis to stop for petrol, a drink, an ice cream, anything. He could think of nothing else but how much longer he could hold on.

At a junction, Dennis took the exit to Colchester, Bishop's Stortford and Stansted Airport. Luckily, London was now off the possible destinations. Dennis hadn't carried a bag to the car when he left the house, so Tom thought the airport seemed highly unlikely too.

He had to concentrate hard not to lose him as Dennis drove through a couple of roundabouts before taking the B1004 heading towards Bishop's Stortford. "Please stop there, Dennis, please, for Christ's sake!" Tom shouted. And five minutes later, after almost an hour and a half of driving, he did just that, pulling into a small car parking area.

Beginning to worry that Dennis had noticed him, Tom drove up the street, well past the car park and then back again, before parking his car on the street about 40 yards away. Here, he had a clear view of Dennis' empty parked car. Unfortunately, Tom hadn't seen where Dennis went but was in no state to care. He hurriedly undid his seat belt and his pants, grabbed the apple juice container, and took an urgent look around to make sure he was not going to be noticed.

More comfortable now, Tom settled in to wait – again. He couldn't get out of the car in case he was spotted, so he pulled out his camera, ready to fire off some photos when Dennis came back. About half-an-hour later, Dennis emerged from a parked car several cars up from his own. No one else got out, and as Dennis walked back to his car, Tom snapped a series of photos quickly, framing both cars in the photo with their number plates visible. He watched as Dennis drove off and headed back in the direction he'd come. There was little doubt that Dennis had driven to meet whoever was in that other car. Rather than following Dennis again, it made more sense to Tom to stay and watch this other car. It was impossible to see who was inside the silver Toyota sedan due to its tinted windows.

The driver of the Toyota reversed and headed out of the car park in the direction of the M11 with Tom following behind. Shortly after, it turned left. Tom smiled and said, "Thank God" as he watched it pull into a petrol station. He stopped on the road outside and pressed the window down to wait for the car to pull up at a bowser.

A man got out and Tom grabbed his camera again. He stared at the man, making sure he wasn't mistaken. He pointed the telephoto lens at the man's feet. *Two-tone leather shoes?* Edgar Morrow's preferred choice of footwear.

Tom snapped several photos as Edgar filled up the tank, then he rested the camera in his lap. He shook his head as he watched him walk into the shop and pay. *Dennis and Edgar? It doesn't make any bloody sense.*

* * * *

On the drive back, Tom was confident that neither Dennis nor Edgar had seen him. He tossed over the facts that could be reported to Penny. It was clear the two men had met between London and Norwich, not quite halfway but near enough. And Edgar had returned to London. Edgar Morrow and Dennis Whitcombe weren't old friends catching up for an ale. They didn't want to be seen together.

By the time he got back to his mother's house and picked up his phone to call Penny, he realised he now had more questions than answers. He began to worry how Penny might take it all with everything she had already been through.

The conversation was brief. He said nothing of any of these apparently incongruent facts. She told him she'd be home after 2 pm the next day if he wanted to come by and he said he would fill her in on some 'developments' then.

* * * *

Tom felt a desperate need to be clear headed for this meeting with Penny. He wanted to have some sort of plan – a way forward – but it was a struggle to come up with anything. He fought back concerns that this news would come as another body blow to her. Her husband's secrecy had just gone to another level with a possibly sinister, or at least, unsavoury connection.

Penny let him in. He uttered a nervous hello but barely met her eyes. With his laptop under his arm, he went inside with a purpose to his step and sat on the same couch as before.

"How are you?" he asked as he placed the laptop on the coffee table.

"I'm okay. Are *you* okay?" A resilient half-smile appeared on her face as she sat next to him.

"I'm fine."

"Well, that's good," she said.

"How's your morning been?"

"Not great. I went into work for a few hours, but then my brother, Michael called, and I came home. It's difficult to focus on work. So, I left. Can I get you anything, Tom? Tea?"

"No, I'm good, thank you. Unless you want some yourself."

She shook her head. "What can I expect you to tell me, Tom? You looked worried when you came in. What are you worried about? Why didn't you want to mention anything on the phone?"

"I'm sorry, if I worried you." He paused. "I suppose I am a bit concerned about what we are going to do with the new information I have."

Penny now looked at him with a familiar expression on her face. He knew it was guarded curiosity; she was bracing herself for what she was about to hear.

"You have bad news, you mean, is that it?" she said. "And you have your laptop. That must mean you're going to show me something."

He didn't respond at first. He moved closer to her, closer than he'd ever been to her before. He could feel the air from her nostrils exhale onto his cheek.

"Should I be getting a glass of wine, Tom?"

Surprised, he withdrew a little and smiled.

"I'm serious," she said without breaking her gaze. "Would you join me?"

He saw that she wanted, or maybe *needed* him, to say yes. As always, he could never say no to anything she wanted. "Alright."

She went into the kitchen and poured two of the largest glasses of white wine he'd ever seen. She came back to sit next to him once more, handed him his wine and said, "Here's to good news not bad news – one day. Maybe one day," and she touched her glass with his. She took two long sips before placing her glass down. "Should we look at what's on your laptop first?"

"Well, we can," he said, thinking it would lead into what he needed to say. He powered it on and placed it on his lap. Their heads were almost touching as they peered at the screen together. He flicked through a series of thumbnail photos, clicked on one and enlarged it.

"That's Edgar. What's that, a petrol bowser?" she said. "What am I supposed to be seeing, Tom? I know he's an adulterer and a bastard. But why the photos? I'm in the process of throwing out a lot of photos of him. Did you think I needed to see more? Have you got a photo of him with her? Is that it, because I don't need to see—"

"No." Tom closed the laptop, placed it on the coffee table, then turned to her.

She took another large sip of wine, clearly for medicinal effect, and sat back.

He braced himself. "I … I ah, was staking out Dennis, yesterday. I'd had enough, to be honest, and I was just about to leave. But he came out of the house, finally, and drove away in the girlfriend's car. I followed him. About an hour and a half later, he pulls up in a car park in Bishop's Stortford. He got into another car that was parked there – a silver Toyota. He stays in that car for about twenty minutes, then he gets back in his own car and drives off. I then followed the Toyota to a nearby petrol station. The photos that I just showed you, *that's* who Dennis met in the car park."

"Edgar? What?"

"Right."

"What are you … saying? I don't understand!"

"I don't get it myself, Penny. Edgar was the last person I expected to see – the last person who would be meeting up with this loser, Whitcombe. I'm struggling to make any sense of it, but … he met him in Bishop's Stortford. They went out of their way not to be seen together."

Penny started to shake. She covered her face with both hands. Tom placed his hand gently on her back.

She got up, all of a sudden. "Are you telling me … my husband and this … this Dennis person you've been staking out, have something to do with my missing brother? Is *that* what you are telling me?"

"I can't say for sure. Remember how I told you I put a note under Dennis' door a few days ago to rattle him? Obviously, it worked. They tried to have a meeting in person, so they didn't have to talk on the phone. There's some sort of connection there but I don't know what it is. That's all."

"That's ALL! I can't get my head around this, Tom!"

"Nor can I! I was as surprised as you. Penny—"

"I just don't understand. Christ!" She collapsed back on the couch. Tom knew she needed to digest what she'd heard. But he had barely digested it himself.

"I don't know exactly what to make of it, Penny. I was really expecting nothing at all to come out of chasing up Dennis. Why he would be meeting with Edgar a few days after I paid him a visit and slipped him the note has me beaten."

Penny sat up again, her mind suddenly alive. "Is my mother safe?" she said, as though talking to herself, not to him.

"What do you mean?"

"Tom, she had a brick thrown through her window this morning! That's why my brother called me at work."

"What? Did you say she lives alone?"

"Yes!"

"I think you should get in touch with your brother! And she should be with him, not by herself, until we know more."

Penny jumped up from the couch again and began pacing the room.

"Is there anything that you can think of now?" he said.

"No. It doesn't make sense." After a while, she turned and said, "I should call my brother. Who else should we talk to, Tom? I feel like you and I should go and see Edgar, now. Right now!"

"That's the thing, Penny. Hang on a minute. What we do with this information is absolutely crucial. We need to think about it. That's the main reason I wanted to be here – so we could talk it through."

"Shouldn't we go straight to the police?"

"Well, I've thought about that, but I'm not certain we should just yet. So what, that Dennis and Edgar met. It doesn't mean the police can do anything. Once we tell them what I saw, it's largely out of our hands. I want us to have control for now."

"What do you think, Tom? What should I do? I trust you."

"I think *whatever* they talked about in the car, they made a decision between them. I'm a bit concerned what that might be. I don't know whether the brick through your mother's window is related or not. I'd like to track down this mistress of Edgar's. She's somewhere in London now, I think. The shop in Norwich has been closed for weeks."

"I'm starting to feel scared, Tom."

"I can stay close by."

"Can you stay with me tonight?"

CHAPTER TWENTY-FOUR

By that afternoon, it was settled that Michael would go and see their mother, help her pack a bag and explain to her that it was best that she stay with him for a little while. Tom went and reparked his car in a long-stay car park, bought some food for them to cook, and a bottle of wine. He hoped the bottle would relax them enough to perhaps come up with a plan, before its numbing effects kicked in.

When he got back, Penny had already opened a bottle and was standing in the kitchen.

"You know, Tom," she said, as he placed the bags of food down. "I'm done with pussy footing around with Edgar. Screw that! We need to go and see him. Get an explanation."

Giving her space to digest the latest developments had worked, but he remained uncertain her suggestion was the best thing to do.

"Well, maybe, but not now," he said, noticing half the bottle sitting on the counter had already gone.

"Why not? I know exactly where he is. I don't know where he lives, but I know where he is now! It's 4.30. If we go now, he will still be at the shop in Mayfair."

"I think it's best we wait, Penny. You need to ... *we* need to just think about it a little."

"Look, if that bastard ... He's been lying to me, Tom!" she said, starting to cry.

Tom took the glass out of her hand and placed it on the bench. He held her gently, without thinking. It felt safe yet dangerous all at once, but he knew it was the right and only thing to do.

"Look, I'm going to pour us another glass of wine, we're going to cook dinner and both get an early night," he said. "I want to think, Penny. We both need to sleep on this." He let her go and backed away from her. "If we go and see him, and I'm absolutely okay with that, I want it to be because we've thought about it. But I want to try and see his lady friend first. It's important to do this in the right order. I know it's not what you want to hear, but it's what you're paying me for."

As he said that, it occurred to him he would do it all for free because of the way he felt about her. There had been no discussion of money. "Trust me," he added. "I think I'm right."

"Oh, Tom. What would I do? What would I do without your help?"

He cooked dinner and she fell asleep on the couch shortly after eating. After he cleared the dishes and cleaned the kitchen, he touched her gently on the shoulder and she went to her bedroom. Tom retired to the spare bedroom where he jumped under the covers with his laptop. He tracked down Amelia Briskett on her brand new website, taking note of her stylish, new upmarket address.

* * * *

At breakfast, Penny was quieter than Tom expected. The fire she was prepared to light under Edgar's shoes had gone and he noticed she was in a calmer, more reflective state – exactly what was called for if they were to come up with a plan. He had a decent night's sleep and as he sipped coffee at the kitchen bench, he was pleased to see the wine bottle he had bought sitting there unopened. He had achieved his goal of the day before to have a clear head today.

"This morning," he said. "I think I'll go and see young Amelia first thing, then come back and collect you so we can both visit Edgar. What do you think?"

Penny looked fresh after a shower. She sat opposite him, dressed in brown bootleg trousers, low-heeled shoes and a beige long-sleeved shirt with a shawl. For the first time, he noticed, she had removed all of her rings.

"How old is she?" Penny asked.

"Amelia?"

"You said 'young Amelia'."

"Oh, it's just an expression I use sometimes, even if someone isn't young. About 35, I think. I haven't checked for certain."

She nodded and took a sip from her cup. "What are you going to say to her?"

"I'm going to hit her between the eyes – not literally of course. I'm going to tell her who I am and ask her what she knows. She won't tell me anything, I'm sure. But I'll let her know that we know about her. At the very least, it will throw her into a spin. I like the sound of that. She's obviously of questionable morals. Maybe even a little selfish."

"Where is she?"

"According to her website, the new shop is in Bloomsbury."

"How nice for her," she said sarcastically, with more than a hint of underlying disdain. "Are you thinking of the same strategy for Edgar?"

"Probably. I think they will feel very uncomfortable about being put on the spot. When Edgar sees you and I walk in, he's going to have a fit. He can't sack me this time."

"He won't be in the front of the shop. He'll be in his office out the back. Perhaps I should go in first."

"That might be a good idea." Tom glanced at his watch and downed his coffee. "It's coming up to 9. I'm going to make my way over there now. I'm hoping to be back by say, 11. Certainly, no later."

"Are you taking the Tube?"

"Yes. Are you going to be okay by yourself? I think it's best you stay here. I don't recommend you see her. Not yet anyway."

"I don't want to see her. I'll be fine. What does she look like, Tom?"

He took out a pen and small notepad, wrote something on a piece of paper and handed it to her. "Here is the address of her website if you want to look at it. Her photo is on there."

He put on his coat and grabbed an umbrella. It was raining and the ground was icy and slippery underfoot as he walked to the station.

He was glad that somehow the loose ends might be coming together, although whether his discovery had anything at all to do with Benny was far from certain. The connections might be coincidental, but his gut, once again, was telling him otherwise.

After he got off the train at Russell Square, he walked to the shoe shop. He knew there was a chance she wouldn't be there but he was determined to see her today. He could say he was a salesman with a special offer expiring at the close of business that day and ask when she would be back. And if she *was* there, he would be charming, but if the opportunity arose, he was ready to become a smiling serpent and sink his venomous fangs into this woman who had hurt Penny. He hoped she would not remember him but even if she did, he didn't care. It might just annoy her more.

When he hovered for a brief moment out the front of the shop, he spotted her standing behind the small counter with her head bent over some paperwork. There were two customers inside and a shop assistant who was helping them. He knew the time was right; not quite an ambush, but at least she was there.

She was still engrossed in what she was doing as he approached the counter and cleared his throat. She glanced at him and sighed, annoyed that he was interrupting her. "Can I help you?" she said, in a tone that said anything but that.

"Yes. I hope so. My name is Tom Greer. I'm a private investigator."

She pushed the frame of her slim reading glasses down a fraction to examine him.

"You are Amelia Briskett?"

She stayed silent, but glanced to her left and right to see if anyone had heard him. "I was hoping to have five minutes of your time to ask some questions concerning the disappearance, some years ago now, of a person by the name of Ben Longmire."

"Ben who?" she said.

It quickly occurred to him that question may very well be asked to buy time, just for a split second, while she thought. He felt confident that was true, so he wasn't about to give her any. "He was known as Benny. Benny Longmire. He had a business in Norwich. He was last seen in

Norwich, oh … about five years ago. *Surely*, you know of the man. The man who owned the record store. The young man who went missing."

Amelia threw her pen down, removed her glasses and shook her head. She looked him up and down. "Who did you say you are?"

"Tom Greer. I don't have a card at the moment." He pulled out his wallet and showed her his driver's licence. "I'm investigating his disappearance."

"Well, what's it got to do with me? Why are you here, talking to me? I don't know any Ben Longmuir."

"Are you sure you haven't heard about him? And it's Longmire. Didn't he operate a second-hand music shop in Norwich, five years ago, from the very same shop *you* then rented, Amelia, and that you left just after Christmas? Surely, you heard he went missing."

"I don't know what the hell you're talking about!"

"Sorry?" It was his turn to look around this time, exaggerating his movements, mimicking what she had done a moment before. He leant in and said softly, glaring at her. "Sorry, let's just keep this quiet. Just between you and me. You don't *know* what I'm talking about, when I say you were renting in Norwich? I saw you there, in that shop."

"I meant, I don't know what you're talking about with this Benny person."

"Well, I find that hard to believe." He stepped back. "That you haven't heard of him, even though when he went missing, the police became involved *and* you rented the same shop his business was in. Seems a little odd to me, if you don't mind me saying."

"I don't care … what the hell you find hard to believe! How dare you. You think you can come in here and start …" Stepping back from the counter now, she became aware that the assistant and the two customers were motionless, staring right at them.

Tom saw his chance. "*You* had an affair with Edgar Morrow." No use in holding back now. His volume went up a notch. "Edgar is Benny's brother-in-law. Did you know that? I think you do know something and perhaps the police may be very interested in asking you some questions, if you can't answer mine."

"Get out … get out of my shop!"

"Oh, I will. But, let me ask you, Amelia, before I go. Where's Benny, have you heard?"

"Get out! Get out now, or I'll call security!"

"Is everything alright?" the young assistant approached, looking at her boss.

"No, actually, it's not, miss. That's fine, though. I'll go, for now. But have a little think about these questions, Amelia. Have a *good* think. You have a nice day, now."

On the train back to Penny's, he knew it was highly likely Amelia would be on the phone to Edgar. That would be a traceable call and could be used as evidence that call was made to his number from her number, that day, at that time. Trying to imagine what she might say brought a smile to his face; the first time he'd ever smiled on the crowded Tube.

It was well before 11 when he got back to Penny's flat. "That was quick. How did it go?" she asked, as she let him inside.

"Quite well, I think. She said she'd never heard of Benny at all. She didn't like it when I told her I found that hard to believe. Mind you, I didn't hold back. If it's any consolation, you can bet your bottom dollar I have ruined her day, if not her whole week. She might even be feeling a little ill at the moment." He filled her in on all the details, taking pleasure in her reaction.

"She'll be on the phone to Edgar, for sure," she said.

"That's what I think. So, let's go see him, now, before he has too much time to absent himself this afternoon. Strike while the iron's hot. What do you think?"

"I'm nervous," Penny told him as they made their way to the shop near Mayfair in the rain.

"Don't be. I'll do the talking once we're in his office."

When they arrived at the shop, she said, "Come in. We'll do this together." They collapsed their umbrellas and placed them in a rack by the door.

"Hello Donna," Penny said to the girl at the counter.

"I didn't think you were coming in today, Penny," she said, looking a little surprised.

"Oh, I'm not staying. Is Edgar in?"

"Yes."

"Okay. I'm going to go through, Tom. Come this way." Opening a door, she led him down a narrow hallway, stepping around a sliding ladder that serviced tall shelves stacked to the ceiling with shoeboxes. She reached the entry to Edgar's office. "Wait," she mouthed to Tom, holding up her hand, as he stepped around the ladder. He stopped as she disappeared into the office.

Edgar was on a call and he looked up as Penny entered the room, leaving the door ajar so Tom could hear what was said. "Hang on, John. I have to go. I'll call you back in a minute." Then to Penny he said, "I thought we had an arrangement?"

"What arrangement?"

"That I would look after this store and you would look after Soho?"

"I'm not here to *look after* the shop, Edgar."

"What are you here for then, Penny? To tell me to get the hell out of here, as well?"

"No!"

Outside, Tom crept a step closer to hear better.

"Well, then, what?"

"I want to ask you some things."

"I sent you an email last night with the figures. Didn't you get it? The stock—"

"Shut up for a moment! I'm not interested in that."

"Oh, right. You want to ask me questions, but I have to shut up. You have some—"

"Look! I'm going to ask you some things, things that you bloody well need to tell me the truth about. Can you do that?"

"What are talking about?"

"CAN YOU?" she shouted.

"Calm down, would you! This isn't the place. I've told you about her. I'm NOT seeing her!"

"I don't care about her! I *care* about my brother! You've been seen, Edgar – seen meeting someone who could be a suspect in my brother's disappearance."

"What?"

"Yes. WHAT indeed! You were seen at Bishop's Stortford. Why were you meeting him, Edgar? The truth!"

"I don't ... I don't know what the hell you want from me anymore. It wasn't me. I never ... who told you?"

"Tom. He *saw* you! And, he has photographs. I've seen them, Edgar!"

At that moment, Tom appeared by her side. "I think we need an explanation, Edgar. That's all," Tom said. "That's all she's asking. Nothing more," he added, lowering his tone.

"What is this? You're ganging up on me now? I'm not going to continue this. Put up with this shit! Get the fuck out of my office, Greer. You little slime ball!"

"No, Edgar! He's not leaving, not until you explain yourself. I'm paying him, not you! You've lied to me before. How many more lies are there? How bloody many? What did you do? Why did you meet that man? Tell me!"

"Well, if you're not going to leave, then I'm leaving," he said, and got up.

"No, you're not," Tom said, blocking the doorway.

"How dare you! Get out of my way, Greer!"

"Edgar, just answer her questions."

"I said, get ... the fuck ... out ... of ... my ... way. NOW!"

Tom positioned himself better to block the doorway but in one swift, brutal, double-handed shove, Edgar sent Tom flying out the door, his shoulders and head heavily smashing against the wall of the hallway, before crumpling to the floor. Edgar stepped over him and glared at him for a second, before storming angrily up the hallway, past the ladder and out the door.

"Tom, Tom ... are you alright?" Penny said, bending over him. "What a bastard, oh, God! I'm so sorry, Tom! Are you hurt? DONNA!" she yelled, holding Tom's head in her hands.

Donna came rushing down the hallway. "What happened?" she said. "Is he alright? Should I call an ambulance?"

"Yes, get one on the phone!"

"No. No, I'm fine. Just … just … whoa. Help me up a bit. Ouch!" Tom said, trying to struggle to his feet.

"Tom, you shouldn't move. Just stay there, please."

"I'm okay. Just take my arm and help me up a bit …" He stood up before she could protest further and put his weight on her arm.

"Tom, let's call the police. I'm not putting up with it anymore. I can't do this anymore!"

"Let me sit down," he said and staggered into the office. He sat in the chair, took a deep breath and felt the back of his head. "I'm gonna get a bloody lump," he said.

"Get some water please, Donna," Penny said. "You might be concussed, Tom."

"No. I don't think so. I'm just winded. Hey, I've had worse playing rugby. I'm fine, really."

Donna appeared with the water and he took a sip.

"Would you mind looking after the shop please, Donna?" Penny asked.

"Thanks, Donna," Tom said to her as she left. "Well, that, as they say, went well. Ha! He's taken off, has he?" He rotated his arm and shoulder. "He got me a good one."

"Yes. Oh, Tom, you didn't deserve that."

"Don't worry about it, Penny. I'm not the victim. It's all part of the job. Nothing is broken. I'm okay." He stood up and twisted his head sideways, back and forward, then felt the back of his neck. "I'll be sore for a few days but I'm fine."

"Are you sure?"

"Yes. I am. We should go."

"I want to call the police," she said.

"I agree."

Penny told Donna that if Edgar didn't come back, she should close up the shop at the end of the day. The rain was bucketing down when she and Tom left, so they hailed a taxi to take them back to her flat.

"You should eat something, Tom. You haven't eaten since breakfast. Can I make you a sandwich?"

"That would be great, Penny. Thanks," he said, rotating his shoulder again.

After eating, he seemed almost back to normal. "I'm going to call Donovan," he said.

"But he's based in Norwich. I want the police to talk to Edgar. You should press charges for assault."

"No. I'll tell him about that. About everything. But, Edgar will be able to say we effectively gave him no choice. That we falsely imprisoned him in his own office."

"That's outrageous!"

"Maybe, but he was entitled to leave."

"Is he entitled to keep lying? And he wasn't entitled to assault you."

"Let's focus on what we need to do, not on what he did to me. I'm not certain I can do anything more but give them everything I have. There's quite a bit to tell them, now."

"You can do that over the phone? To Sergeant Donovan?"

"Possibly. I have to get through to him first. He's the one who knows about the case."

At 2.30 pm, after calling the enquiry line, Tom was put through to Norwich Police Station. He left a detailed message for Donovan. Donovan returned the call at 3.30 pm.

"If what you are saying has any truth to it, and I have no doubt you're telling me the truth Greer, then maybe there is something in this," Donovan said, after hearing a rundown of the events since they last spoke.

"Do you need to speak with Penny? She's with me. I'm at her place now."

"No. I'm going to get in touch with the boys at the Metropolitan Service and I'll be down there in the morning. You can tell Mrs Morrow I will look into this and send some boys out to have a little chat with Whitcombe. I'll be in touch after that."

"Thanks, Sergeant."

"Oh, and Greer. Leave it to us from here, would you? You've been helpful. But, time to stand aside now."

"No problem. Are you going to pick Edgar up and bring him in for questioning?"

"As I said, Greer. Leave it to us from here."

CHAPTER TWENTY-FIVE

The rain had gone the next morning but not the pain in Tom's shoulder. But his physical pain was no match for Penny's emotional pain, and he would say nothing of it at breakfast if she asked.

Tom's mother called as he went into the kitchen. Penny handed him a cup of coffee and couldn't help overhearing his conversation. "Fine, Mum. How are you? That's good. Yeah, I'm staying with … someone, assisting her with a case."

When Tom ended the call, she said, "That was your mother? She's like me. Worried about you."

He rolled his eyes. "Why don't we go out for breakfast this morning?" he said.

"Okay."

They walked to the nearest café and he ordered his favourite full English version and a large black coffee. She ordered only toast and tea, saying it was all she could stomach. "How's your shoulder?" she asked.

"It's fine. How do you feel today?"

"I feel like … like I just want to stop not knowing what happened to Benny. I've wanted to know so badly, for so long, it physically hurts every day. For the first year, I would get up in the morning with a pit of emptiness in my stomach. It made me sick. Now, I don't know, I just feel numb, in a way. Like, the answer is maybe close but maybe it's as far away as it ever was. I want to know, but I'm now scared of knowing as well. With all this going on with Edgar, it's … I just have no idea anymore."

"That's understandable. I think Donovan is now motivated again. That's something."

"Do you think we'll hear from him today?"

"I hope so. And if not today, then soon, I think. The boys at the Met wouldn't know much about the case. He'll have to get them up to speed. It could take time."

"I hope he brings Edgar in and grills him. What am I going to do if it turns out like it's looking, Tom?"

"You're going to get on with your life, Penny. You're one of the strongest, most remarkable people I've ever met." He paused, wanting to say so much more. "You'll be fine. I'm sure of it."

"I don't know," she said, looking away while cradling her tea in both hands to warm her fingers. "It's overwhelming. My mother doesn't deserve this, at her stage of life. She's already lost a son. I try to stay strong for her, but it's hard. I wonder if the police really understand what an impact it has on a family when someone goes missing."

"Donovan tells me he's aware of a lot of things. But I guess, like most things, unless it happens to you, it's difficult to fully appreciate. The police have to stay detached."

"Does your family worry that you're in a dangerous job, Tom?"

"My mother does a bit. But, it's not *that* dangerous. I don't need to carry a gun. You do develop enemies, though. People don't like being snooped on, let alone caught out doing something they spend a lot of time trying to hide."

"What made you choose to go into private investigation?"

"Originally, I thought it was going to be interesting – fun. But I got a reality check and quit."

"Do you still want to quit?"

"I want to keep working on your case."

When they returned to the flat, Penny asked, "What do we do now? Are we just supposed to hang around for a phone call from the police?"

"Maybe. Do you want to go to work? Would that make it easier?"

"I could. What will you do?"

"I can go and see my friends. Or I can go and move my car. I can even do some shopping for dinner. But maybe I should check into a hotel."

"No, you will not! I need you here. I don't want to be by myself at the moment. I will pay you, or make sure you are paid, for every single second you are here. Your support, Tom, has been so important to me."

"Penny, I don't want you to worry about the money. I don't need ..."

"Tom. This is not just about me. It involves my whole family."

"But with the divorce, it's going to be burdensome for you. I'll discount my time. I won't charge—"

"Tom! I won't have that. I've told you my mother is quite well off. She will help. It's not an issue at all. You're working for my family."

"Maybe if you go to work, it might make the time pass quicker."

She looked at her watch. "I'll go to the Soho shop but be back here before 5. I'll let the girls close up."

"Perfect. If you hear anything, call me. I don't know if Donovan is going to call you or me."

"I hope he calls today," she said.

Within twenty minutes they had both left the flat. She gave him a key and said to come back when he wanted. She went to the shop and he went to his car. After paying for an extra two nights parking and wandering around Hyde Park for an hour, he decided his mind was too preoccupied to see Paddo or Bessy. Besides, it was still working hours and he was working too, albeit waiting on the police to do their work now he'd given them some tasks.

He rang Marzena for a chat, then walked back to the high street, where he bought a photography magazine and had a late lunch. At 4 pm he bought some food for dinner and by 5 pm, he was back at Penny's flat. She wasn't home and he settled on the couch scrolling through the news on his laptop.

By 5.45 pm, Penny had not arrived home. Starting to worry, he picked up his phone to call her, and just at that moment his phone rang. He was relieved to see her name displayed on the screen. "Hello, Penny. I was just about to call you. Is everything okay?"

"I've just received a phone call from Sergeant Donovan," she replied, also with relief in her voice. "I've just left the shop."

"Yes. Excellent. What did he have to say? Has he made it to London yet?"

"He's at the police station. They've been interviewing Edgar. And Amelia, apparently. He wants me to come down to the station. He wouldn't give me any other information. Would you come with me? I'm actually very worried, Tom."

"Yes, yes. Of course. Where?"

She gave him the address. He told her he could be there within half-an-hour.

Tom jumped up, shrugged into his coat and was out the door in a flash. Automatic pilot took over as he walked swiftly to the train station, his head spinning with one thought after the other. The fact that both Edgar and Amelia had been brought in for questioning seemed an interesting move and he wondered whether they would still be there when he arrived. And just what was Donovan going to tell them now? Was the Met involved, ready to take over the investigation? And, if Donovan was in London, calling for Penny to come in, there must be something of significance happening, but what?

He met Penny on the front steps. As they walked into the police station together, he saw Penny had a sense of purpose now. There was an urgency to her stride, unlike anything he'd seen before. Whatever she was about to hear, it was clear that today was the first positive breakthrough for her since her brother had gone missing. At the counter, Penny introduced herself, and then introduced Tom as her 'friend'. They took a seat and waited. A young female constable approached them after a few minutes and asked them to come through. She took them past a series of doors and then to a room where she asked them to wait. The room was sparse but large, with a long table and lots of chairs. Donovan appeared with another female constable and they both took a seat. Small CCTV cameras pointed to the centre of the room.

"Good of you to come down, Mrs Morrow. How have you been?" Donovan said, resting his elbows on the table. "Hello, Mr Greer," he added politely.

"Fine, thanks," Penny said, eager to dispatch with niceties.

"This is PC Delahunty."

Penny and Tom both said hello to her.

"I don't mind you being here, Mr Greer. But in a moment, I'm afraid, I'm going to have to ask you to leave, or at least go to the waiting section," Donovan said.

"Why is that, Sergeant?" Penny asked, surprised. "I'm entitled to have someone with me – a support person."

PC Delahunty looked at Donovan, as if she might agree, but Donovan continued. "Yes. You are. We're all well aware of that, Mrs Morrow. However, we're going to ask you to come and sit in with Mr Morrow. And it would be, let's say, a bit inappropriate that Mr Greer be there, at that particular time."

"What about her solicitor?" Tom said.

"You can call your solicitor, if you want," Donovan replied.

Penny turned to Tom and said, "Do you think I should?"

"Maybe. What's all this about exactly, Sergeant?" Tom asked.

The sergeant sat back and let his belly have some room. "We've been interviewing Mr Morrow for more than two hours now. He co-operated with us when we asked him to come in, eventually. Ms Amelia Briskett has been interviewed separately and that interview concluded, what would you say, Constable, half-an-hour ago?" he said, looking at PC Delahunty. "We think we have made some significant breakthroughs in the case of your missing brother, Mrs Morrow."

Penny exuded a loud sigh of relief and met Tom's eyes before she returned her gaze to Donovan. "What can you tell me? What is it?" she said, an urgent tone in her voice now.

"Mrs Morrow," The sergeant glanced at PC Delahunty again, measuring his words and seeming to enjoy Penny's expected reaction. "Your husband has told us some useful things which Ms Briskett has independently corroborated, but he's refusing to say any more until you are present."

"What!" Penny said loudly, and shook her head, shocked and angry.

"Mr Morrow said that he does not want us, the inspector and I that is, or anyone else for that matter, to be the ones to tell you. He wants to tell you himself. It doesn't bother him if we are there, but he doesn't want you …" he paused, and looked at Delahunty again, "… he doesn't want *you* to hear it for the first time from anyone but him."

Penny sighed again, put her hands to her face and rested her elbows on the edge of the table as she covered her eyes. Then she took her hands away quickly. "What do you want me to do?" she said, exasperated.

"If you are up to it, we want you to come in and sit with him. He's promised to tell you, and *us*, everything if it was done that way. We said we would call you."

After a pause, she looked at Tom. He could see she was scared yet there was determination in her eyes. Tom nodded.

"Alright, let's go," she said.

"Let them know," Donovan said to PC Delahunty. He then turned to Penny and Tom. "Mr Greer. I want you to stay here. When PC Delahunty returns, she will escort you to the waiting area."

Penny followed Donovan down the hallway, into a room cluttered with various documents and computers where another male officer was working at a computer. Donovan asked her to wait a minute. She caught a glimpse of herself in the reflection from a large, darkened glass panel on the wall. Lifting her shaking hand to tidy her hair, she refrained, realising she didn't care. When Donovan reappeared, he held open the door into a connecting room and ushered her in. Edgar was sitting at a table opposite another male officer who rose to his feet when he saw her. "This is Inspector Holden," Donovan said as he followed her in.

Holden extended his hand and said, "Mrs Morrow," with a nod. "Thank you for coming down." He resumed his seat opposite Edgar.

Donovan motioned her to a vacant seat next to the inspector and then took the other. At first, she found it difficult to even look at Edgar, but when she finally did, she noticed how tired he looked, as if he hadn't slept for days. She sat down and examined him more closely. She could not recall ever seeing him look so bad. Being unshaven was never his style. His suit looked crumpled too, as if he'd slept in it.

She swallowed, realising that sitting opposite him in that foreign sterile room was unquestionably the most uncomfortable experience of her entire life. Her heart pumped rapidly, every blood vessel feeling like it was working overtime. Nausea filled her stomach.

"We've done what you've asked of us, Mr Morrow," Holden said.

"Thank you," Edgar said. He turned his bloodshot eyes to her. "Hello Penny."

She stared at him, incapable of speaking.

"Just before you begin, Mr Morrow, you understand you are not under arrest." Donovan said. "And that you are giving this information voluntarily of your own free will. Also, that you have been explained all of your rights. These are questions for the record. On the record. That you have insisted that it just be the four of us in this room. Yes?"

"Yes."

"You have refused to call your solicitor. That's correct?"

"Yes."

Penny bent her head and clutched her small handbag so hard the whites of her knuckles appeared. She looked up again into the eyes of a man she no longer loved and now doubted she ever knew.

"I ..." he started to cry a little.

"Oh, stop it, Edgar! Be a man, for Christ's sake," she said, with utter contempt. "If anyone should be in tears it should be ..."

"It's not what you think," he said, interrupting, swallowing the tears back.

"Edgar!" she said loudly.

"Just wait," Donovan said softly, putting his large hand on her shoulder gently for a second.

"I met Amelia some time after Benny went missing," he began, composing himself.

"Back to Amelia again," she said with a shake of her head.

"Let me finish, *please*." Edgar focused on her face, as if Donovan and Holden weren't even in the room. He sniffed, dried an eye, and leant back. "I don't know when it was, not exactly. She – as I told you – she was at a trade fair in the city. I actually can't remember the date; so much has happened. It doesn't matter I suppose. You didn't go. I wish you had. But you and I weren't talking much then. Amelia and I started an affair. I'm sorry. I really am. I was weak. I don't ... expect your forgiveness."

She shook her head, continuing her deathly stare.

"We didn't see each other very often. She wasn't working at that time, so she would come to London. Sometimes, every second week. Sometimes, on weekends. It went on that way for about six months." He stopped to take a sip of water. His hand shook, making the glass wobble on its return trip to the table.

"Do you really think I want to know the details of your affair? Is that what you think?"

"No, Penny. Just wait and I will tell you. She had a brother, *has* a brother."

"His name?" Donovan interrupted.

"Wait," Inspector Holden said. "Continue, Mr Morrow."

"Her brother was from Norwich, as she was. He'd been in jail. It was his first time and it was just minor. Nothing too serious, but he got six months for driving without a licence for – I don't know how many times – plus high-range DUI. Anyway, he did his time and hadn't been out long when he told Amelia something. Amelia was living in Norwich, trying to get into shoe retailing."

Edgar's gaze switched for a second to Holden and Donovan, then back to Penny. "At the time of his release, it was still in the news in Norwich that Benny had disappeared – but it was old news." He cleared his throat. "Amelia had heard about it but thought nothing of it. We never discussed it. I never told her about it or said who he was. I also didn't tell her anything about you Penny. It was one of those things, where each time I saw her, I thought it would be the last."

"Spare me," she said.

"One night when Amelia's brother was drunk and out of his mind, he told her that another prisoner had told him that he did it. He told Amelia that prisoner's name. She didn't ask. He just told her."

"Did it?" Penny said. "What do you mean, *did it*?"

"This prisoner said it was an accident. And that, he'd got away with it. Her brother was scared of this fellow. Everyone was. He'd heard about him on the outside and knew what he was capable of."

"Are you going to tell us this prisoner's name now?" Inspector Holden said.

"Yes. In a minute. Amelia's brother – his name is Adam. Adam Briskett. When Adam got out of jail, he moved into a flat in Norwich. He was released about a week *after* the prisoner who told him he did it. This other fellow was also in for some minor offence but he'd been in jail before. He waited for Adam to get out, and then he went to see him."

"Why did he do that?" Donovan asked.

"Because, Sergeant, he realised that he'd made a mistake by opening his mouth to Adam in jail! He was paranoid Adam would tell the police. At that stage, Adam had only told his sister, Amelia, when he got drunk. He hadn't been anywhere, except to the bloody pub. He regretted telling her though as everything started to snowball."

Penny sat motionless. She could feel her emotions boiling under her skin, ready to explode. She wanted to ask him again what he had meant by 'did it' but just then, he continued his story.

"Penny, this thug prisoner turned up at Adam's demanding to know if he had told anyone, either when he was in jail or since he'd got out. He held a knife to Adam's throat, demanding the truth."

Donovan began to interrupt again but Holden held out a flat palm, indicating he should stop.

"Adam was petrified of this bloke. Still is. His name is Charlton Anton Moss. But, the fool had told his sister. He confessed that he didn't tell a soul, except his sister, when he was drunk. He promised he would never, ever say a word about it again, to anyone. And Amelia wouldn't either. Moss was furious. Threatened to kill him on the spot. Adam thought he was going to die that day. He begged for his life, Penny."

"Charlton Anton Moss is his name?" Inspector Holden asked.

"Yes. Moss went to see Amelia then, and that's when things got worse. That's when they turned into a living nightmare."

"And you've held on to this information?" Donovan said.

"Yes, but I can explain. Look, I had a good reason. You might sit there and judge me for being unfaithful to my wife. Well, guilty!" he said, looking at Donovan. "But the price *I've* paid for that and the decisions *I* had to make, well Sergeant, you just put yourself in my shoes."

Donovan refrained from making any comment about shoes for fear of chastisement from Holden and let Edgar continue.

"Moss told Amelia that if she went to the police, if he even *spotted* her near the police station, he would either kill her, or arrange for her to be killed, in an instant. He said he'd killed before and could kill again without blinking an eye. And he wouldn't stop there, because if he was going to go down, then he'd take her brother as well. He instilled the utmost fear into her that … that …" He stopped again and shook his head. "She told me everything the next day. She was a complete mess and didn't know what to do. That was the first I'd heard of it. I couldn't believe it. I was in shock and didn't know what to do at first. She cried for days, upset that Adam had told her and how his drinking problem had basically destroyed her life. Right! So, I told her then who Benny was. And we had to make quick decisions."

"What happened to my brother, Edgar? What are you saying, for Christ's sake!"

"Look. I have to get it all out first. I made the stupid mistake of going to see Adam about it. Of course, I wanted to get the facts about Benny. All the facts. What he was told, how he was told. What really happened to him. That was my motivation, Penny. You have to believe me. I was in a state of chaos myself, at the time. I hadn't really thought it through.

"Adam can't stay sober. I found out not long after that he told Moss about me knowing. He put both Amelia's life and mine in danger.

"Moss then paid me a visit in London one day at the shop in Mayfair. He told me that if I told one person – if one more person finds out about what he did to Benny, let alone the police, he would kill me and Amelia. He said he would find out; that he had friends who got paid to kill, and also, if I had any family, he might take care of them first."

"You're saying this Moss thug killed Benny? Is that what you're saying? SAY IT!" she said.

"Adam said Moss told him in jail that it was all Whitcombe's fault. Adam didn't know Whitcombe at that stage. When Adam and Moss were sharing a cell, Moss said something about him and Whitcombe being into petty crime, breaking into people's houses, dealing in drugs."

"Edgar …"

"Adam said, that according to Moss, Whitcombe just wanted to rough Benny up after work one night but Whitcombe was a coward. He couldn't do it himself. He had some sort of stupid grudge against Benny, some trivial, imagined thing and was prepared to pay Moss a couple of hundred quid to rough him up for him. Just that – nothing too serious. Moss and Whitcombe pushed their way into Benny's flat late one night – the night Benny went missing – and next minute, Moss had Benny in a headlock."

Edgar extended his hand across the table in her direction. "This … this is why I wanted you to be here. I wanted to be the one who told you. I've held so much from you already. Please, could you hold my hand?" he asked, lowering his voice and his palm face up.

"No," she said.

He sat back upright on his chair and retrieved his arm. He looked at the wall, then back at her. "It … it happened in less than a minute, apparently, after they pushed their way in. They wore balaclavas. Benny put up a fight. There was a struggle for a split second and then a twist and …" He paused, looked away again. "And … his neck snapped and he fell, dead on the floor. Moss didn't mean to kill him, but he did. For nothing. Just a stupid, trivial—"

Penny erupted into tears. Her wail was utterly harrowing as she held her hands to her face. Donovan was on his feet immediately. PC Delahunty quickly entered the room and knelt down by Penny, putting her arm around her shoulders as she wept.

After a minute, she composed herself and said to the constable, "I'm fine. I want to stay." She returned her gaze to Edgar. "You utter bastard! You knew for years and let me suffer. Let my mother suffer, my brother, and all the time you were sleeping with her … how could you possibly—?"

"Penny, I had no other option! I had to keep it from you! It was too risky. You *have* to believe me."

"You talked to her, your mistress, and not *me*!"

"It wasn't like that! I did it to protect you."

"Protect me? Oh, come on!"

"Penny, he would have killed you, if I told you. And I couldn't tell you! How was I going to explain it to you? How I found out? It wasn't going to bring Benny back. I got paralysed with the whole situation."

"Why did she go into that shop that Benny had? Why would Amelia do that, Mr Morrow?" Donovan asked, resuming his seat. "You'd already hurt your wife enough. Why?"

"This is the thing, Sergeant. You don't understand. None of you do! Moss didn't just leave Amelia alone. He told her he would keep an eye on her. He got hold of her number and started calling her. Told her she'd better stay in Norwich, where he could find her. Otherwise, if he had to come looking for her, he'd be angry. As she'd already told one person, he would have to monitor her. And if he was angry for too long, he'd find her and kill her. She was out of her wits, and so that's when we decided she needed to keep busy. Doing nothing was not a very good idea. Right? I helped her set up shop in Norwich and the vacant premises that Benny once occupied seemed as good as any. It … I didn't think too much about it; we didn't have the luxury of time and choice, you might bloody care to understand. It didn't seem to matter, given everything else that was going on at the time. She needed to work. We needed to make a quick decision, for everyone's benefit."

"Mrs Morrow," Donovan said, "so that you know, we have our boys in Norwich picking up Whitcombe now."

Inspector Holden spoke quietly to Penny. "I'm sorry, Mrs Morrow, but I have to ask your husband some questions. Mr Morrow, do you have any other information? Information about the whereabouts of … what they did with the body?"

Penny started crying again.

Edgar gathered himself. "You have to understand some of this evolved over time. Amelia and I would meet Adam occasionally, to discuss whether Moss had been in contact. And whether to go to the police, but, we would always decide not to.

"Moss told Adam that he and Whitcombe waited in Benny's flat until after midnight. Whitcombe stayed with Benny while Moss went and got a car. They put the body in the boot of the car and buried him late that night. I don't know where. Adam doesn't know where. I don't think he was told much more."

"You better be telling the truth, Morrow. It's pretty close to accessory after the fact. If you're lying, you'll go to jail for a long time," Donovan said.

"I'm not lying. Amelia will tell you the same. Do you think we wanted to be told all this? That we wanted to keep it secret? That I didn't *want* to tell you Penny, but couldn't?"

"Why didn't you come and see me earlier? That would have helped," Donovan asked.

"You think so? Easy for you to say. I was scared. Not so much for myself, but for everyone else. I didn't have any doubt at all that Moss would carry out his threats. Adam told Amelia lots of things he knew about Moss. If Moss had killed even one person, I could never live with myself. I thought if we told you what we knew, there wouldn't be enough time to stop him hurting someone. He'd kill someone first, before you got to him, because he knew he was going down. He made it clear that he had contacts, so even if he was in jail, we wouldn't be safe. He was already paranoid about how many people knew, and telling just one more, could well have sent him over the edge. Moss told Adam, then Adam told Amelia, then Amelia told me. I wasn't going to be the person who told someone else, not even you Penny, not when he had held a knife to someone's throat. As I said, it wasn't going to bring Benny back. It was a choice between you not knowing, Penny, and your life."

"But now, you are not so concerned," Inspector Holden said.

"As time went on, Moss went quiet. No one knew where he was. We thought he might have moved on. We decided to get Amelia out of the shop in Norwich. To try and move on - get her to London, end the relationship. Adam got a job and he stopped drinking. We stopped meeting. We all tried not to think about it. Just to forget it. It would have been better to have never known and just get on with our lives."

"And this meeting you had with Dennis Whitcombe, why?" Donovan asked.

"Moss also threatened Whitcombe, as you would imagine. Moss let him know about Adam and Amelia and me. He told Whitcombe he would kill him first, just to demonstrate to all of us how serious he was about carrying out his threats. That his body would be found in a dumpster out of town somewhere. I know that because Whitcombe contacted me and Amelia. He made similar pathetic threats that were laughable and told us that Moss had threatened him. It was best we all now shut up, permanently. He insisted I meet with him in Norwich, which I did once years ago. I told him to never contact me or Amelia ever again."

"But he did?" Holden asked.

"Yes, he did. The thing is, we hadn't heard from Moss for over a year. But then, Penny, you started to get Greer involved. After *years* had passed. You didn't tell me you were going to do that. I came home one night, and you told me you'd hired a PI. Well, I played along at first, as I felt I had no choice. Why do you think I rang up his firm and complained? I tried to shut it all down because I *knew* what had happened! To protect the lot of us! That was the only priority! But then, once Greer started digging and the focus turned to me and Amelia, it was only a matter of time before word was going to get back to Moss. Whitcombe rang me after Greer tracked him down. He shouted at me on the phone, saying he also got some bloody note under his door and demanded we meet somewhere as he didn't want to talk on the phone."

"So, you agreed to meet at Bishop's Stortford?"

"That's right. Whitcombe wanted to know how a private investigator had become involved. He didn't know about you, Penny. So, Whitcombe was paranoid, in a panic and wanted to know what was going on and if I knew anything. I wasn't sure it was Greer, but from the description Whitcombe gave me, I figured you had engaged him again. I told him I didn't know anything about it. And he should just shut the hell up about it. Let it go."

"If you'd come and seen me straight away, protection could have been arranged," Donovan said.

"You weren't the one threatened, Donovan! What are you going to do about Moss and Whitcombe now? Are you listening to what I'm saying!"

"Our men are looking to bring them in for questioning as we speak," Inspector Holden said. "Is that everything? Have you told us everything, Morrow?"

"Yes. That's all I know and it's all Amelia knows. Can you get police officers outside our doors tonight? All of our doors, including Penny's?"

"Yes," Donovan said.

"I need to leave. This is … I've heard enough. Can I go?" Penny said.

"Yes. Follow me," Donovan said. "You stay there, Morrow."

They left him sitting in the room by himself. Donovan returned twenty minutes later.

"Can I go and see my wife?" Edgar pleaded. "I need to see her. To say I'm sorry."

"She doesn't want to speak to you. It's far too late for all that. You got more than you bargained for, Morrow, when you had that affair. But Ms Briskett is downstairs, waiting. I'm sure she'll comfort you. You're right that idiot prisoners talk in jail. Just lucky this time we've got some back up and don't have to rely on the single testimony of an inmate. It's kind of ironic in a way. If you never dipped your wick, your wife may never have known what happened to poor old Benny. Now, out you come."

CHAPTER TWENTY-SIX

Tom had not pressed for any details when she emerged from the interview room. "They're dropping me home. Please, come with me."

He nodded. Once they were in the back of the police car, she started to cry. He placed his arm around her, holding her, watching her, as she gazed out the window of the car. Shortly before they arrived at her flat, she smiled at Tom through her tears, took his hand and held it tightly.

"It's just here on the right," Tom said to the driver.

A bobby stood guard at the front. "Evening, Ms Morrow … Sir," he said. Tom nodded and Penny thanked the young policeman.

Tom opened the door with his key and helped Penny remove her coat, placing it on the coat stand inside.

"Excuse me," she said.

* * * *

"I thought you might like some tea," he said, when she returned. "I've made a pot and there's a tray of biscuits." Eager to hear her say something about what happened, he felt it was best to wait until she was ready.

"Yes. That would be lovely."

He watched her walk to the window at the end of the lounge room, where she pushed the curtain aside and peered out for a moment. It had been difficult to catch her eye since she had come home. They both sat on the couch together.

"Are you alright?"

"I'm okay. I'm just very tired now."

"I hope Donovan treated you properly. He can be a bit gruff," he said, as he poured both cups.

"Yes." She took a sip of her tea, still not meeting his eye. He reached for a biscuit. After a while, she said, "You know, when I got in there, Edgar said, 'Hello, Penny,' as if he'd run into me in the supermarket. Just like that." She blinked and shook her head.

He waited. Then took another biscuit. He was hungry now, so he was happy that he'd put ten on the tray.

She turned to him. "He told me … in front of Donovan and Inspector Holden … what he'd known … what he'd *actually known,* Tom, for all these years. He kept it to himself, despite everything … *everything* he'd seen me go through. He said … it was to protect me."

"To protect you?"

"Yes. And everyone else."

"What did he know?"

And she told him. He forgot all about the biscuits.

* * * *

That night, after Penny had gone to bed, Tom went for a walk in the night air, just to think. He walked aimlessly, with no particular destination in mind until he found a late-night café where he had a meal. He returned to the flat after midnight and chatted to the bobby until another arrived to relieve him of his shift. Back inside, he felt wide awake, like he never needed to sleep again. It felt strange, somehow sad yet uplifting all at once. But overall, he felt relieved – a door had been closed and another had opened. Penny could walk through that door now.

* * * *

The next day, Penny's head felt lighter. At 11 am, Sergeant Donovan called her and told her they had arrested both Whitcombe and Moss; Whitcombe at his flat in Norwich and Moss, somewhere just on the Suffolk side, outside of Bungay. Edgar called her shortly after, but she refused to answer.

It was late that evening when Donovan called again, saying he wanted to come over. She agreed, knowing this time, Tom could not be asked to leave. At 9 pm he arrived, greeted the bobby at the front, and told him his job was done now. If he waited, he would give him a lift back to the station.

Donovan knocked on the door. Penny let him in and led him down the hallway.

"Hello, Sergeant," Tom said, as Donovan entered the room, took his police hat off and held it in his hand. *Cap in hand, this time*, Tom thought.

"Greer," he said softly, acknowledging him with a nod.

"Please, Sergeant, take a seat," Penny said. They all sat around the table. "Can I offer you some water, or some tea or coffee, Sergeant?" she said softly.

"No. Thank you."

"You have something more to tell me, no doubt. It seems like every day now I'm being told something new," she said.

"I do," he said. "Your husband—"

"Please don't refer to him as my husband anymore, Sergeant," Penny said. "My divorce will take some time to go through, but I certainly regard him as my ex-husband already."

"What Morrow told us is true. At approximately five o'clock this afternoon, after four hours of questioning, Whitcombe admitted he was at Benny's flat. He put Moss in. He said it was an accident. Blamed the whole thing on Moss. He was to give Moss a miserly £300 from the proceeds of his next drug sale, just for helping him rough your brother up. But it all went wrong and Moss threatened to kill him if he didn't help cover it up."

"I see," she said, as if it was all so clear now, so matter of fact.

Tom could see it may be clear but it was still shockingly raw. He noticed how she clenched the table tightly.

The sergeant continued. "Earlier today, Moss put up a bit of a fight down in Bungay, on the edge of The Broads. It took several of the good men of The Broads to round him up and get him on the truck. He was dragged in by his feet, kicking and shouting. But we got him."

"He's in custody?" Tom asked.

"Yes. Charlton Moss is well known to us but, up until now, we've only known him to be a petty criminal of sorts with a vicious and violent streak. I'm telling you, Ms Morrow, if we knew, I can assure you, we would've acted earlier. But, be that as it may, it's going to be investigated. Dare I say it, there will be an internal review on all of this. But I wanted you to know, he's been told there will be a total of four people – including Adam Briskett – who will testify against him. He was also told to think hard about his position, because then there is Whitcombe who told us everything and who is going away for a long time. Then there's Amelia, who told us yesterday, he had personally threatened to kill her. And then of course, there's your husband."

"Ex-husband," Tom said.

"Ex-husband. And finally, he was told that he should tell us where the body is." He stopped and waited for her reaction, but she remained silent. "He should do so because he's going to jail. It's in everyone's interest that he assist us. That the truth be told. That the Coroner be engaged. And if it was an accident, if it wasn't *murder*, then he'll fare better in front of a judge. There can be a big difference between a sentence for manslaughter and murder."

"You are *bargaining* with him?" she said.

"No. We just told him the facts, Ms Morrow. Your friend here, Mr Greer, he knows what I mean."

"And what did he say? What happened?" Tom said.

"He told us where the body is."

They both looked at Penny who closed her eyes for a good ten seconds. When she opened them again, she said, "And?"

"He's being taken across to Thetford at 7 am tomorrow morning. Whitcombe has confirmed what Moss said already. And that was, that they buried your brother in the forest there about 3 am that night. Whitcombe said he would have no idea where it was now, but Moss is sure he can take us there. There'll be a whole team from the Forensics Department and they'll meet another team from Norwich."

Penny gazed at a picture on the wall just above Donovan's head. It had been taken of Benny when he was twelve, wearing a football shirt, and smiling at the camera. "Can I be there?" she said, turning her gaze back to the sergeant.

"It's not something we recommend, Penny," he said. It was the first time he had used her first name. For all of his lack of tact at times, Tom noticed in him a sense of humility now.

"Just what *do you* recommend, Sergeant?" she said, defeat apparent in every way.

"It's something … well, you would have to seriously consider it before making up your mind," he said.

"Penny, I know how you must feel, but I tend to agree with—" Tom began.

"NO ONE KNOWS HOW I FEEL!" she snapped back at him. "No one!" She shook her head and looked at them both. No tears now. "I'm sorry," she said, hanging her head, looking down at the table.

"You don't have to apologise, Penny," Tom said. "Not to anyone."

She raised her thumb and finger, and rubbed her red, completely shot eyes. "Okay, I'm not going to go. Don't … worry yourselves. Sergeant, would you come and see me, please? After it's all done? Or send someone to see me. I don't care."

"I think that's wise, Penny," Donovan said. "It's a crime scene and … it would be better if you did not put yourself through that."

"Is there anything else, Sergeant?"

"There is one other thing. We haven't told the press any of these developments. But it will come out soon, most likely and charges will be reported. We might have to make a statement. I just want you to be pre-pared. I thought it was important to keep you and your family informed of these significant developments and let you know you are entitled to support."

"Well," she said in a determined tone now. "I want you to do some-thing for me, *Sergeant*, if you speak to the press." Sitting more upright in the chair, she gathered herself and swallowed.

"What is it?"

"Tell them about *this* man – this man here!" She pointed to Tom. "YOU TELL THEM that it was *his* good work, *his* lack of giving up, that meant my brother's killers were brought to justice!" She paused, staring at Donovan as tears began to fall. "Would you do that?" she said, softly this time. "For me?"

"Yes. I will, Penny. I will."

CHAPTER TWENTY-SEVEN

Tom checked into a hotel for two nights before returning to Norwich. On the last evening, he had dinner with Marzena but didn't mention the case. By the time he had returned to Norwich, news began to filter through that there had been a breakthrough in the Benny Longmire case, but the police remained tight-lipped. Not until later that week did Penny receive the call from Donovan to say the police had recovered her brother's body.

The day after that, the news appeared in the newspapers. Tom's mother asked if he had heard about the case, not knowing that his name would soon appear in the press, and he would be credited with assisting the police and enabling the ultimate laying of charges. He gave her the barest of details, telling her about how relieved he was that it was over, and how glad he was to have been of service to a lovely family, and to the sister, in particular. Several reporters got hold of his number and requested an interview and when he refused, they asked for a statement instead. He declined to comment at all, except for asking that they respect the privacy of Penny and her family.

Tom didn't hear from Penny until two days before the funeral.

"Would you sit beside me and my family? It will be a small family service and a private burial. I would like you to come to his final resting place, if you can make it."

"I would be honoured."

In the days that followed the funeral, Tom remained in London and stayed a few nights with Marzena. She wasn't getting on with her flatmates and was ready to move to a new location. She asked if he would consider finding a place with her. He said yes as he had finally decided to move back to London and set up his own office.

* * * *

Three weeks later, he was in residence at his new office in Camden within walking distance to some of his favourite pubs. A call came in from Alister. "My boy, my boy. Wow! I never got any press coverage like that!" he said. "Young, green-around-the-ears PI stakes out killer and tells police where to find him!"

"Well, he wasn't the actual killer," Tom replied. "And, I was lucky. If I hadn't seen Edgar that day having lunch, I'd be sitting on a beach somewhere in Australia now. I was ready to run away."

"I know you were. And I was disappointed. But, if it wasn't for your good follow-up work, Mr Longmire would still be lying in the cold ground of Thetford Forest. I'm very proud of you."

"Thank you, Alister."

"You know, I've started to set up a scrapbook of clippings from the papers for you. It's really for me. I've been telling everybody, 'That's my student!'"

"Ha! Well, keep it up until you get to my obituary, Alister. That might be in the paper one day soon, if I'm not careful."

"I think that's a way off yet, my boy. I'm so glad you've set up by yourself. You'd have been making a big mistake to have given up the job. I tried to tell you that! Anyway, are there any good Middle Eastern restaurants near your office? I'm missing Edgware Road."

"I'm sure there are, Alister. I'll investigate it," he said.

"Well, you take care, my boy. I just wanted to give you my congrats. Bye for now."

"Thanks, Alister."

Tom had never been one to seek praise, but it kept flowing in for some time and the phone started to ring with potential clients. It was Cathy who took the initial enquiries. "Please tell me you need someone,

Tom! I'm so ready to quit! Jason is driving me bonkers," she had said. He was only too happy to rescue her from Jason. Tom wondered exactly what his ex-employer was thinking now.

The new office was really an old office, nestled on the first of two floors above street level. Although very small and basic, with timber panelling and an old oak desk the previous tenant had left behind, it felt warm and inviting, ready for its new life.

Paddo and Bessy arrived late one morning to take him out for an early lunch, the same day that a man arrived to display the office signage. One sign was to be placed behind Cathy's desk at reception, one on the street and one on the door of his office. He admired the tasteful design – warm yellow printing on a cedar backing, in keeping with the timber panelling inside.

The red cedar bowl that he had bought in Australia at the Eumundi markets was now back on his desk and filled with a handful of paperclips. His office was large enough to accommodate a bookcase. His diploma in its cedar frame with new museum glass hung on a wall.

Bessy stood in reception watching the man install the sign. 'Thomas J Greer, PI' it read. She turned and said to Paddo in earshot of Tom, "I didn't know he had a middle name."

"Me either," Paddo said.

Cathy smiled and looked at Tom. "What *does* the 'J' stand for, Tom?" she asked.

"I don't have a middle name, actually. I just thought it would look a bit plain without a middle letter. I asked my mum, 'Why the bloody hell didn't you give me a middle name?' I feel like I'm missing a middle finger. 'I'm going to have to go and adopt one, now,' I told her. I might be asked by licensing one day what it stands for. And if they hassle me about it, I'll just give them the middle finger."

"Not recommended, Tom. And what are you going to choose for your new middle name?" Bessy asked.

"I don't know yet. I'm thinking maybe 'Jay' as I've always liked that name."

"Don't you mean Jason?" Cathy said.

"Ah, *no*, Cathy. I don't like that name much at all," he said with a smile.

Tom discussed Whitcombe with Paddo briefly. Paddo was still amazed he'd been involved. But out of respect for Penny and her family, Tom kept the details of the case to the bare minimum when over lunch, Paddo asked how he felt about the press coverage.

"They seemed to be very hard on the police, particularly the tabloids," Bessy said.

"That didn't come from me. I didn't talk to them. And I don't think it would have come from Penny or her brother. It's too easy to be critical of the coppers. They have to deal with a lot. So many cases. It looks bad when they miss stuff, but it happens," he said.

"Why don't you come out to Exmoor next weekend, Tom? The weather is looking better. We can pick you up. I'd love to show you the place," Paddo said.

"Sure," Tom replied. "I'd love to. We can walk the moors. I've always wanted to do that."

"It's beautiful, Tom. Very good for the soul," added Bessy.

After a slow walk back to the office after lunch, Tom shook Paddo's hand and kissed Bessy goodbye. He bounced up the stairs and into reception.

Cathy gave him a pointed look, motioned to the right with her eyes and a slight tilt to her head. He turned around and found Penny and her mother sitting, waiting for him to come back.

"Penny! Hello, Mrs Longmire, how are you? Lovely to see you both," he said, somewhat surprised to see them.

"Can we come in, Tom?" Penny said. "I'm sorry we didn't call in advance."

"Of course, of course, please do," he said, and led them into his office.

As they took their seats, he noticed that Penny looked relaxed and colour had returned to her cheeks. But Mrs Longmire had aged, even in the few weeks since he had last seen her. Her hands shook as she settled in her chair.

"Tom, you know I don't ever want to waste your time," Penny said. "And today is no different."

Feeling he could say a lot more about spending time – any time – with her, he of course respectfully refrained. "Penny, don't be silly. You never have and never will waste anyone's time."

"My mother insisted that we come," she added.

"Of course, is there a problem?" he asked.

"Yes. She's not happy with you."

"Mrs Longmire, is there something I've done?"

"No," she said, in her soft, frail voice. "It's what you *haven't* done, young man," her diminutive, wrinkled, ring-covered fingers clutching her purse.

He looked back at Penny. She smiled and winked, hinting to him to be patient with her mother.

"You haven't sent me a bill, so I've come in to pay it," Mrs Longmire said.

"I just haven't got around to it, Mrs Longmire. You don't have to—"

"Well, *I'm* getting around to it," she said, trying to open her purse.

"Here, Mum, let me help," Penny said and took the purse from her.

"Mrs Longmire, it's really not necessary," Tom said. "I haven't got it ready."

"Now listen here, Mr Greer," Mrs Longmire said. "I won't have this! What you did for my daughter … and I don't mean just standing behind her at my son's grave." She paused. "You did more than that. You gave her – you gave *me* – the truth. Hand me the chequebook, Penny," she said.

"Mrs Longmire—"

"Tom, just *let* her do it. It's important," Penny interrupted him.

"Mr Greer, I want to know what the rent is on this place for one year," she said, looking around and up at the walls, now she had the chequebook in front of her.

"Oh, Mrs Longmire, you can't do *that*. I absolutely refuse, I cannot—"

"You listen to me!" she said, raising her voice, almost as high as was possible for her to do. She cleared her throat and swallowed. "I'm not leaving this office, young man, until you tell me, and you tell me the truth, because, by God boy, I'll find out if you've lied! And I know you're a good liar. I mean *good*!" she said.

He looked at Penny. She smiled again. "Do it, Tom. Do it for her. And do it for me. Tell her, please."

And when she said those words, he knew how impossible it had always been to refuse anything she requested of him.

"I have to ask Cathy," he said, as Penny stared him down.

He picked up the phone. "Cathy, what's the rent on this place again?"

"For a year," Mrs Longmire added.

"Annually," he said to Cathy. He put the phone down and said, "It's £18,500 but—"

"That's not enough," Mrs Longmire said immediately. "Give me that pen. I'm rounding it up to 20. Will that be enough?" She looked at him.

"No, no … please, Mrs Longmire, I'd rather—"

"I'd like to know Mr Greer."

"That … that is far too much," he said.

"Good," she replied and proceeded to write out the cheque to him. He couldn't look as she managed to steady her hand long enough to write, then she tore the cheque off and pushed it across the desk. "Now, my daughter wants to say something to you," she said.

"I just wanted to say, Tom, that … no amount of money can properly thank you for what you did for me and for my family. We want you to know that. We will forever be grateful. I never got a chance to properly thank you at the funeral, particularly for staying with me those days. So, thank you, Tom."

For a moment, he didn't know what to say. He had run out of words. But he could feel that this was perhaps a goodbye. That he may very well never see her again.

"It was a privilege to be able to help. I'm just so pleased, if that's the right word, that I was actually able to help."

"Tom, I was ready to give up, not just on ever finding out what happened to my brother, but on everything. You saved me."

Her mother looked at him with her sad eyes. He got the feeling that she would never have been able to cope with a second loss. He said, "I was honoured to be there."

But Tom knew for certain, it was that day, which seemed so long ago now, when he had sat spinning in his chair, ready to quit, and Penny had come to see him, that resulted in him sitting where he was now. *She* had also saved *him*.

ACKNOWLEDGEMENTS

Thanks to Michael Charlwood for his cover artwork and to Patrice Shaw from PS Editing and Kirsty Ogden from Epiphany Editing & Publishing, Brisbane.

ABOUT THE AUTHOR

Carl Spence was born in 1965 in Sydney, Australia. *Thomas J Greer, PI* is the second novel in a short series, although it is a standalone story and can easily be enjoyed independently. His fiction involves an entertaining blend of drama and humour, with emotions and events often intersecting. This novel adds mystery and intrigue to an evolving repertoire.

For more information, please visit www.carlspenceauthor.com.